B.A.M.
An Arlon Grey Novel
Book 2

Josef Peeters

Edited by: Rosemary Hillyard

Editing Services, rmhillyard@aol.com

ISBN-13: 978-0-6450288-2-9

OTHER BOOKS BY THE AUTHOR

Fiction:

Dumped (action/adventure)

Daintree Denizens (thriller)

Mt. Moulamein (sci-fi)

Transience (magic realism)

Black Heart (psych. thriller)

Horror Series:

Eat What You Kill (Book 1)

Non-Fiction:

Wood Whisperer Volume 1

Wood Whisperer Volume 2

Wood Whisperer Volume 3

Giving Up (Short, autobiographical)

Don't Let The Bastards Win: Live. (Short, autobiographical)

Visit Josef's web page for all purchase links and detailed book descriptions;

http://lakesidecaravanpark.wixsite.com/josef

ACKNOWLEDGMENTS

My sincerest thanks and appreciation to my editor, Rosemary
Hillyard, for her generosity and skill.

ONE

After a long day of travelling, from the picturesque Shute Harbour on the central Queensland coast to their destination on the equally idyllic Cid Island in the Whitsunday group, Arlon Grey was quite willing to go straight to bed. He did not take well to water of any variety, other than a hot shower. He didn't even like having a bath, if truth be told.

Not since he was a child growing up in a small seaside village, where he encountered a rather large shark, had he ventured into or onto the water. Though he never showed an emotive response to his aversion of water because of his condition, he baulked at the possibility if it was mentioned or became necessary.

The smallish island did not offer an airstrip or any other means of ingress other than by sea, so Arlon was forced to accept the bothersome journey. Clarice Manning, the woman whom he had recently agreed to marry, on the other hand, enjoyed the experience immensely. Though her café au lait complexion did not tan as readily as she would have liked, she seized the opportunity to bask in the glorious sunshine on the bow of the dual-hulled powerboat as they crossed the Coral Sea, allowing the wind to whip through her golden, curly locks.

After Arlon had been given basic instructions and taken through the safety aspects by the elderly owner, they had loaded their provisions and personal belongings for the expectant week or so on Cid Island in the home of Gail Sandringham, Clarice's sister. Later that day, the 1994 34ft Devil Cat, which the pair had hired from the private operation, lay at anchor within the sheltered bay. Gail had inherited the island home from her late husband's mother. Ben Sandringham, Gail's husband, had passed away only a year earlier under strange circumstances.

Gail adored her island sanctuary, despite the tragedy that had taken her husband such a short time ago. Clarice had grieved with her sister for her charismatic brother-in-law. She had read the long letters her sister had written of the happy times they had shared on the island in the home her mother-in-law owned, but no longer frequented because of ill-health. Ben was her only son, so, when Patricia Sandringham passed away, the home went to her daughter-in-law.

While it was heartbreaking enough that her husband had passed away prematurely under a cloak of mystery, Gail informed Clarice of other strange occurrences while she stayed at the island home. Events had progressed to such an extent that Gail had decided to move back to Sydney. When Clarice informed her sister of the new direction her employer had taken with his business; namely, the newly-formed and renamed Bizarre and Mysterious Detective Agency or B.A.M., as it was shortened to, she leapt at the opportunity to hire the detective to investigate the goings-on at their island home.

It had taken all of Clarice's considerably persuasive powers to convince her husband-to-be to take on a new direction following the semi-successful conclusion of their previous assignment. Arlon's unique qualities made it a perfect fit in Clarice's mind. While their previous engagement would have been a spectacular disaster in the eyes of most, it had turned out in their favour financially and fortuitously, as far as Clarice was concerned.

No longer viewed in the conservative light he would have preferred, Arlon came out of the debacle with a new reputation and a strange following among the darker, more obscure proponents of the macabre and mysterious who frequent the internet to chat among themselves. Introduced to the underworld of the occult and other happenings in which he was a fledgling virgin, Arlon was convinced by Clarice of the lucrative business to be made from that niche.

The Bizarre and Mysterious Detective Agency was born shortly thereafter, with Arlon accepting their first brief to investigate the suspicious circumstances surrounding the death of his fiancée's brother-in-law. Clarice also saw it as an excellent opportunity to test the waters of their unproven relationship.

Her proposal to him had come at a vulnerable moment when he was caught completely off-guard. The acceptance arrived at an equally vulnerable moment; post-coitally, while deep in the throes of ex-virginal ecstasy. She'd held slim hopes for her chances of ever luring the man she secretly loved into bed, let alone convincing him of marriage. Because of his condition, he was unable to respond in a normal sense. Alexithymia prevented him from expressing or experiencing emotions; both a curse and a blessing at times. It was a rare piece of the autism puzzle and Arlon was rated in the highest percentile among the afflicted.

If Arlon kept hold of his tongue he could be mistaken for a dashing film star, with his blue-black wavy hair and cobalt-blue eyes that pierced the soul of any female who happened to come under their gaze. But opening his mouth was usually sufficient to sour the opinion of the most ardent admirer.

"I'm off to bed," said Arlon, the moment they entered the stylish beach 'shack'.

"Arlon! No, you can't mean that!" exclaimed Clarice as she followed him through the front door.

"You should know better than that."

"Yeah, I get it, you always say what you mean. I was just voicing my shock, that's all. It's two o'clock in the afternoon and you want to go to bed? Arlon, we've arrived at possibly one of the world's most idyllic destinations for romance and pure tranquillity and all you can think of is going to sleep?" Clarice asked in desperation, as she struggled with some of their luggage.

"I thought we were here to do a job?"

"That, too," she admitted. "Here, take this through to the bedroom, would you? How come you gave me your heavy case while you took mine?"

"I didn't give it to you. You almost shouldered me out of the way to get hold of it, if my memory serves."

"How was I to know you loaded *my* suitcase with *your* gear?"

"You weren't."

"Exactly!"

"Your point?"

"Why did you?"

"Yours is bigger than mine and I needed the space more than you," he explained in a deadpan tone.

"How come?"

"How come, what?"

"Why did you need more space than me?"

"I have more stuff. I would have thought that was obvious."

"Don't tell me you brought all your safari suits and that ridiculous pith helmet?"

"Of course," said Arlon, as he proceeded to relieve Clarice of the heavy case, which he transported to the main bedroom of the three-bedroomed house.

"Well, why, for goodness sake?" she asked, following him. "Arlon, we're on an island, completely alone, secluded in our very own little bay. Why would you need to bring your Livingstone costume?"

"It's a practical ensemble for venturing into the wilds. I prefer to be covered and protected at all times, Clarice."

"It doesn't bother you that you look like a fool wearing that silly outfit?"

"Of course not. Nothing bothers me, you know that."

"I thought we might have some fresh fish for dinner tonight," suggested Clarice, boldly changing the subject.

"That sounds fine. What's stopping you?"

"You haven't caught it yet."

"Caught what?"

"Dinner!"

"You can't be serious."

"Why not?"

"Me? Catch a fish?"

"Haven't you ever gone fishing?"

"You know how I am about the water."

"I don't get that. I've seen you face up to some pretty tough dangers without blinking an eye. You say you don't have fear because that is an emotion, so why are you afraid of the water?"

"I don't *fear* the water. I don't even fear what's in the water. I just don't wish to be on the menu, that's all. The sharks don't come on land where I live and I, in turn, do not enter the water where they live."

"It's the fishing *line* that goes into the water, Arlon, not the fisherperson. Are you saying you lived on the beach as a child and never went fishing?"

"No."

"Well, then?"

"What?"

"Off you go and catch our dinner. You'll find all the equipment you need in the shed at the back of the house, according to Gail. Bait is in the freezer. Apart from a decent sunhat, I want you out there in some shorts and a T-shirt, Arlon. Thongs on your feet if you must;

other than those items, nothing. I want you to get some sun onto that magnificent body of yours."

"Is that the shed where...?"

"Yes, but don't even think about starting work yet, mister. I want you all to myself for our first day here. Tomorrow you can begin your investigations."

"I don't think your sister is paying us to have a day off."

"Gail told me we should have some leisure time while we investigate her husband's grisly death. The police haven't gotten any further, and she needs us to bring her some closure, but she expects us to enjoy some of our time together on a pristine island. Besides, she has oodles of dosh coming to her from her mother-in-law's passing. This island home is only the tip of the iceberg."

"Does she own the entire island?"

"No. In fact, she doesn't own anything. She inherited the remains of a ninety-nine-year lease on this bay. It has less than thirty years left on it, with the option to renew once it expires. The home was built by Patricia Sandringham and her husband, Conrad, in the fifties as a holiday getaway. When her husband fell from the rocks on the point fifteen years ago, she seldom ventured back here. Ben began visiting the island on his own. When she became gravely ill, she never returned."

"Then one year ago Ben Sandringham dies in...unique circumstances?"

"Uh, uh, not going to happen, Mr Detective. I have to get us squared away in here and you are on strict orders to provide dinner and get some sun. In other words, relax. Shoo!"

Arlon managed to snag hold of a straw hat as he was unceremoniously ushered out of the back door after changing. It was only when he placed the hat on his head that Arlon realised it was about three sizes too large. He had to hold his head back at an awkward angle to see where he was going. He walked along the shaded, sandy path toward the large shed at the rear of the property housing the diesel generator, miscellaneous machinery and a mechanical workshop. It was where Ben Sandringham's body was discovered. At least, what was left of it.

Lining the pathway on either side were the ubiquitous collections derived from frequent beachcombing expeditions: clam shells, driftwood in interesting shapes and sizes, rocks and other items, presumably found by the Sandringham family during their regular visits. Interspersed between the odd assortments were the solar bollards lighting the path at night in differing hues to create a festive atmosphere, so Arlon was told. He did not understand how coloured lights could add anything of value to any situation. Parties, festivities, gatherings...*holidays* (albeit working holidays) were completely lost on him. Arlon's condition deprived him of many normal associations taken for granted by everyone else. He derived no pleasure from the company of others, no enjoyment of his surroundings nor any other emotions of a positive or negative kind.

Arlon recalled his parents' sadness and frustration when they were unable to receive love from their only son. His time spent with them at the seaside residence of his youth did not conjure happy memories, nor even laughter and enjoyment where his parents were concerned. The harder they tried to gain some emotions from their son, the worse it became for them: they sank further and further into depression. Rather than accepting their son's condition and learning to live with it as best they could, they had made it their impossible mission in life to break through to him.

The shell did not crack, the emotions did not flow, and their family fell apart. They provided for him, saw that Arlon had the best schooling they could afford, but grew sullen with their disappointment, eventually blocking him out altogether. They no longer felt guilt that they had somehow contributed to their son's condition. That had been disproved by the diagnosis. However, when they refused to accept that they could not get through to him, it caused them more and more grief.

The large, insulated shed of corrugated iron exterior and sound-proofing interior, loomed at the end of the path. Gail Sandringham had sent a mechanic to service the generator and ensure that all was in working order before her sister and Arlon arrived. Arlon could hear the dull thrum of the generator, despite all the effort to suppress the noise. He felt the vibrations through the soles of his Dunlop Volleys as he approached the heavy, latched door.

A pair of seagulls in the treetops above him squawked their protest at his intrusion into their midst. Arlon peered up through the dappled light, wondering if the birds had built a nest above him. Then he wondered if seagulls nested in trees at all. He felt sure he had read that they nested on the ground, mainly among the low shrubs and other vegetation adorning the dunes. This was just one of the many useless facts running around Arlon's mind, garnered from a troubling childhood spent almost entirely on his own, reading everything of a factual nature he could lay his hands on.

To either side of the doorway rested a sentinel pair of large, barnacle and oyster-encrusted boulders. It would have taken quite some effort to move the rocks there from where they were presumably found on the beach. Arlon pondered the possible reason anyone would go to all the trouble to line the path with debris and to haul huge rocks from the sea. It didn't make any sense to him. As he drew near the door, reaching out to release the latch, Arlon suddenly retracted his outstretched hand.

He peered about him with a look of concern creasing his handsome features. If asked to describe what he was experiencing, he would have had some difficulty. It was as if there was a drop in pressure about him. He wondered if perhaps it was the precursor of an impending earthquake. He had read that some people claim to experience an increase or decrease in seismicity before an earthquake. It was very brief and Arlon dismissed his initial assertions. He unlatched the door, stepping through into the gloomy interior, where the deafening sound of the generator pulsed and pounded the senses.

While he was sorely tempted to poke around to get a head start on his investigations, he dismissed the notion in favour of appeasing his wife-to-be. She could get very upset if Arlon chose to ignore her wishes to relax and catch dinner. He found the light switch on the inside of the door frame and flicked it on.

To the left of the entry was a small area given over to housing fishing rods in overhead racks, benches and sinks for cleaning fish and tending to tackle and other assorted paraphernalia. A chest freezer gave off a pungent fishy odour when he lifted the lid. He retrieved a plastic bag of frozen prawns from it. He then chose a suitable beach rod with a side casting reel. He was familiar with the operation of that particular type, which resembled a handheld reel mounted on a rod.

A wicker creel, a small tackle box with sufficient hooks and sinkers, along with a filleting knife and a hook remover, completed his provisioning. He gave one last look around the cavernous interior before switching off the light and closing the door as he exited the shed. Relieved to be away from the imposing noise, Arlon made his way along the path, then veered around the house to head for the beach.

Things had certainly changed for Arlon since his last assignment for a long-time friend and client. The job had not ended well. In fact, it spelled the final days for his conservative detective agency. While he had rescued a woman and been paid handsomely for the effort, the notoriety he gained did not bode well for that kind of business any longer. Once he had agreed to marry Clarice, his secretary and assistant of a couple of years, she nudged their agency into a very new and, to Arlon, totally foreign, direction.

Clarice had been an aficionado of the bizarre and weird for some time as she trawled through the internet for stories that few believed. Her hunger for the obscure involved her in many chat groups with fellow conspirators. When it seemed obvious that Arlon's conservative agency would no longer gain sufficient contracts to keep the business afloat, Clarice threw him in the deep end with his first serious client seeking answers to a grave mystery.

The entrance onto the grand vista once he was over the dunes cut short Arlon's reveries. The sun was high in the sky. The snow-white sand leading down to the mirror-like waters of the tranquil bay would take anyone's breath away. For Arlon, it did nothing more than affirm his wish to be anywhere but there. From under a coconut palm marking the beginning of the path to the house through the dunes, Arlon retrieved a lightweight, foldable, reclining chair.

He made his way down to the water's edge, where he set up his chair at the appropriate angle to relax while keeping an eye on his fishing rod. He deftly baited the single suicide hook with a decent-sized, sufficiently-thawed prawn, twisted the reel to face the tip of the rod and then let fly with the weighted line to a distance of some thirty metres from the shoreline. From one of his shirt pockets, he retrieved a tube of zinc cream to spread onto his nose.

He placed the handle of the rod into the metal rod holder he had spiked into the soft sand beside his chair, then reclined comfortably. The boredom hit him almost the moment he sat down, with his eyelids beginning to sag. The warm sun lulled his body into an immediate snooze. Fortunately, he had had the foresight to set the drag on his reel correctly, for, moments after he subsided into slumber, the reel began to scream as the line ran out.

Reflexively, Arlon's hand shot out to the rod and reel, which he removed quickly from the holder. Before he had time to consciously decide upon a course of action, he reared back on the rod to set the hook firmly into the mouth of the fish. Rising from the recliner, Arlon began the process of raising the rod to drag the large fish in by a metre before winding up the gain as he dropped the tip once more. This action was repeated many times as the large pelagic was brought slowly to the shore.

The GT, or giant trevally, weighed about fifteen kilos and Arlon was feeling the strain on his muscles after landing the fish. Satisfied that he had caught dinner, he set about returning to the house. The heavy fish and the other fishing gear made the trip back a slower one with a few rest stops.

At the shed, he placed the fish on the stainless steel sink, ready for cleaning, filleting and deboning. Unlike their non-pelagic cousins, from which a nice clean, boneless slab of flesh was possible, a pelagic had to have a centre, lateral line of bones removed.

Arlon placed the rod and reel back into its rack, then distributed the remaining gear to the places they belonged. He then washed down the fish with fresh water. He decided that Clarice would have the honour of dressing the fish, as he had done all the hard work in catching it. As he left the shed he once more felt that WHUMP he had experienced earlier, only intensified. It was a gut-somersaulting feeling almost like the experience of descending quickly on an elevator. It lasted only milliseconds, yet made him look about uncertainly, wondering if he was imagining it.

Glad to be out of the noisy shed once more, Arlon made his way back to the house, where Clarice was still packing clothes into a chest of drawers.

"Back so soon?"

"You asked me to catch dinner; I did. You didn't say anything about staying out there a certain length of time."

Clarice stared at him to ascertain if he was telling the truth.

"You telling me you already caught our dinner?"

"Yep."

"Well?"

"Well, what?"

"Where is it?"

"In the shed, waiting for you to clean and fillet it."

"I don't believe it."

"Why would I lie?"

"I can't believe you would leave it to me to clean and fillet the fish. Why wouldn't you do it and bring in for me to cook?"

"Surely I don't have to do everything?"

"Ooh, you're sounding more like a husband every day," she sighed. "Go on, then, wipe that silly cream off your nose and I'll go out and slave over *your* fish."

"Aren't *you* eating any, then?" he asked pointedly.

"Arlon, I swear..."

"You do not."

"I bloody do!" she admonished, before stomping off through the rear door to the shed.

When Arlon returned from the bathroom after cleaning his face, Clarice was in the living room.

"Well, that was quick. See? I was right to let you clean and fillet the fish if you were that quick," suggested Arlon, as he sat heavily on the cane sofa with coastal pattern print cushions.

"Very funny. Why don't you take up comedy as your next gig?"

Arlon looked at her with surprise, "I don't get it. Why would I want to take up comedy? I have a perfectly good job..."

"Give it up, Mr Funny Man. I knew it was too quick for you to be back. Did you decide against fish for dinner?"

"What are you talking about, Clarice? I caught..."

"Hey, enough with the jokes already. I'm not amused, Arlon, okay? I was hoping we could have a lovely fresh fish dinner out there under the stars. I think there's even a full moon tonight."

"Well?"

"Well, what?" said Clarice, with an angry face and her hands on her ample hips.

"What's wrong with the fish I caught?"

"Where is this mysterious fish you caught?"

"Clarice, have you been drinking? I left it on the sink in the shed. If you really don't want to clean it up, then just say so."

"On the sink?"

"Clarice, are you getting hard of hearing? Yes, on the sink."

TWO

Resting on the stainless steel sink in the noisy, intensely hot shed was the object causing consternation for Arlon and Clarice. Before leaving the shed earlier, Arlon had marvelled at the fish's tenacious grip on life, still gasping for air and flopping about atop the sink. As he stared at the fossilised form that replaced living flesh only moments ago, he began to wonder what they had stumbled upon.

"Where the heck did you manage to get this thing, anyway?" asked Clarice, shouting to be heard over the thrumming generator.

"From the ocean, like I told you," answered Arlon reluctantly.

"What, you found it?"

"I wasn't fibbing, Clarice. I caught it. It took some effort to land this monster."

"Arlon, that's just not...you *have* to be fibbing."

"Clarice, examine the inside of the mouth."

Clarice bent lower to peer inside the wide maw. When she could not quite believe what she was seeing, she looked a little closer.

"Well?" asked Arlon.

"Something metal in there."

"Right, stainless steel actually; namely, a fish hook. How long do you think it takes for a fish to become petrified like that, Clarice?"

"I don't know. Thousands of years probably?"

"Probably. Way before stainless steel came about, don't you think? I couldn't quite dislodge the hook embedded in the fish's mouth, so I cut the line. You can still see the end of the line hanging from the hook's loop. Even if the hook was around for all those years, the nylon line would no longer be there. It would have disintegrated. How possible is it to even get a perfectly preserved modern fish like that? Were giant trevally around back then?"

"Can we get out of here? I can't think for all the..."

Just then the generator stopped and the lights blinked out. The sudden and foreboding silence had Clarice wishing for a return of the noise. They exited the shed through the heavy door into the dappled sunshine once more.

"Well, that was freaky. Gail said she had a mechanic come in last week to service the generator and top up the fuel."

"Somehow, I don't think this has anything to do with the condition of the generator or the fuel supply. Something odd is happening here. I sensed something before the onset of these occurrences. I felt it before and just now again."

"What was it you felt?"

"Not that I have any experience in it, but it felt like a sudden drop in pressure. People are said to feel it before an earthquake."

"And you think it has something to do with what happened to Gail's husband?" asked Clarice with rising concern.

"He was found just inside the shed there, you said?"

"According to the police report."

"Yes, I read the report."

"Ghastly way to go."

"Impossible, I would have said."

"Not impossible if it happened and we have the proof. You saw the photos, heard what Gail said on the phone when she discovered..."

"Half a body?"

"Yes. How could that even happen? I mean sliced like that, so cleanly?"

"Puzzling, to say the least. Even laser implements leave evidence of their use, such as searing. The surgical precision of the bisection is not possible, according to the medical examiner. It would be difficult enough to perform a horizontal bisection of the human body in the manner it was done, let alone the perfectly divided vertical separation that occurred. The flawless cross-section is indicative of a specimen sample in normal circumstances, something we would see in a forensic laboratory for the study of human organs and the like.

"What's more perplexing, however, was the *missing* half. According to the experts, there was no sign of the right side of the body, none. The amount of blood discovered around the remaining half accounted for approximately half of the average human content for a man the size of your brother-in-law."

"I'm scared, Arlon."

"Really? I thought you enjoyed the macabre and mysterious? Don't you venture into the realms of the inexplicable in your nightly forays on the web? Isn't that the direction you wanted for our little agency, even calling it that ridiculous name?"

"You didn't think it was so ridiculous when it landed us our first lucrative case."

"Something tells me we would have secured your sister as a client without the name. Bizarre and Mysterious Detective Agency: I mean, really? It makes *us* out to be the bizarre and mysterious ones, not the cases."

"Well, where you're concerned it's not so misleading," Clarice barked.

"Wow, that was a low blow."

"Ooh, sorry..."

"No need for an apology. It didn't bother me. I just made an observation about your character, that's all."

"No one forced you to accept the name, and I was only trying to help," said Clarice sadly.

"I probably deserved the criticism, Clarice. I know I'm not an easy person to like. God only knows why you asked me to marry you."

"Arlon, it just seemed to me that you have a positive quality for the type of clientele we are likely to meet. Your cynical, logical mind and total lack of emotions mean you're perfect to handle these types. They have nowhere else to go. No one else believes them, or they get judged so harshly that the clients drop the cases altogether."

"Nutcases, in other words."

"If that's how you choose to see me and my sister, that's up to you, I suppose."

"In light of the evidence and our own experiences within such a short time of landing here, I'll retract that statement, if you'll take my word for it that I caught that fish from the ocean only a short time ago, alive and kicking?"

"Could be a stonefish," suggested Clarice with a smirk.

"How droll."

"What now?"

"I don't know. Why don't you call your sister and ask her if there's been any seismic activity in the area? Ask her how long it's been going for if she gives a positive reply."

"You think it could be building up to a big one? That these signs are precursors?"

"Following one line of thought only, Clarice. Don't read too much into it."

Just as Clarice was about to answer a loud rumble signified the generator starting up automatically. Although muffled to a degree by the heavily insulated shed, it was uncomfortably loud following the total silence. Clarice marched through the shed door, returning soon after with fishing equipment.

"Where are you going?"

"Wow, and you call yourself a detective. Someone has to catch our dinner and I guess that's me."

Clarice tromped past Arlon, who was staring at her with a look of bemusement. Clarice had changed from her floral frock to a pair of cut-off jeans and a white T-shirt. Arlon had noted earlier that she wore no bra beneath. He could feel the now-familiar stirring in his groin as he watched her plentiful behind in the tight shorts, strutting past the house.

Clarice's figure could arguably be described as 'big-boned', rather than be labelled obese. Arlon supposed she was pretty in a rough, tomboyish way. She certainly wasn't genteel and delicate, but exuded warmth and affection, which was ultimately wasted on Arlon. She represented his sole venture into the world of sex. If she hadn't instigated their first act of love-making he would still be a virgin at an age which some would have deemed impossible in the modern era.

He still found it odd that his body responded at all. He had mistakenly believed that without emotions involved it would not be feasible for him to perform the act. He'd discussed it with Clarice a few times. He ardently adhered to the principle that it shouldn't be possible for him to make love to anyone, only to have her prove otherwise as she deftly manipulated parts of his body to respond to her seductive touches.

Arlon still didn't understand anything about relationships or how they survived the vicissitudes of human behaviour. Clarice had demonstrated this only a few moments ago. One instant she was angry and pious, the next smiling and compliant, then seemingly indifferent to anything Arlon said.

Then he heard the scream.

As he reached the top of the dune he wondered what could have occurred in the short time they had been apart. If it kept up, there would be no such thing as the relaxation she had planned for them.

Arlon saw Clarice backing away from the edge of the water, leaving the rod on the beach with the gentle waves lapping over it. Arlon could not immediately see the cause of her distress. She was alone on the beach, as was expected. It was only when he looked out into the bay that Arlon learned the reason for the scream.

Shark!

Well, sharks, plural. Hundreds and hundreds of fins slicing through the calm waters of the bay, joined by hundreds more as they crossed the outer reef from the open ocean. By the time Arlon reached Clarice's side, there were thousands of sharks of every variety churning the water with their frenetic movements.

"Good luck getting a fish out of there in one piece."

"That, that's not funny, Arlon," said Clarice, clearly shaken by the sight.

"I'd better get that rod before the..."

"Arlon, no!"

"Why not?"

"Th-them! That's why not. Look at them all."

"They're not about to come ashore, Clarice."

"Ooh, I've seen the documentaries of those buggers washing themselves upon the shore to get the baby seals," whispered Clarice.

"Clarice, they were killer whales and there aren't any bloody seals here."

"No, there are big juicy humans for them to eat. Arlon, they're massive, some of them."

"They still can't walk on land, though."

"Nothing would surprise me at the moment. Forget the fish. I'll cook us up a T-bone steak on the barbeque, with some fresh salad."

"You'd be missing an amazing opportunity to witness something truly unique, Clarice."

"This is not unique, Arlon. It's...unnatural, is what it is."

"You think sharks are unnatural?"

"No, just this behaviour."

"There are many recorded incidents of sharks gathering in large numbers, Clarice. Besides, if it was something out of the ordinary, wouldn't you be excited by that? I thought you liked all that sort of weird stuff."

"I, I don't like sharks."

"Well, neither do I. That's why I have no intention of going for a swim right now. It's why I don't like being on the water at any time. But I'm not worried by them while my feet remain on terra-firma."

"I don't like what's happening here, Arlon. Can we leave, please?"

"Exactly how do you think we can accomplish that task?" asked Arlon cryptically.

"What do you mean?"

"Notice anything missing?"

Clarice screwed up her features in consternation, "Arlon, make sense, would..."

That was when she realised what Arlon meant. She scanned the water with the profusion of shark fins swirling about the uncommonly calm bay. With dismay, she understood their predicament, but did not understand how it was possible.

"What could have happened to it?" whispered Clarice.

"Why are you whispering?"

"Someone could hear?"

"Who, the sharks?"

"No, dear, whoever took the bloody boat, of course!" exclaimed Clarice in frustration.

"If someone took the boat then they wouldn't be here, would they?"

"Oh, to buggery with your calm logic, this is serious, Arlon."

"I thought you said my calm logic is exactly what was required for our new direction?"

"This is different."

"I see. So I should be panicking?"

"No."

"Then?"

"Arlon, stop it! I'm frightened, show some...oh, stupid me. You can't. That's right. What are you going to do about finding our boat, Mister Smarty-pants?"

"Nothing."

"Nothing? Giving up already?"

"No. Simply that investigation is not required in this instance."

"Why, for goodness sake?"

"Because I know where some of the boat is," explained Arlon.

"Some of it? What the hell does that mean?" cried Clarice.

"Calm down, Clarice. You'll burst a blood vessel or something.

If you go to the top of the dune there, you'll understand what I'm saying."

"Just explain it, Arlon. I'm not in the mood for guessing games right now."

"Ever heard the expression that a picture paints a thousand words?"

When Arlon saw the murderous glint appear in Clarice's enigmatic eyes, he backed off a step and raised his arms in surrender.

"Okay, okay, don't get your knickers in a knot. At the bottom of the bay rests what remains of our hire vessel. I estimate about a third at most."

"You mean our boat blew up or caught fire? I didn't hear or smell anything."

"No, nor would you. Cut clean through by the look of it. If you have a gander at those rocks over there you'll note the oil slick? Much less than you would expect from the two Mercury outboards, I would imagine. Only a third is visible at the remains of the transom. The cabin is gone completely. That's probably why nothing is floating around on the surface."

"We're completely alone here with no way off?"

"We still have the tender," replied Arlon, lifting his chin toward the small landing craft resting at the highwater mark.

"No way am I getting in that tiny thing with all those sharks out there."

"I wouldn't have suggested it even if there were no sharks. Gets pretty rough between here and the mainland, even on a relatively calm day."

"What are we going to do?"

"Finish our job and earn our fee. It's not like we're marooned, Clarice. We have our mobile phones if they're still working. All we need to do is call up the owner of the boat so he can get some insurance going and make arrangements with them to get us off the island."

"You mean you want to stay here?" Clarice asked incredulously.

"Aren't you intrigued? I haven't heard of any scientific breakthrough into converting the molecular structure of organic matter..."

"Ah, English, please?"

"Turning fish to stone."

"You couldn't just say that?"

"I just did."

"Go on," said Clarice, sighing impatiently.

"Well, it would be a great discovery to find out how that was achieved, wouldn't you say?"

"If we don't get cut in half in the process, sure."

"Let's go back up to the house. I want you to give your sister a call and find out if anything changed from before her husband met with the...incident. Ask her if she has before and after pictures we could examine. She may not know what to look for."

"And we do?"

"Not specifically, no. It might help if fresh eyes looked at it from that angle, though. I'm pretty sure the police won't have thought about it from that point of view. It's not the sort of thing that was drilled into us at the academy."

"That's right, you were a copper once, weren't you?"

"Yep. I think they had a party among themselves when I was finally told to leave."

"Aww, poor Arlon. Did they give you a hard time?"

"Oh, I got the usual snickers and derogatory comments that I get from everyone I meet. No one knows how to handle my condition and my bluntness almost always sees me saying the exact wrong thing at the worst possible time."

"No shit, Sherlock," said Clarice, with a roll of the eyes.

"You still want to get married?"

"Yeah."

"Keep that up and you'll be waiting a bloody long time!"

Arlon did his best to keep a straight face as he twirled about to march off in the direction of the house, leaving Clarice behind with a stunned expression.

"Arlon? Arlon?" she called as she hurried to catch up with him.

THREE

"Isn't there anything you can remember that was different, sis?" Clarice asked her sister Gail on her mobile that was tuned to speakerphone so that Arlon could join in.

"You've seen the photos. I took the first set about three months before Ben passed away..." There was a brief silence as Gail's voice caught in her throat. "The others I took after all the police tape and everything was taken down and the whole place was cleaned up. I thought about selling it."

"Why didn't you, Mrs Sandringham?"

"Oh, is that you, Arlon? I didn't realise I was speaking to both of you. About time I met this man of yours, Clarry. Um, to answer your question, Arlon, I just couldn't. Ben and I lived there for about six months after he semi-retired. It was probably the happiest time of my life until... I couldn't bear to part with it, Arlon, but I also can't go back there without some answers."

"Mrs Sandring..."

"Now, Arlon, we're practically family. Won't you call me Gail?"

"Oh sis, I have a hard enough time getting him to call *me* by my first name. Don't hold your breath, okay?"

"That's not a very kind thing to say, Clarry. Where have your manners gone?"

"Arlon isn't offended, Gail. Spend more than the length of a phone call with him and you'll wish he was calling you by your formal title again. You would probably lose your temper before the conversation ended."

"I'm happy to call you by your first name, Gail. Pay attention to your sister, though, I'm much worse than she makes out. I am not a people person, that's for sure."

"Why on earth are you two getting married? Oh, that was rude of *me*, now. None of my business; please don't answer that. Anyway, I can't think of anything different, Arlon. Nothing that would explain the incident."

"I didn't ask you that. I don't want you to use your inadequate judgement to eliminate anything. I asked if there was anything,

anything at all different from the first time you stayed on the island to the time your husband was cut in half."

"Arlon! How dare you?"

"What?"

"See what I mean, sis? He's a fabulous man until you spend some time in his company and he opens his bloody trap to remove his size ten foot."

"I was just..."

"Being you, yes, I know. Doesn't excuse it, though."

"It's all right, Clarry. I have to get used to it sooner or later. I've done all the crying I aim to. He's right; it's time for tough, no-nonsense questions if we're going to get to the bottom of this. Arlon, there is nothing that I can think of."

"It was a long shot. I just wondered if we might explore the possibility that something you guys did or saw might give us a clue."

"We didn't do much at all while we were there the last time. Lazed about and went for long walks down the beach, mostly. The time before that we collected all the stones and driftwood to line the pathway at the back of the house. That was fun. We painted them white last year, Arlon. Does that help you at all?"

"Not unless you acquired some radioactive paint or something."

"From our local hardware store in Sydney? Not unless he gets his supplies from Chernobyl. Besides, last I heard, radiation poisoning won't do what happened to Ben."

"As far as I know there is nothing at all capable of doing that, Gail," explained Arlon carefully.

"Well, I have to disagree with you there. There *was* something capable of doing that and much more, according to what you said happened earlier. Do you need me to send a rescue ship?"

"Not necessary yet, Gail."

"Speak for yourself, bucko!"

"No one's stopping you if you want to go, Clarice."

"You mean you're staying?"

"Absolutely. I wouldn't be much of a detective if I ran away each time something odd occurred."

"Odd! Jeez, that's understating it."

"She's right, Arlon. I wouldn't want anything to happen to either of you. Losing my husband was more than enough."

"If you honestly thought that way you wouldn't have asked us for help. Considering how your husband perished, there was always going to be an element of danger involved."

"Holy crap, Arlon! That's going too far."

"He's right, Clarry. It was inconsiderate of me to place you in harm's way. I wouldn't go there and yet I said my sister could. It's on me if something happens. I'll send a ship..."

"No, only if Clarice wants to go. I was hired to do a job and we allowed ourselves a week to investigate. I intend to stay until at least then."

"I should have warned you that he's as stubborn as a mule as well, Gail."

"Arlon, I understand and respect your conviction and the fact that you're honouring our contract, but I'm releasing you of all obligations. I don't want anyone to get hurt on my behalf, especially now that you tell me other strange things are happening there."

"If we come across anything too dangerous for us to handle we'll take you up on your offer. I'm fascinated by it all, to tell you the truth."

"Take care of my sister, Arlon. She's the only sister I have left. I need her on my side when it comes to our brothers. And I want to see a niece or nephew sometime soon."

"Jeez, sis!"

"Bye."

"Bye, Gail."

Clarice shut down the call with a sigh. They were sitting in the living room, which was decorated in a bright coastal motif of palm tree wallpaper and seagrass matting. The cane sofa on which they sat sported similar coastal prints on the oversized, comfortable cushions. Large ceiling fans circulated the fresh sea breezes wafting in through the front door and open windows. Shadows crept into the home as the sun began to descend.

Clarice rose and walked to the open-plan kitchen with its large island bench surrounded by cane stools with rattan backing. Without a word, she started preparing the night's meal. She was no longer excited about the prospect of their first night together signifying the sharing of a home. In Brisbane, where they both lived, she still maintained a small flat near Kangaroo Point, with a view of the iconic Story Bridge.

Arlon owned a small, neat home in Indooroopilly and had not

yet invited her to move in with him. On their last assignment, she had asked Arlon to marry her. While he had agreed to the request, he had not yet named a date nor made any effort to welcome her to his life. She peered over at the handsome man, tall, wiry and very strong, with the most striking eyes she had ever seen. She knew he didn't love her. She knew he was incapable of love or any other emotion. She had forced herself to deflect notions of that ilk. She had to constantly remind herself that she should never entertain the notion of him changing or of her attempting to bring out his feelings. He'd had that with his parents and did not deserve more of the same from his future wife.

To look at Arlon, he appeared to be the stuff of every woman's dreams. She became hot and moist just thinking about him being with her, feeling that superbly-toned body on and in her. She had admired him in their office for over a year before she invited herself out to a property inspection for a long-time client and solicitor friend. The job had been a bust from the start. It turned out the prospective owners had already purchased the property and everything Arlon was hired to do was completely unnecessary. The fact that their lives were endangered by the assignment, and that Arlon had heroically saved them all, did not prevent them from being forced to abandon their regular activities because of the bad publicity.

She watched surreptitiously as Arlon remained seated on the sofa, oblivious to the embarrassing comment made by her sister about children, unoffended by anything that happened or was ever said about him or to him, and obnoxious in most of his responses to other human beings. Not for the first time did Clarice seriously question her motives and her impulsiveness in asking him to be her husband. Not for the last time, she conceded that what she felt for him was something she had never experienced before. It was powerful and overwhelming at times.

When Arlon turned to look at her with a slight smile, it immediately melted her heart.

"You're crying," said Arlon, in a matter-of-fact tone.

"Onions," explained Clarice falsely.

She had shed many a tear lately when she thought about their complicated and ridiculous lives. It seemed all too preposterous on occasions, while at others it seemed as though they were made for one another.

Arlon had a brilliant mind, honed to a sharp degree in the school of hard life, and by endless hours spent reading everything non-fiction he could lay his hands on. It was his way of escaping the torture of coping with being a freak from an early age.

It was never easy for anyone meeting Arlon for the first time. His total lack of any emotion, empathy or sympathy usually attracted all the wrong responses, especially when he opened his mouth. Arlon admitted to her that he had to learn from an early age to defend himself against physical attacks. He poured his energies into the martial arts and could pretty well beat most of his opponents by the age of five. He was a black belt in many disciplines, often having reached the highest rank possible.

Clarice ruminated on all the benefits and disadvantages of being hopelessly in love as she cooked their simple fare of steaks and salad. Arlon had told her he liked his meat 'dead' before he deigned to eat it. This meant he preferred a well-done steak, whereas Clarice loved her meat seared and sealed to leave a pink perfection within. She placed Arlon's steak in the griddle pan a good five minutes before her own, ensuring that both would be ready at approximately the same time. Just as she was about to pick up her raw steak, her eyes were drawn to the large window in the front of the house which she and Arlon had recently unshuttered.

Arlon turned suddenly when he heard the small yelp escaping Clarice's lips. The fork fell to the concrete floor with a loud clatter. Clarice stood frozen to the spot behind the large island bench while staring agape at the window. When Arlon turned his gaze onto the window, he could see nothing alarming.

"Clarice? What is it? What's wrong?" he asked calmly.

"A face! A man. I saw..."

There was a light knock on the door. Arlon rose to answer it.

"Arlon, don't," cried Clarice in alarm.

"Why not?"

"It could be dangerous. He might have a gun," she warned.

"If that was the case I'm pretty sure he wouldn't be knocking on the door, Clarice."

"We're supposed to be alone here," said Clarice, picking up a knife with which to defend them.

"Obviously that isn't the case. Put the knife down, Clarice, you'll end up hurting yourself. Whoever it is wouldn't be politely knocking on the door if their intentions were evil," declared Arlon, as he walked a couple of paces to the front door and opened it.

Standing in the halo of the exterior light was a man of advanced years with a dishevelled appearance. His long, lustreless hair hung to his shoulders in unkempt bangs beginning to take on the look of dreadlocks. His weather-beaten face told the tale of an outdoorsman who toiled for a living. His clothes were all but rags hanging loosely on his emaciated frame. Arlon recoiled at the smell emanating from the filthy man.

"Sorry, folks. Didn't mean ta barge in like and startle ya. Saw ya comin' in this arvo on that boat. Hopin' I could maybe get a lift back with yiz if ya going anytime soon?"

"Probably not, as our boat is resting on the bottom of the bay. What's left of it, anyway," replied Arlon, stepping back a pace to be out of the way of the horrendous odour.

"Got ya, too, did it?" asked the man, wringing his gnarled and calloused hands.

"Did what get us, too?" asked Arlon.

"The island. Got me a month ago, or near enough. Took me bloody boat! All I had in the world, that fishing boat."

"Why don't you come in...?"

"Clarice, no! He pongs to high heaven."

"Arlon Grey! Stop being so rude. Sorry, mister...?" said Clarice, as she moved around the bench.

"Can call me Freddy, miss. He's right enough, though, miss. I am on the nose. Haven't washed for all the time I bin here."

"Plenty of water out there," suggested Arlon.

"Oh, Arlon, really! You'd best ignore everything he says, Freddy. He only opens his mouth to change feet. The worst case of foot-in-mouth disease you've ever come across."

"Ya see them sharks, mate? Come in every afternoon they do, when they aren't circlin' the bloody island makin' sure a body don't have no ideas about leavin' the cursed island. Not gonna have no wash with them in there, no way! Rather go dirty than dead," declared Freddy, with a proud shake of the head.

"You look positively starved, Freddy."

"Yeah, miss, I am that n-all. Smelled them onions a-cookin' way afore I got here. Been livin' hard, I has. Nothin' but grubs and a few bird eggs. Normally I'd catch a mess-o-fish for me supper, but me lines all got took with the boat. Lucky ta be alive, I is."

"Well, how about you have some dinner with us then?" asked Clarice generously, with a huge smile.

"Not smelling like that he won't, Clarice. I'm just about vomiting in my mouth now!"

"Well, a bath and some fresh clothes will soon sort that out, won't it?" said Clarice, showing a ramrod straight back that brooked no defiance from Arlon.

"I'd be right obliged if I could get cleaned up, miss..."

"Clarice. My name is Clarice Manning and this is Arlon Grey, the rude one."

"Freddy. Freddy Boggs, ma'am, "said Freddy, knuckling his brow in the way of old seafarers.

"C'mon then, I'll show you where the bathroom is. I'll have to get some Solvol, Freddy. I know my sister keeps a few bars around here somewhere. Nothing gets through grit and grime quite like a bar of Solvol," declared Clarice, as she led the rake-thin man through the house to the rear.

"I hope you're not thinking of giving him any of my clothes?" asked Arlon on her return.

"Already got him some duds from the master bedroom. Must have been my brother-in-law's. I'm surprised Gail hasn't got rid of them yet."

"Won't fit that bloke," mumbled Arlon.

"Well, I don't think his own clothes would fit him anymore. He's lost a lot of weight pretty quickly. He said he's been here a month. Poor bugger."

"Moments ago you didn't want me to open the door: now you've invited him in for dinner and a bath?"

"Only the right thing to do for a person in need."

"If he is."

"What's that mean?" asked Clarice, as she retreated to the kitchen, where she proceeded to cut up the two steaks into equal parts so that they each had approximately a third.

"Well, we only have his word for it, don't we?"

"You think people go around starving themselves deliberately just to get on someone's good side?"

"Well..."

"Arlon!"

"You don't find it strange that someone who claims to have been marooned here for a month hasn't broken into this house to get food or shelter? He had to know it was here."

"Maybe he has better manners than that. Not everyone's a criminal, Arlon," said Clarice. She shoved some dishes and cutlery toward him. "Here, make yourself useful. Put some lights on, too. Getting dark in here," she ordered kindly.

FOUR

A warm ocean breeze blowing in through the open window washed over the trio as they sat at the dining table just off the sitting room. Freddy Boggs appeared almost human again in clean clothes, with his hair washed and bound back with one of Clarice's hair ties. His weather-worn face wore a friendly smile, but his bright green eyes held a portion of the fear he had expressed earlier.

"Have you had enough to eat, Freddy?" asked Clarice, in a chipper tone.

"Oh, miss! Stuffed ta the gills, I is," he replied.

"Probably because of all the time you went without, I reckon," added Arlon. "Strange that you never thought to break into this house, if you were that hard up?" suggested Arlon, with more than a hint of suspicion.

"Give it a rest, Arlon," Clarice lamented.

"No, no, he's right to be askin', miss. I would too 'n-all. Tried, I did, Mr Arlon. Tried everything I could to break in here, more-n-once. Shuttered and locked up to the billy-o, it were. Me with no tools and nothing. I woulda only borrowed anything, mind? I'd-a paid it back."

"You said earlier that the island got me, too? What did you mean by that?"

Freddy looked at the pair in front of him with a discerning eye, measuring their ability to accept his far-fetched notions. Real as they were for the old fisherman, they still didn't seem believable even to him.

"Cursed, it is. The whole bleedin' island, like it's alive or somethin'. Shoulda known, I shoulda. Heard tell the Spanish were runnin' off the Cid an' I got me lotsa good customers for em if I can get gooduns. Shoulda known. In all me years-o-fishin' I ain't never seen no Spanish runnin' off Cid. Too shallow for the big ones, ya see. They usually like the deeper water with plenty-o-baitfish schoolin'."

"Spanish?" queried Arlon.

"Spanish mackerel. Biguns they was, too. Never seen em so big this close in. Had me springer line out on either side-o-me bondy..."

"Bondy?"

"Arlon, let him finish, would you?" cried Clarice impatiently.

"Ah, I'm old school, I is, Mr Arlon. Bondwood boat. Not like these flimsy tin things everyone's scootin' around in these days. I had me that solid bondy for over fifteen years. Good boat, it were. Bloody good boat," Freddy said sadly.

"How about a beer, you two?" asked Clarice, to brighten up the evening.

"Aww, miss, don't count me ungrateful, like, but you wouldn't have a tot for an old salt, by any chance?"

"A tot?" asked Clarice, looking confused.

"I think you'll find he's talking about rum, if I'm not mistaken?"

"Sorry, shouldn'ta asked," admitted Freddy.

"Nonsense. I'm sure we have some rum here as well. Arlon?"

"A beer would be fine, thank you," said Arlon.

"Go on, Freddy, tell us what happened," begged Clarice, as she rose to fetch the drinks.

"Well, like I was tellin' yiz. I had a bunch-o-customers from the posh hotels lined up for Spanish if I could get 'em. Well worth me while, too, to come out all this way from the mainland. Had springers out for me second run through the bait ball after landing two beauties worth about fifty bucks each. Was gonna make me a month's worth in one day, I thought. Then the island had its way. Didn't like me takin' nothing, it didn't. Sent up a monster to swallow me whole.

"I was tendin' to one-o-me springers when I suddenly look up and see this shimmerin' in front-o-me boat, about half a mile away. Next time I look up I seen this...kraken or something, big as a whale, about to swallow me whole, boat-n-all. I abandoned ship, I did."

"What happened then?" Clarice asked as she returned with the drinks that she handed out, keeping a glass of white wine for herself.

"Nothin', miss."

"Nothing?"

"Weren't nothing to see when I came back up spittin' saltwater. No boat, no monster, no bait ball, no fish, nothing. Everything gone deathly quiet and even the waves died down. Looked under the water. No bondy down there. Gone, just like that. So I had to make a swim for it. Just as well I didn't know about them sharks what come back here every day since then."

"You swam back to this bay then?"

"Yeah, got here, just. Not a crash-hot swimmer. Cheers," said Freddy, as he sipped his straight Bundaberg rum.

"What makes you think it's the island? The sea has all kinds of monsters of the deep."

"Weren't nothin' like I ever seen. And I seen it all, most like, Mr Arlon. Thirty years I bin on the sea and never saw nothin' like that thing. Then gone, just like it never was. When I couldn't get inta this house, I went explorin', tryin' ta find a way orf the island. Never seen nothin' like what goes on here. Take me shoes orf to air me toes one night and wake up with half a shoe lyin' next ta me in the mornin'. Terrible sounds and howlin' winds fit to make ya skin crawl.

"Coupla weeks in I saw a young woman with a girl, dirty and raggedy they was, walking through the scrub toward me. Went right past me without a word, like I wasn't there. Her eyes all glazed over like she had the life frightened out-uv her. Never saw them again. Bin livin' off bugs and roots mainly, some oysters and a bit-o-crab when I could for nigh on a month, maybe more. Don't know what day it is."

"Would you like to use our phone to call someone, Freddy?" asked Clarice.

"Nah, no one ta call. Not at night, anyhow. Might call the insurance mob termorra, if ya let me. Least I can claim me bondy and maybe get off here at last. If the island lets me," he whispered with a haunted expression.

"Well, as you guessed, we were...'got' at by something that cut our boat cleanly. One-third of it is at the bottom of the bay. We're here to investigate the mysterious death of Clarice's brother-in-law over a year ago. Presuming that all was normal before then, it would appear that an escalation is taking place."

"Escalation?" voiced Clarice.

"I assume, Mr Boggs, that if anything like this with the fish and the sharks you describe, was happening for a longer period, that you would have heard about it?"

"Too right. Thing like that don't go unnoticed by fishermen for too long, I can tell ya."

"All fantasy and creative imagination aside, I would say that something happened around a year ago to upset the balance here.

Have you heard rumours of anything, Mr Boggs?"

"Freddy. Call me Freddy. Don't much care for me last name. Nah. Never heard of nuffin' goin' on. I'da known through the grapevine, just like I found out about the Spanish runnin'," attested Freddy, with a confident nod while stifling a yawn.

"Boring you, are we?" asked Arlon

"Arlon!" cried Clarice.

"Ya don't hold back, do ya?" asked Freddy, with more than a hint of annoyance. "I'll get going..."

"You'll do no such thing, Freddy. I'm afraid you'll have to forgive Arlon. He has a condition that makes him possibly the rudest man on earth. He can't help himself. No emotions, see? None!"

"Really?"

"I'm afraid so. I'm about the only person who can put up with him. We're engaged."

"Hmm, sorry for yiz, I am, miss. Nice lookin' sheila like yiz should have no trouble findin' a decent bloke what don't upset ya like."

"He has his good points. Just takes a whole lot of digging to find them, Freddy. And a whole lot of patience to put up with the rest."

"I am still here, you know," offered Arlon.

"You said you can't be offended, so I'm taking you at your word, Arlon."

"Doesn't mean I'm deaf."

"Never said you were. I'm just giving you some of what you dish out."

"You're holding me accountable for my condition?" he asked sincerely.

"Not the cause, just the symptoms. I think, if you applied yourself, you could learn to curb your rudeness. I believe you're intelligent enough to work it out. All it takes is some effort, which you seem reluctant to make most times."

"I learned to shut up in school. Would you rather I employed that tactic?"

"That is also the lazy way out. No, I don't want you to shut up. I want you to distinguish between rudeness and inquisitiveness. You simply cannot expect to say whatever comes out of your mouth without consequences."

"I really think I should go, miss."

"Don't you start! Where would you go, anyway? Don't be silly. You're staying here, and we'll sort you out with your insurance company tomorrow and arrange for you to leave the island. I will not hear of you wandering about out there on your own. Arlon, tomorrow we're going to look for that woman and her child after we've sorted Freddy here. Freddy, I've already made up the bed in the second bedroom and laid out some extra clothes for you. Now, do you want to go to bed, seeing as you're tired?"

Freddy blinked in surprise. Arlon smiled.

"She can be quite feisty when she gets her dander up, can't she?"

"Yiz can say that again, mate," agreed Freddy. "If yiz don't mind, miss, can I trouble yiz for another tot before I go ta bed?"

"You can have the whole bloody bottle for all I care. Men!" she harrumphed before heading off in the direction of the bedroom.

An eerie sound drifted over them, a haunting, pained cry emanating from the direction of the bay. It had a familiar singsong quality to it that had the hairs standing up on the back of Clarice's neck.

"Crikey!" exclaimed Freddy. "That sounds like whale song. Them humpbacks make that sound, don't they?"

"I think you're correct, Mr Boggs...Freddy. Coming from the bay, most likely. Shall we take a look? Clarice, I think we have some torches under the sink?"

"Yeah, saw them earlier. You really want to go out there?"

"Why not?"

"The island."

"Not you, too?"

"Well, how do you explain what's happening?"

"I've heard of sharks being drawn by geological events disturbing the magnetic polarity of an area. It could presumably work with whales as well," explained Arlon.

"Don't rightly explain none of the other shit...pardon, miss, happenin' round here. No bloody magnetic disturbance ever cut a man's shoe in half before."

"We're on the extreme edge of the Ring of Fire, you know? What we are experiencing may be the precursor to a major upheaval about to happen here. All animals react to such things, marine and otherwise."

"Weren't nothing normal what took me boat," said Freddy

defiantly.

"I admit there are some things I can't explain at the moment. Doesn't mean that anything overly mystical is happening, though," said Arlon.

The mournful tones filled the air once more.

"Don't sound too peaceful, like ya hear on them nature shows," observed Freddy.

"By rights, we shouldn't be hearing them at all. As far as I know, whales don't usually make any sounds unless they are submerged," explained Arlon.

"I hear 'em often enough when I'm fishing the outer reefs late at night," said Freddy. "Like with a full moon we got tonight. Seems they like ta frolic in the moonlight," he added.

"Shall we take a look?" asked Arlon.

Without waiting for an answer, Arlon went to the kitchen to retrieve a couple of torches from the cabinet under the sink. He then nodded at the other pair before marching off to the front door, which he opened quickly. Freddy and Clarice had to scramble to catch up with him as he moved down the sandy path to the top of the dunes.

At first, nothing could be seen to indicate what was making the sound. The moonlight sparkled off the calm waters in the bay. The many shark fins from the afternoon had vanished. Out beyond the reef protecting the bay from the worst of the prevailing weather came the distant sound of the whale song, plaintive and hauntingly beautiful.

Then a fountain appeared in the middle of the lagoon, followed closely by another smaller jet of water. It was almost impossible to distinguish the dark leviathans from the inky black water, but the phosphorescent trails marked their passage.

"A female and her calf, by the look of it, and that's the mate out there trying to coax them back out of the bay," ventured Arlon.

"How you s'pose they got in here past that reef, Mr Arlon?"

"Hard to know for sure. Sudden tidal surge, perhaps. Caught them in the wrong place? Not sure how they are even swimming about in there. Isn't it too shallow for them?"

"Oh no, Mr Arlon. Deceptive it is. All that white coral on the bottom makes it look shallow during the day. Reckon it's close to thirty metres in the middle."

"That's very deep for a lagoon like this, isn't it?"

"Me granddad said he heard a science fella say this bay was most likely formed by a meteor. That there is a crater. Probably used ta be much deeper. Filled up with sand and dead coral over the ages."

"You think that's true?" asked Arlon.

"Couldn't say, Mr Arlon, couldn't say. Don't like them whales' chances-o-survivin' in there. Nothin' for em ta eat. Calf might be okay on its mother's milk for a time but that'll run out soon enough. Shame," said Freddy with a sigh.

"Can't we do something?" asked Clarice in alarm.

"Sure, I'll just jump in there and scoop them out with a fishnet and toss them back over the reef, shall I?"

"Smart-arse! I was just asking," she replied sulkily.

"Whatever happened to allow them access to the bay will have to occur again to release them, I would imagine," explained Arlon.

"Better happen afore termorra," said Freddy gravely.

"Why's that, Freddy?" asked Clarice, concern creasing her features.

"By next afternoon them sharks'll be back like every other afternoon I bin here. Mum might manage to stave 'em off for a bit, but bubs is a gonna for sure. It'll be a feasting frenzy in there. Bay'll be awash with blood and guts."

Before anyone could react to Freddy's ominous statement, a total silence descended on the trio as the dull thumping of the generator within the shed died, taking the house lights and exterior spotlights out with it.

"Shit! What now?" cried Clarice.

"Diesel," said Arlon.

"What?"

"Diesel is what now. I probably had to fill it up earlier."

"Arlon, Gail said the mechanic was just here servicing and filling the generator. She said it should run for at least two days on a full tank."

"Well, maybe it'll come back on again as it did before. I don't know anything about generators, do you Mr...Freddy?"

"Bin around marine diesel motors all me life, mate. Want me ta have a look-see?"

"If you wouldn't mind?"

"Is that a good idea, Arlon, considering?"

"What's that, miss? Something wrong there in that shed?"

"Just...that's where my brother-in-law died."

"How, if ya don't mind me askin'?"

"Chopped in half. Cut clean through the middle vertically, like he was sliced open with a surgical laser or something."

"Crikey, just like me shoe!"

"Perhaps more of a concern than with your shoe?" said Arlon drily.

"Don't be takin' no offence, Mr Arlon..."

"I wasn't. It's impossible to offend me. Now, would you like to take a look...?"

The generator kicked in again just as it did earlier. Behind them, a sucking, gurgling sound drew their attention. When they turned they were surprised to find a creature struggling on the beach. Neither Arlon nor Freddy recognised the animal immediately, though, with the limited light available, that was not entirely strange. The sound it made resembled a breathing sea turtle when it surfaced. Arlon pointed his torch beam at the animal. None of them wanted to get any closer to inspect it.

From the top of the dunes, in the torch beam, they saw the creature struggling to get back into the ocean. It had the general shape of a large seal with an enlarged head. Arlon played the torch beam over it and they gasped in unison. Its lower half seemed to be missing and it was bleeding out quickly on the pristine white sand. That was strange enough to warrant their concern, but what worried them more was the colour of the bodily fluids staining the sand. The eerie fluorescent blue shone brightly when they averted the torch beam.

"We get any seals in these parts, Freddy?"

"That's no seal I ever seen and no, we don't get no seals hereabouts."

"Shall we have a closer look?"

"Not goin' nowhere near it. It's a gonna, and nothing we can do for it."

"Aren't you interested to find out what it is?"

"Probably one-o-them mermaids ya hear tales about," whispered Freddy fearfully.

"Superstitious claptrap! Next, you'll be regaling us with tales of sirens and such luring men to their deaths."

"Shouldn't oughta make fun, Mr Arlon. Plenty-o-unexplained

things happen at sea."

"Unexplained, yes. Not explained by old wives' tales and fishermen's yarns. Sailors are notorious for being a superstitious lot."

"How'd ya explain that thing then? How'd ya explain them whales in here and the sharks and me shoe?"

"Are you on about your shoe again? It must have been a very special shoe, Freddy. Did you get married in that shoe, or something?"

"Scoff if ya like. Tales, even fairy tales, are based on fact."

"Arlon, what is that thing?" asked Clarice to belay the certain rebuke from Arlon.

"I don't know, Clarice. I'm not a marine biologist. There are probably plenty of animals in the ocean I have no clue about. Just as our last assignment had nothing to do with the supernatural or fairy tales, I feel certain this will end up being no different. Just because we aren't knowledgeable of the subject doesn't make it extraordinary in the mystical sense. There are times when I count my blessings that I'm not disadvantaged by emotions like the rest of humanity. It makes everyone go a little loopy and susceptible to flights of fancy," said Arlon calmly.

"Can't we see if we can at least put it out of its misery? Not nice to leave an animal to suffer like that," she said with passion.

"While I don't subscribe to the mystical and whimsical, I do acknowledge the presence of danger, Clarice. Whatever happened to that creature could happen again. Do you want to be in the vicinity when it does?"

"Not on your nelly!"

"No. Well, neither do I. I think it might be wise for us to retreat to the house and start over in the morning, don't you?"

A last look back at the grisly scene revealed the twin sprays from the humpback whales as they rose to the surface once more. The plaintive cry from beyond the reef by the male calling for its mate and calf had Clarice choking back a tear.

FIVE

The sun was just appearing over the horizon when Freddy Boggs approached the dune's crest before it angled down toward the beach where they had witnessed the strange event the previous evening. It was just after five in the morning, according to Freddy's internal clock. He never grew tired of watching the sunrise over the ocean after he had been fishing for most of the night. He knew from experience to watch for the signs; 'red sky in morning, sailor take warning'. It had saved his hide on too many occasions for him to ignore it.

On the beach below his position he watched the odd man, Arlon Grey, dressed in some sort of floppy white pyjamas, going through a series of stylised movements, followed by a lightning-quick succession of martial arts manoeuvres. Freddy guessed that's what they were, as he couldn't be certain. He became mesmerised by the slow-motion portions of the ritual. They seemed so balletic and serene.

He continued to watch unnoticed as Arlon stripped to the waist, dropping his top to the sand. Even from his distant viewing platform, Freddy marvelled at the bristling musculature of the man, glistening with sweat despite the coolness of the morning. Freddy assumed that Arlon had been exercising for some time already. Arlon demonstrated his superb athleticism by going through a rigorous routine that had him kicking, extending, leaping, punching and balancing perfectly on either leg to deliver precise kicks to his unseen opponent.

After the exhausting routine, Arlon slowly descended to the sand to a sitting position Freddy recognised as meditative. Freddy marvelled at the rate of the man's chest expansions decreasing so rapidly. He imagined the same amount of effort on his part would see him huffing and puffing for an hour. He made his way quietly down the beach to join Arlon without disturbing him, keeping well behind him.

"Good morning Mr Boggs...Freddy," said Arlon suddenly, without turning.

"Shit! Startled me, Mr Arlon. I had no idea you knew I was

here."

"I smelled your presence about half an hour ago."

"Fair go! I had a shower 'fore I came," explained Freddy, sounding hurt.

"Which is what I detected. A strong soap smell. Why must everyone I speak to automatically assume that I am speaking about them in a negative sense?"

"Well, I guess it's easiest ta assume that most people are talkin' about body odours if they say they smelt you. I thought yiz was out here in ya pyjamas when I first saw ya."

"Karategi, or judogi, which is most often shortened to just dogi. It's not ideal, in my opinion, but I wear it out of habit. It does soak up the sweat quite well," explained Arlon, while continuing to face the sea with his back turned and his eyes closed.

"Ya got one-o-them black belts, eh? Ya some kinda fighter, then?"

"I have achieved the highest ranks in many disciplines. These have taught me many self-defence strategies which, unfortunately, I have had to employ on too many occasions over the years. Not a fighter, though: a defender. I have no trouble dealing physically with anyone who threatens or attacks me, however, I don't ever use it to inflict harm on someone without sufficient cause."

"Could call that overkill if you learnt a heap-o-fighting things when one woulda done."

"I like to learn. As with languages, I found I had a natural aptitude and so continued with my education, and the physical regimes keep me healthy and fit."

"You know a lot of languages?"

"About a hundred or so."

"Crikey! You some kinda...what they call it? Like that Rainman character...Dustin Hoffman."

"Savant. No, I don't think so. I do have some natural abilities, but everything I learn comes from hard work and disciplined habits."

"They got a name for what's wrong with ya?"

"Nothing is 'wrong' with me, Mr Boggs. I have a condition called alexithymia, a rare form of autism which prevents me from expressing or experiencing emotions. I have never known them so it doesn't bother me, much like a blind person from birth cannot miss sight."

"Didn't mean no offence," Freddy offered.

"I just finished explaining that I was incapable of emotions, therefore I can't be offended, Mr Boggs."

"Oh, rightyo. Handy, that."

"Not always."

"You get a look at that...thing from last night?"

"No, got washed back out to sea, I assume. Pity. I would've liked to examine it in the daylight"

"Them whales still in there?"

"Yes."

"How are they doin'?"

"Not good from what I can see. The mother is unable to feed and, in turn, will find her milk diminishing. It will be very stressing for the animals."

"How'd ya think they got in there? That reef shoulda kept 'em out, far as I can tell."

"You probably have more of a clue than I do where that is concerned. Are we experiencing king tides at the moment?"

"Might be, but I wouldn't be thinkin' that was enough to see them big fish gettin' in there."

"Not fish, Mr Boggs. Air-breathing mammals, like us. Would have thought you'd at least know that much."

"What's that supposed ta mean?" asked Freddy, bristling.

"I sense an altered tone in that question which leads me to believe I have offended you. It's impossible for me to deliberately offend someone unless I truly apply myself. If you take offence at something I say or ask, it's your problem, not mine. I won't apologise for something I am virtually incapable of. I simply meant that as a fisherman with a supposedly wide knowledge of the ocean and her inhabitants, that you would know more than most that a whale is a mammal, Mr Boggs, not a fish."

"I see the miss was right. Most people will end up...not liking ya much after spending some time with yiz. She warned me fore I come down here."

"Very perspicacious of her."

"Dunno what that means, neiver," admitted Freddy sullenly.

"Nothing a decent dictionary wouldn't solve if you had the inclination."

"Don't need no fancy education to go out fishing like me dad or granddad."

"Quite right. You wouldn't need to know Pythagoras' theorem to work out where to catch fish, but even a rudimentary education would provide you with enough knowledge to understand what the word perspicacious meant. Still, some like to learn and others don t. Where did you come across them?" asked Arlon suddenly.

"Where...what?"

"The woman and the child. How long ago and where?"

"Few weeks ago, inland of the next bay over."

"How long for us to get there?"

"I ain't goin' nowhere."

"I don't hold out much hope of finding them without you to guide me, Mr Boggs."

"Couldn't survive, anyhow."

"You said they were looking the worse for wear when you came across them, didn't you?"

"Yeah, so?"

"That would imply that they have survived for long enough to get to that state."

"All right, suppose they did, then. They was walkin' past me headin' further inland. Won't catch up to 'em or find 'em now!"

"Why not?"

"Well, they got too much of a head start, is why not."

Arlon swivelled around to face Freddy. "If they were as run down as you suggest, they would most likely not have gone far. She had a young child in tow, after all."

"Not my problem."

"You weren't our problem last night, either. We could have easily left you outside, stinking to high heaven and starving."

"You was gonna do just that,' accused Freddy.

"Too right I was. However, Clarice had the good sense and graciousness to open her home to you. She now wants to locate the woman and her child because she has a kindness of heart that cares for stray puppies like you and these other two. We need your assistance to help us locate them."

"Bin here for over a month. I need ta get home. Call the cops if ya wanna locate them two. I ain't no tracker or nuffin'."

"You're free to leave at any time. Start swimming," Arlon offered, with an arm extended to the bay behind him.

"Yiz said I could call me insurance?"

"That was last night."

"Yiz saying ya won't let me use ya bloody phone this mornin'?"

"You're getting aggressive, Mr Boggs. I wouldn't if I were you."

"Ya threatenin' me?" warned Freddy, getting louder and angrier.

"I'm cautioning you. I've had to deal with ignorant people like you all my life, always taking offence at what I say, getting irate and eventually thinking they have a right to get physically aggressive with me. I did not say that we would be withholding the phone from you or disallowing its use. I am saying that it's of no use this morning."

"Hey?" asked Freddy, calming down somewhat.

"No bars."

"Come again?"

"No bars. On the phone. No reception, no way to make a call at the moment. At least, not when I woke at four this morning."

"Oh," said Freddy, relaxing his shoulders.

Freddy considered his situation. He was wearing clothes that were about three sizes too large and hung loosely on his emaciated frame. He was never a large person. A healthy diet of seafood had kept him lean and trim. He was getting on a bit in years and had nothing to show for all his hard work. A shanty on a little coastal block next to a tidal creek, where he kept his boat moored at a small private jetty, was all he needed, he supposed.

The strangers had taken him in the night before and provided him with clean clobber and a feed, even a tot of rum and a comfortable bed. He supposed he was being churlish and selfish in light of the generosity the woman had shown him. If his mum were still alive, she would not be impressed with him at the moment. He owed it to his fellow humans to offer his assistance, such as he could. Without a phone or a boat, he wasn't getting off the island any time soon, anyway.

In truth, he admitted to himself that he wanted to get off the island as quickly as possible because he was shit-scared. He'd seen and heard terrible things and he didn't want to dig too deeply into the origins of those occurrences. He was afraid of what else they might find if they went looking for the woman and her kid. He was scared they would be too late to find them alive. He didn't want to find their corpses or what was left of them. He certainly didn't want to find them if they had suffered the same fate as his shoe or the creature from last night.

He ran a hand through his freshly-washed, longish grey hair, worrying at a stubborn knot, which eventually he untangled. He wandered away a step or two to think through it all without having to look at the bloke making him feel guilty. He sighed heavily, knowing that he would have to capitulate in the end. He knew he had to do the right thing, the decent thing, as much as he feared the possible outcome.

"S'pose I hafta do the right thing by them two, specially the little tyke. Seein' as I can't call no one now," he agreed.

"Good on you. Have you had some breakfast yet?"

"Nah, come straight down here after me shower ta watch the sunrise like I do most mornin's."

"Well, I haven't had my first cuppa of the day yet. We won't be going anywhere if I don't have my heart-starter, and you need all the food you can get. I'm sure Clarice will be cooking something up for us."

Arlon picked up the top of his karategi and led the way. Freddy sighed as he followed resignedly. They covered the short distance to the house without speaking. Arlon, who had gone barefoot, wiped the sand off his feet with a towel hanging by the side door. Freddy peered at him doing this, looking down at his own sandy feet as he did so. He had discarded his remaining canvas shoe when the other was destroyed. He didn't think he would be going too far without replacements.

"Go on through to the shower, Arlon. Breaky ready in five," said Clarice, looking refreshed and buoyant. She wore a pair of loose jeans and a white, long-sleeved cotton blouse.

Freddy admired her lovely, addictive smile and was quite attracted to her full-bodied figure. It had been a very long time since Freddy had been in the company of a woman or romantically inclined. He wondered what she could possibly see in the horrible bloke she was with. He'd never met a more unpleasant man in all his years.

"Yiz was spot on," he said, after Arlon had exited the room.

"About?" enquired Clarice, as she prepared their breakfast.

"I don't like him one little bit. Was he tellin' the truth about the phone?"

"Arlon doesn't lie, Freddy. He may be a lot of things when he opens his mouth, but a liar isn't one of them."

"Was *hopin'* he was, is all. Wadda ya see in him?" said Freddy, as he pulled up a stool to the island bench. Clarice handed him a steaming mug of coffee.

"Hope you aren't a tea drinker, Freddy. I don't know how to make a decent cup of tea. His lordship likes his tea a certain way and I just can't seem to get it right. We both drink coffee in the morning, anyway."

"Coffee's fine. Well?"

"It's a hard question to answer simply, Freddy. I mean, look at him for a start. He has drop-dead movie star looks and a superb body."

"I'll give ya that. Looks like he can use it, too."

"You bet. Don't mess with him if you fancy staying on your feet. I admit it's bloody hard to truly love him unconditionally. He says some things...well...that leave you struggling, that's for sure. He has some amazing qualities. Old-fashioned qualities that young men don't seem to have these days and young women don't necessarily want any more. He has honour, integrity, reliability and dependability. He's a proper gentleman, opening my door and things. He would defend me with his life and has done."

"No flowers though, huh?"

Sighing, Clarice said, "No, no flowers. No romance at all. Not a single sentimental word has ever passed his lips for anyone, I don't think. He isn't wired that way, Freddy. He can't display any type of emotion unless he manufactures it, in which case it's artificial and I don't want it," she explained wistfully.

"So, no love then? Sorry, that's personal, I shouldn'ta asked that."

"No, no love. He can't love...or hate. That's why you shouldn't take offence at whatever he says, no matter how blunt. He doesn't have an emotion behind it. He is completely innocent of all the reasons for making inflammatory remarks. He holds no malice, no grudges and has no other hidden meanings or innuendos in his words. He's also unpretentious, generous and extremely protective of the underdog, especially me. It may sound as though I'm sacrificing a lot to be with him, but I'm not really. I'm too old to be worried about all that romance stuff you read about in crappy books. I've woken up about some of those things. They just aren't as important as the other qualities he has. Don't get me wrong. He drives me up the wall sometimes: he really does. But I have to remind myself that he doesn't want to start a fight, he is just being him."

Clarice placed a plate of bacon and eggs in front of Freddy. She then placed hers and Arlon's plates on the bench and poured his coffee. Arlon reappeared from the hallway.

"Oh no, Arlon! Not the Livingstone suit!" exclaimed Clarice in embarrassment.

Arlon was dressed from head to toe in a replication of the attire worn by the early English explorers to the African continent; a khaki safari suit, complete with pith helmet, and a brown leather utility belt cinching in the waist, resplendent with many pouches and sheaths. He wore long socks and sturdy leather hiking boots. Clarice had seen the outfit before, on their last assignment. She had hoped she would never see it again.

"I suppose you have the fly nets again?"

"Of course," he said simply, as he sat down to his breakfast, unperturbed by the outburst.

"If you aren't a bloody sight!" mused Freddy.

"I didn't realise you two were fashion aficionados. We're going on a hike, are we not? Through some pretty rough scrublands by the look of it. I'd like to come out of it relatively unscathed. I assumed you would be staying here, anyway, Clarice?"

"Oh, what gave you that idea?"

"Didn't you learn your lesson from our last...adventure? It could be dangerous."

"Yeah, I guess there isn't much danger here, is there? Unless you count getting chopped in half while in your backyard shed?"

"Well, I wasn't suggesting you wander into the shed, Clarice I would have thought that was obvious."

"What I learned from our experiences is that the safest place to be in any situation is usually by your side, Arlon. And that's where I intend to be."

"You realise that we'll have to do this off our own bat? That we can't very well charge your sister for the time we spend searching for a couple of lost persons."

"She won't know and she has plenty of money," argued Clarice.

"All the same, we will not be charging her for any time we spend not directly connected to her husband's case."

"If you insist."

"I do. Now, I am going to eat this fine breakfast and then make some preparations for our departure. Mr Boggs has kindly offered to assist us in our search, despite being trapped on this island for a long time and feeling quite exhausted and run down by the experience."

"Oh, that's very generous, Freddy. I'm sure it would have been difficult for us to find them on our own, but you're more than welcome to stay here until reception comes back to the cell phone," offered Clarice.

"Ah, n-no, that's okay. Glad to be of help," Freddy managed through a beet-red face, glancing sideways at Arlon.

"So, Arlon, do you have an idea what might be going on around here yet?" asked Clarice.

"No," he said simply.

"Not like you. No theories, no possible explanations, nothing?"

"I didn't say that," said Arlon between mouthfuls.

"Well?"

"I still maintain that we could possibly be looking at a major geological event here. The drop in pressure that I felt is endemic to seismic activity."

"You mean, like an earthquake?"

"Yes, or volcanic."

"You can't be serious?"

"We're on the edge of the Pacific rim here, Clarice. The Ring of Fire harbours some 450 dormant and active volcanoes, 75% of all the volcanoes in the world."

"That doesn't explain a man cut in half or that creature we saw last night," said Clarice.

"The Bougainville Trench is just south of New Guinea. Deep-sea eruptions could disturb whatever creatures reside down there that we are as yet unaware of. I haven't been able to tie the incident with your brother-in-law into this scenario yet, I admit. That's why I haven't said anything until now. I don't have any answers, just questions and some theories at present. Trying to be scientific and logical."

"Are there volcanoes around here, or them plate things?"

"Tectonic plates? There are no major tectonic fault lines right here that I'm aware of, or volcanoes. I could be wrong; I haven't done any major geological studies during my reading. I assume they exist because continents are floating plates. We are on the Australian plate and it has a border on the Ring of Fire, essentially a product of two lithospheric plates colliding."

"Ya know all that without havin' studied nothin'?" enquired Freddy, with a look of astonishment.

"No in-depth studies, Mr Boggs. I know some basics only. What about you, do you think that creature we saw could have come from a deep-sea environment?" asked Arlon.

"Hard ta say. Didn't see it close enough. What I did see in the torchlight was eye-shine and that don't seem right. Them deep-sea critters are all blind. Don't need eyes in pitch black, they don't."

"Hmm, I didn't think about that aspect. Maybe not deep-sea then. Maybe just an unidentified species. We haven't discovered all the animal life there is on our planet yet," suggested Arlon, taking another mouthful.

"You want me to make up some food for us to take along, Arlon? I suppose you want some curried egg?"

"That'd be fine, Clarice. How about some chicken and salad sandwiches as well, using that cooked bird we bought from the supermarket? Wouldn't pay to keep that too long without refrigeration," replied Arlon.

"What're you talking about? The fridge is working fine."

"I intend to turn off the generator and shutter up the house while we're gone," he explained.

"Why?"

"Just a precaution. Could be away for a few days, and the generator would probably run out of fuel, anyway."

"Got solar," suggested Clarice.

"Maybe enough to get by, maybe not. I wouldn't trust it and I think we're in for some bad weather."

"Not a cloud in the sky and weren't no red in it this mornin', Mr Arlon," offered Freddy, who was struggling to finish his large breakfast.

"You swear by that old sailor's myth, do you?"

"Done right by me all me life, it has."

"Never let you down?"

"Well...not...perfect, like," he admitted sheepishly.

"I wouldn't push that plate away if I were you. You're going to need all that energy for the day ahead. Not a walk in the park we're planning, is it?"

"Too right, Mr Arlon! That scrub's a lot thicker'n it looks."

"Clarice, I want you to find those plastic ponchos we brought with us, and add some extra clothing in case we find those two. You can put it all into my knapsack. Find some bottles of water for us all and make sure you pack plenty of food."

"What will you be doing?"

"I have a decent knife with me, but I'd like to scrounge around to find something else."

"Something else?"

"Like a weapon of some sort," he replied.

"A weapon?"

"Must you repeat everything? Yes, a weapon, Clarice."

"What do we need a weapon for?"

"In case, Clarice, in case. I want us to be prepared."

"I don't like the sound of that at all. There should be nothing on this island to pose a danger to us, Arlon."

"Tell that to your brother-in-law."

"Ooh, that was...uncalled for," said Clarice sadly.

"Now, Miss Clarice, I think maybe ya oughta take ya own advice and not take no offence. He's right to think we might need some protection. I'd feel a whole lot better if we had something."

Freddy smiled and nodded at Arlon to let him know that he was repaying the earlier kindness. He wasn't at all sure if Arlon understood, because he frowned in answer.

"You should know by now that I like to be prepared, Clarice. It's better to have a weapon and not need it than the other way around. Now, let's finish eating and then we can get ready. Mr Boggs, are you comfortable enough in what you're wearing?"

"Good as anything, I s'pose, but I need something on me feet because..."

"Yes, yes, yes, please don't start with the shoe story again. I have a pair of runners that might fit you, otherwise you might find Clarice's sister may have left something of her husband's. You'll need a hat and probably a long-sleeved shirt. I have fly nets for us all if they are required. Clarice? I think a comprehensive first-aid kit might be needed."

"Hmm, saw one earlier in the bathroom. Not sure how 'comprehensive' it'll be, though."

"I just thought we might have more than simply dehydration and starvation to worry about if we should find our quarry."

"You mean scratches and so on?"

"Yes, but it's the 'and so on' that's more of concern."

"Ya sound like ya know somthin' ya not tellin' us," suggested Freddy.

Arlon stopped eating to look directly at Freddy, then Clarice, weighing up the pros and cons of speaking his mind. Much of what he had swirling about his mind was pure conjecture, highly debatable. He wasn't sure how much of that he should reveal. While he had no personal concept of fear, he had witnessed it often enough in others. It was a particularly unstable emotion that saw the exponents acting erratically and irrationally. He didn't want to scare them any more than they already were.

"I feel that we have a diminishing window of opportunity."

"Well, that makes everything clear as mud, Arlon," Clarice stated with a groan.

"Ya talkin' time-wise, is ya?" asked Freddy.

"Yes. Not only that, though. If, as I predict, we have a major seismic event building in this region, it's escalating in intensity and duration, as well as the nature of the occurrences. Several unexplainable events are occurring simultaneously; these may or may not be connected. As you mentioned earlier, Clarice, a seismic event does not adequately explain the severing of organic material, as in the case of your relative and the creature we saw last night.

"Super tides caused by mid-oceanic tectonic movements could conceivably explain the two whales finding their way into the lagoon. Underwater disturbances could be responsible for the destruction of the two vessels, at a stretch. If a major shift in the tectonic plates is imminent, we will experience a range of other proceedings, ranging from possible lava eruption to sulphur pools and other lethally noxious gases permeating the area.

"In the short time we've been here I've noted the rapidity with which these new events occur. The chances of our survival decrease exponentially the longer we remain here," Arlon explained in his quiet, unemotional manner, causing his audience to squirm with ominous fear.

"Arlon, it sounds...impossible."

"Just because a volcano hasn't popped up and blown its lid in the last century or more here in Australia doesn't mean it can't happen, Clarice. Any major movement of two plates can cause devastation on a global scale. Think of the ash cloud from the Icelandic eruption not so long ago. It halted all air traffic for a time. A blast like Krakatoa or Mt. St. Helens had lasting global implications. A large enough ash cloud could blanket the entire earth, effectively blocking out the sun for who knows how long. Things like that have caused the type of layers we see in archaeological excavations all the time," he argued reasonably.

"Why are you talking about the earthquake and volcanic eruption in the same breath? Aren't you mixing the two up?"

"I am conflating the two elements because they are so closely linked at times. Major tectonic movement was the cause of the Ring of Fire. It's not impossible to think a dual event may happen here."

"That's bloody scary!" said Clarice with a shiver."

"Quite."

"You aren't, though?"

"Scared? No, of course not. Do I want to make it out of here alive? Absolutely! I'm not stupid, just unemotional."

"I'm suddenly not that hungry," she confessed.

"Well, I believe that you never know when your next meal will be available or when you might have the time to eat it, so I'll be making the most of this breakfast while I can," claimed Arlon, as he reverted his attention to the remainder of his meal.

"Dunno if I signed on for all that," whispered Freddy.

"Don't know that you have a choice. If you're unable to leave the island, or contact anyone, you have to be a part of it. Whatever it is, it will probably affect the whole island, maybe the entire eastern seaboard of Australia, even the world! No escaping it, really," said Arlon in his annoyingly calm tone.

"Ya could be wrong," accused Freddy.

"Sure. Everything I said could be nothing but a load of codswallop. I'm all ears if you two have anything better to offer," enquired Arlon. "What's indisputable at the moment is the fact that we've had at least one fatality and two boats gone under mysterious circumstances. We also have a pair of our fellow humans wandering around out there, and their lives could be in jeopardy. Clarice has pointed out to me that we have a moral and ethical obligation to conduct a search for them. I'm inclined to agree. You might possibly be the best one to comment on the suggestion of an escalation, Mr Boggs. Have you noticed diminishing periods between events?"

"I haven't noticed no *events*, 'cept what we saw together last night," he said.

"Oh, so you often come across lost women and children after losing your prized fishing boat, which you abandon just before being swallowed by a kraken? You told me you knew about the sharks coming into the bay every afternoon. Is that normal? No, I think you said that was decidedly unnatural. And the 'Spanish' running off the island which brought you here? I think you alluded to the fact that it was most uncommon for that to happen?"

"Ya sure remember a lot," said Freddy sulkily.

"Sticking my head in the sand to pretend that nothing untoward is occurring around me has never been my style, Mr Boggs. I much prefer to face up to whatever it is that causes problems or obstacles for me or my investigations. I find it pays to be proactive rather than reactive. Clarice? Perhaps you should fry up the rest of the bacon as well?"

"Thought I asked ya ta call me Freddy?" he asked sullenly.

"You refer to me as 'Mr Arlon', which is entirely incorrect. It should be Mr Grey if you are going to use a title. Kindly make up your mind to use a title properly or not at all...Freddy," Arlon replied.

"Now, now, you two. No need to get snippety at each other," warned Clarice, with a patient smile. "What did Arlon say to you on the beach to make you dislike him, Freddy?"

"No need for that, Clarice. Water under the bridge, I'm sure."

"No, no, she's right. Shoulda come clean right away. Fact is, miss, I didn't volunteer ta guide ya. I didn't want no part of it. I just wanted ta skedaddle outta here quick as. And he made out I was a bit of a stinker for thinkin' like that," Freddy explained.

"I said no such thing."

"Ya didn't have ta. Came across clear as day and I took it ta heart. Felt guilty. Then he made out like I was bein'...noble or somethin'. Sayin' I volunteered ta guide yiz ta them two when we came ta breaky. That were wrong, miss. Shoulda told the truth then. Thought ya said ya man can't lie?" added Freddy after a moment.

"Strictly speaking, I wasn't lying. In the end, you did volunteer to take us back to where you came across them," admitted Arlon.

"Only when I was pushed, like."

"Freddy, it doesn't matter how you reached the decision, only that you did. No one is perfect. You had every right to be reticent about remaining on the island after everything that's happened to you. How *are* you feeling, by the way?"

"Full as a goog after that meal. Thanks, Miss Clarice. Umm, hope ya don't mind me callin' ya that? Still bloody tired, but okay."

"If you're comfortable calling me that, I'm more than happy. Arlon is perfectly comfortable with Mr Arlon as well, aren't you dear?" she asked with a beatific smile.

"I don't care one way or the other. It's him that objects to his last name being used."

"He still calls me Miss Manning in the office, Freddy. Suppose he'll start calling me Mrs Grey when we're hitched. That's just his way."

"Ya really gonna get married?"

"Yes."

"No...eventually," came the joint replies, with Arlon receiving a look of surprise from Clarice at his negative reply.

"Arlon? Sick of me already?" she asked.

"I would have thought the opposite to be true, Clarice. What's it been? A little over six months since you proposed?"

"*She* proposed!" exclaimed Freddy.

"And just why shouldn't I? Are you about to stumble right into a sexist comment, Mr Boggs!" she bristled.

"Whoa, sorry. Didn't mean ta get ya back up. Bit of a surprise, is all," Freddy ventured in mock surrender.

SIX

Several hours later, with the sun high in the sky, the trio sweated profusely as they hiked along the sandy beach to the northern point of the bay. Every so often Freddy smiled when he turned to look back at his followers, especially at Arlon, who was dressed like an African explorer. It looked so very much out of place on a pristine beach in the pleasant Whitsunday islands. Although it was late in April, and the torrid summer temperatures had all but abated, it was still in the mid-thirties Centigrade.

Clarice, thankful for the broad-brimmed straw hat and dark sunglasses, shading her face and eyes, battled to repress the tears that threatened to cascade at any moment. She had not expected Arlon's thoughtless admission to hurt as it did. If she thought about it logically, she should have been expecting him to back out of the marriage. Not that he had terminated it, as such. He certainly hadn't demanded the return of the engagement ring.

Clarice remembered them shopping for the ring together. Arlon, ever the pragmatic one, pushed for a large rock with provenance and certification as an item of pure investment. Clarice attempted, unsuccessfully, to steer him onto something less auspicious and more a token of their relationship and coming nuptials. She had to remove the ring often to protect it from damage or loss during normal activities, like the present.

She had been so proud to be engaged at long last. Her sister, though older by some years, had ribbed her about possibly being left on the shelf if she didn't put some effort into finding a man soon. Succumbing to an impulse when she proposed, she regretted it afterwards, though she was secretly delighted later on that he had accepted during the occasion of their first intimacy. She almost felt as though she had taken advantage of him whilst he was in the afterglow, if it could be said that such a state existed within the man.

She had been expecting him to come to his senses. After all, she was no beauty queen. That was the way she thought, when, in fact, she could mostly be described as exuding beauty. Her bubbly personality and wholesomeness made up for any shortcomings she believed she possessed as far as most males were concerned. She'd had her share of lovers and found them all to be less than attractive or worthy of love in the light of day.

Arlon was so very different. He epitomised all that she desired in a man appearance-wise and exhibited all the masculine qualities she expected. It was only the love component that was sorely missing in the man and their relationship. She knew and understood that going in. She had been his assistant in the office for a year before their engagement. She had witnessed his brutally unemotional behaviour often, making her gasp at times. Yet he possessed qualities and invoked feelings in her that she had never before experienced, leaving her breathless and pining for him whenever they were apart.

Hearing Arlon say 'no', then changing it to 'eventually', shattered her heart. Every ounce of her brain matter insisted that it would happen sooner or later. But every ounce of her heart was broken, nonetheless. Following behind him, wearing his ridiculous outfit on a sub-tropical island beach, where she had been planning a pre-honeymoon tryst, caused her to smile and want to screech at the same time. He was easy to hate for almost everyone bar her.

Clarice sighed as the troop veered toward the top of the high-water mark to enter the inland scrub before they reached the rocky point at the northern tip of the bay. Freddy had explained earlier that it would be too difficult to manoeuvre around or over the large, slippery boulders. One slip of the foot could spell pain and injury for the victim, slicing himself open on the barnacles and oysters clinging to the lower portions of the rocks where they met the water.

Although the interior of mostly stunted growth offered a modicum of relief from the hot sunlight, it had the cloying effect of high humidity and claustrophobia within the confines of the thickets. The path was barely recognisable amid the twisted, gnarled roots of the trees and grasses underfoot. If Clarice weren't careful, she could easily trip over and hurt herself, so she pushed aside further prognostication over her hurt feelings. She would have to await an opportunity to gain some clarification about Arlon's comment before she made far too much of it. It didn't pay to assume the worst or the best where he was concerned. It was impossible to accurately interpret his meaning or intentions.

Arlon Grey had no self-awareness where fashion was concerned. He didn't care what anyone thought, and that was probably a good thing. However, it got him into trouble when others commented on the odd costumes he wore. After a lifetime of derogatory comments and derision from his peers and others, Arlon no longer ignored them. He now tended to confront anyone taking issue with anything he said, did or wore.

A shattering crack shook the ground and made the travellers look up instinctively. Through the dense foliage, they made out nothing but a clear blue sky. All about them, birds of different varieties, mainly sea birds, took to the air. On the ground, lizards by the hundreds accompanied all manner of insects scurrying about in mad panic, rustling through the leafy litter.

The sound and the resulting activity stunned the trio, who had stopped in a little clearing while the mayhem surrounding them settled. It was a long while before any of them spoke. Instead, Arlon used the opportunity to sit down and take a sip from his canteen. Clarice and Freddy watched, bemused, as he removed his lunch container from his knapsack and began to nonchalantly unwrap a sandwich from it. .

"How can you think of eating at a time like this, Arlon?"

"A time like what, Clarice?" he asked innocently.

"Well, with the lightning and thunder and the animals and all," she replied.

"What lightning? I didn't see any lightning."

"Whatever!"

"No need to get yourself all flustered, Clarice."

"Didn't you just hear what we heard?"

"Of course I did."

"Well?"

"You mean I shouldn't be eating because I heard a noise?"

"Oh, Arlon, I give up sometimes."

"What's gotten into you? A loud noise scares the animals and I should be afraid as well? You know I don't feel fear, Clarice, so I'm a little confused about what you expect me to do right now. I can't control the insects and other animals, and I certainly can't control the weather, if that's what it was," he explained calmly.

"What do you mean, 'if it was the weather'? What else could it have been?"

"Could have been a jet overhead breaking the sound barrier," he suggested in a logically frustrating manner for Clarice.

"And just why would a jet suddenly be flying directly over this island, breaking the sound barrier?"

"I didn't say it was. You asked what else might have made the sound. I gave you an example. I sat down to eat something because I'm hungry and thirsty. Something you should both be doing before we continue. It also gives the animal life a chance to settle down again. Don't want to be stepping on any snakes slithering around here, do we?"

"Snakes?"

"Certainly."

"Here?"

"Where else?"

"You didn't say anything about snakes," she whispered with a shiver as she sat down on a rock nearby.

"Nor would I. Perfectly reasonable to expect snakes in a scrub setting like this, island or not. Whereabouts did you come across the females, Mr Boggs?"

Mopping his brow with his borrowed handkerchief, Freddy answered: "Wouldn't surprise me if this were the exact spot."

"Coming from which direction?"

"Same way we come."

"So you were heading towards our bay at the time?"

"More or less. Caught me a small goanna which I'd cooked on a fire the night before. I was stopping to munch on that when I saw 'em. They was walking towards me in a dream-like state. Mother was holding the young one's hand and both just up and passed me without a word."

"Probably in shock, I should imagine," remarked Arlon.

"Why do you say that, Arlon?"

"Well, you could hardly expect a woman with a young child in tow to be coming to an island on their own. I suspect they were travelling with their husband and father when something happened to take him out of the picture. Maybe the same sort of thing that happened to your brother-in-law, or their boat suffered a calamity. Had to have arrived here somehow. Like our Mr Boggs."

"I hope they're okay. I would hate to come across the body of that young girl."

"So the body of the grown woman wouldn't bother you?"

"I didn't say that, Arlon. That's a terrible thing to think of me.

Can't see as to how you could imagine I might not be upset about that."

"I was asking a question, Clarice. You only mentioned being worried about finding the young girl, not the mother. I was curious why that would upset you."

"A young life taken before her time is a sad thing, Arlon, and I would feel upset because it's a human reaction. A perfectly natural human emotion, which you know nothing about."

"Incorrect. I know about emotions, I just don't feel them."

"So you don't care about them bein' alive or not, Mr Arlon?" asked Freddy reasonably.

Clarice expressed a hiss of regret at hearing Freddy's question, for she knew the answer and knew that Freddy would not like the answer. Nor would she.

"If I didn't care for their livelihoods I wouldn't be here trying to track them down, Mr Boggs. Will I be shedding tears and expressing sentiments about them? No."

Clarice opened her eyes again with pleasant surprise after hearing the almost human response delivered by Arlon, when his usually emphatic reply of 'no' did not make its customary appearance. Before she could make a comment she saw that Arlon was paying particular attention to something flying around Freddy's head. Just as Freddy was about to swat at the annoying insect, Arlon's hand shot out to grasp his wrist in an iron-like grip, making Freddy wince and yelp in surprise.

Arlon held a finger to his mouth to indicate silence, while he peered through his fly net to find the creature again. Before long they all watched in fascination as a purple insect flew around them in lazy circles. Larger than a blowfly and smaller than a dragonfly, it flitted about them with an accompanying buzzing sound made by the wings. Two enormous eyes sat atop its tiny head, followed by a thorax, abdomen and whatever the caboose may have been called on this particular insect, which Arlon did not recognise. It appeared to be more like a scorpion's tail than anything else.

It finally settled on Freddy's knee, where it folded its multi-coloured, gossamer-thin wings next to its body. Standing remarkably still on its eight legs, it slowly lifted its tail into an S, and a long, lethal-looking barb extended from the tip. Before it could sink the barb into Freddy's knee, it suddenly stiffened as if it had been jolted by electricity, then, poof! It more or less imploded, leaving nothing but a slimy purple residue on Freddy's pant leg.

"What the...?" exclaimed Freddy, rearing back.

Clarice also gave an involuntary gasp. Arlon nodded his head sagely.

"Interesting," he said.

"Bizarre, more like," said Clarice. "What the heck was that thing?" she asked of no one in particular.

"That didn't come from no deep-water trench, mate!" cried Freddy with conviction.

"No, it didn't," agreed Arlon.

"Well?" begged Clarice.

"You expect me to explain the unexplainable, Clarice? Yet when I offer some form of logical answer you dismiss it out of hand. Let's say the noise we heard earlier was a fissure opening in the ground here somewhere and it released a captive insect not known to us. Hundreds of unknown insect species waiting to be discovered out there, Clarice. Maybe millions."

"And it explodes. Why?"

"Who knows? Possibly a reaction to sunlight for the first time it's exposed. I don't know, Clarice. I don't have all the answers to every mystery in the world, otherwise, I would be a very wealthy man."

"You still going with the earthquake or volcano theory?"

"I'm not going with anything. What I do know is that insect showed up moments after the noise. Coincidence? I don't believe in coincidences. I have never seen an insect like that. My understanding is that an insect is an arthropod with six legs. Typically, one or two pairs of wings if they fly. They usually have just three sections to the body, being head, thorax and abdomen with an exoskeleton. This 'insect' had four distinctive parts which included that tail, as well as eight legs and four pairs of wings. Whether it was about to inject you with poison or..."

"Poison?" Freddy cried.

"Of course, poison or some form of acid. What is it you think a bee's sting or a wasp's sting is comprised of? Of course, that thing may have had some form of neurotoxin in its arsenal, like a snake or marine stinger. We couldn't be sure."

"Yiz was gonna let me get stung-n-injected with neuro-whatever?"

"No, Mr Boggs, I wouldn't have waited until it stung you. I was about to swat it away when it did that by itself. I'd wipe that slime away if I were you, with a leaf or something. No telling if the toxins might still be active in its body fluids. Of course, it may not have been about to sting you, but perhaps to lay eggs inside you."

"That's bloody worse, I reckon," said Freddy with obvious revulsion, as he swiped away at the wet patch on his pants with some dead leaves he'd picked up from the sandy soil.

"This is all downright weird, if you ask me," announced Clarice.

"Well, as the founding directors of the Bizarre and Mysterious Detective Agency, I would think that falls right into our bailiwick, wouldn't you?"

"Oh, hardy, ha, ha! I still think it's a good name, even if you don't."

Why don't you two have a drink and a bite to eat while we can, then we'll set off again?"

"Fine by me, don't like it here at all," admitted Clarice.

"Too right," agreed Freddy.

"I think we will be just as likely to come across these phenomena no matter where we are," suggested Arlon.

Though Arlon's statement was meant to ameliorate some of their fears for their present location, he did not entirely trust the declaration. The startling sound they experienced had the distinct impression of proximity to the trio. The undeniable, rending crack left him in no doubt that they were dangerously close to whatever made the sound.

The occurrence of two creatures unknown to Arlon, despite his encyclopaedic knowledge of the animal kingdom gained from his extensive reading habits, left him doubting his earlier observations. He truly did not have any idea what might be happening. Nothing in his vast experience compared to the present events. Nothing in his imagination could conjure a guess as to the cause. It was a conundrum, to be sure. Yet Arlon Grey thrived on such things.

His enquiring mind and his condition had led him to bury his nose in books from a very early age. While his dashing looks, even from a child onwards, meant he had any number of female admirers, his condition all but forbade his inclusion in groups or social occasions. The deepest, cobalt-blue eyes penetrated the soul and heart of every female with whom he came into contact, yet the moment he opened his mouth he managed to alienate everyone. To say that he became reclusive as a result would not be entirely accurate, although he did spend many hours alone.

School was a prime breeding ground for hostility towards Arlon. He found solace and comfort in his own classrooms. Arlon poured his energies into physical activities of a defensive nature and into books. He was a rapacious reader and the accumulated knowledge remained with him. He did not retreat into books so much as launch himself into them for the sheer joy of learning. They opened up new horizons and fields of study he had never believed possible, although he never gravitated toward a scholastic career, much to his parents' lamentation and regret.

Arlon had not been back to visit his parents in an age. He supposed he might have to remedy that soon to introduce them to his bride-to-be. It was, perhaps, the main reason for his reticence in pushing forward with plans for the nuptials. He assumed that Clarice would like all the bells and whistles of a marriage in a church of some denomination, and a heap of guests, including his parents. He could not bring himself to summon up an image of him telling his parents about a possible marriage, or them at a wedding of his. If they even attended!

They were a great disappointment to Arlon in a non-emotional sense. They blamed themselves for his condition until it was diagnosed as a rare form of autism. Then they made it their mission in life to break through to him, to bring out his natural emotions with their pure love and boundless energies. They felt slighted that Arlon was never able to demonstratively return their love. No longer indicating that they cared more than as just providers, they came to resent their son when their efforts to conquer the condition failed.

Arlon stayed only until he was old enough to live on his own, just before entering the police academy. Scholastically and physically, he breezed through the academy, then excelled as a policeman right through to graduating as a detective after serving the requisite years as a constable. His consummate skills at reading a crime scene were second to none. His solve rate was in the very highest percentile. His popularity and cooperation as a team member were the worst in the history of the force. His callous manner won him no friends or admirers, even after solving crimes. The victims were often counted among his detractors and even haters.

His superintendent had no idea what to do with his troublesome detective. If he tried to move the man indoors, chained to a desk, he drove everyone around him to distraction and, eventually, resentment. He was also far too close to the super's office. Arlon's objectionable personality finally landed him in hot water when he was asked to explain to a young girl's parents the events that led to her shocking rape, torture and death. Arlon described in graphic detail what had occurred to the inconsolable and distraught parents. He was given his marching orders the same day. The whole precinct cheered at his dressing down and dismissal in front of the entire staff. A party was thrown for his departure, a party to which he was not invited.

He was not sad about such things, though he often mulled over the events of his life, attempting to glean from his mistakes the tools he required to assimilate, to a certain degree. It was impossible for him to completely avoid people, but imperative that he be able to at least communicate and feign a sense of emotional input to place the listener at ease. He most often failed in that regard. He could not abide falseness, even at the expense of cooperation or harmony.

Arlon peered at Clarice and Freddy, chewing on their sandwiches unenthusiastically, each in their own sphere of thoughts. He grasped the opportunity to view Clarice once more. He knew he had possibly hurt her with his comment earlier. He corrected himself, he thought, in time. Yet he sensed a melancholy air to Clarice since that moment. He was unsure how he might mend that bridge if, indeed, he had managed to burn it in his usual club-footed manner.

He wondered if it had been a Freudian slip, that he had inadvertently voiced an inner need to be free from the commitment of marriage. She had helped their agency considerably with her suggestion to take a new direction when the last assignment had ended less than favourably for a long-time friend and client. The lawyer, whose reputation Arlon had saved during his policing duties, was largely responsible for the success of the investigative agency Arlon had set up after his abrupt departure from the force. Robert Granger used Arlon's agency to perform many of the due diligence enquiries required of his law firm as well as other investigations on behalf of his clients. Though the two men remained good friends after the last assignment went sideways, Robert admitted that he could no longer use Arlon in that capacity.

Clarice was an avid follower-cum-admirer of certain areas of the internet that could possibly be classified as somewhat...kooky. She spent much of her spare time involved in the many strange and weird stories out there in cyberspace; alien abductions, ghosts, and all other mysterious and unexplained phenomena. She convinced Arlon that his talents were highly suited to investigative work of that nature, and said there was no shortage of potential clients looking to have their mysteries explained. They were lucrative clients, like her sister, hoping to find some closure.

Arlon allowed himself to be roped into a new name for the agency and a new direction that went against every logical notion he maintained. It was anathema to him to seriously consider some of the stories she related to him, yet here they were. A hefty retainer from her sister, their client, saw them beginning the strange journey that had landed them in the middle of some very disturbing events. Arlon had to find a way to solve several mysteries and also salvage his relationship with Clarice. He shook his head at the wonder of life and its infinite complexities.

Soon, they were once more trekking through the scrubby landscape, following the semblance of a track that Freddy had taken regularly throughout the time he had been on the island. Freddy appeared to be gaining a little weight and a healthier skin tone after his ordeal, though he still felt far weaker than he usually did.

Few words were spoken as the three of them pondered their private opinions and notions on the events evolving about them. Freddy had been on the island the longest and had blocked most of what he experienced from his consciousness. He refused to acknowledge the unusual sounds, sights and ominous impressions he felt at different times. They went against his simple beliefs, so he relegated them to those fabled and mystical notions he had about most things that were inexplicable.

Freddy felt he had been railroaded into leading the search for the lost females. He did not believe they could have survived that long on their own, not with everything that was happening around them. It was a futile search and he still couldn't comprehend how he had ended up agreeing to it. He needed to get off the cursed island, back to the mainland, back to his comforting shack on the beach, with the familiar fish smells.

Thoughts of his home brought with it the troubling realisation that his treasured fishing boat, his bondy, was gone. He wasn't likely to be able to replace his vessel with another like her, that was for sure. He loved that boat. He knew every square millimetre of her. He knew her quirks and foibles as well as he knew his own body. He could fix anything on her that happened to go wrong. She was a stout, all-weather vessel that had served him well for many years, and he mourned her passing as keenly as he would a close relative.

He'd had nothing but trouble and problems since heading out for the Spanish. He knew what he saw before leaping from his boat, but no longer trusted that vision. Once on the island more and more things had happened to make Freddy regret his impulsive actions to make a score. Nothing was worth the worrisome events they were experiencing. *People being chopped in half? Strange creatures suffering the same thing?* It was more than Freddy's simple mind could cope with. Shutting it all away in the deepest recesses of his mind made so much sense to him.

He'd admit to having told a fisherman's unlikely tale or two over his lifetime, but no one was going to believe a word he said if he succumbed to relating his experiences on the island. He vowed to remain stoically silent about any of it, if he survived! He suddenly turned to face Arlon, who nearly bumped into him.

"This ain't right, Mr Arlon, not right. I gotta say it. We's chasin' ghosts, mate. Them two ain't survived out here alone with all these...goin's-on. We should be gettin' back ta the house and gettin' orf the bloody island."

"How do you suggest we accomplish that, Mr Boggs?"

"What?"

"Getting off the island. Last time I checked, I wasn't able to walk on water, and I don't suppose you or Clarice can, either. We've been through this, haven't we?"

"Ya tricked me, ya did. This is wrong. Nothing good'll come of it," said Freddy, wide-eyed with fear.

"It won't if you keep panicking. Unreasonable fear as you are displaying..."

"Unreasonable? Listen here, mate. There's nothin' unreasonable about what I'm feelin'. Just 'cause you're a dead fish what can't feel nothin' doesn't mean others are like that or wannabe."

"Dead fish? Well, that's a first. Not often I come across a new insult for me. Does it make you feel better taking your frustrations out on me? Will it bring you any closer to serenity?"

"We won't find 'em. They're dead, don't ya see that? We're wasting our bloody time."

"It's not me you should be hoping to convince. I didn't want to go looking for them in the first place," admitted Arlon.

Both of them stopped to stare at Clarice.

"Oh, I see. It's all my fault now, is it?" asked Clarice, straightening her posture, ready for a stoush.

"Beg pardon, miss, but them two ain't gonna be alive no more. It were so long ago I saw 'em."

"Well, you would be very wrong about that," she insisted.

"I'm inclined to agree with Mr Boggs on this occasion, Clarice."

"Well, for once, that makes you wrong as well, buster!" she declared.

"What makes you so sure?" asked Arlon quietly.

"You haven't heard it?"

"Heard what?"

"If the breeze blows a certain way, then you can just make it out. I thought I was imagining it earlier, but it comes and goes clear as day."

"Clarice? What comes and goes?"

"The singing," she explained simply.

"Singing?"

"Well, humming, to be more precise," she said.

"Humming?" asked Arlon, with doubt creasing his features.

"Now who's repeating everything? Yes, humming. A young girl's humming, actually," she explained reasonably.

"I haven't heard anything," admitted Arlon.

"Nope, me neither," added Freddy.

"That's because you're too concerned about yourself, Freddy. I can't believe a big strong man like you is too afraid to go searching for an innocent little girl and her mother. From him," motioning towards Arlon with her shoulder, "I would expect a total lack of empathy for a lost soul, especially a child. Not from you. I thought better of you. Seems I was wrong. Go on, then, up it back to the house if that's the way you feel, and you can join him if you like, Mr Grey. I am going forward and I am going to find them both and bring them back."

Clarice squared her shoulders and marched past Freddy, who stood there agape. Arlon was equally stunned by her outburst. Without saying anything, Arlon followed quickly to catch up with her. Freddy, deciding he did not want to be left on his own, trailed reluctantly behind the pair. Clarice stopped periodically to listen for the sound she had heard earlier. Freddy and Arlon strained to hear it, too, without success.

At midday, when the heat within the scrub became almost unbearable, Clarice stopped. Rotating clockwise, she concentrated hard, then headed completely off the track through the brush in an easterly direction. Freddy looked at Arlon, who merely shrugged and followed. It was only as they neared the dunes at the top of the beach that both men finally heard the sound Clarice had described.

At the waterline rested the remains of a luxury motor launch. It was clear from the shattered bow that the stern of the vessel had not suffered the same experience as Arlon's hire boat. The jagged edges of fibreglass and timber were entirely different from the precision-cut edges of the boat at the bottom of the bay that Arlon had witnessed.

Emanating faintly from within the remains of the forward cabin came the humming sound Clarice had referred to whenever the breeze blew into their faces. On the dune before the beach were the smouldering embers of a recent fire. Scattered about the fire were the frames of fish and other assortments of bones, some recognisable, some not.

SEVEN

Eight-year-old Tara Blaze skipped along the gleaming wooden planks, polished to a high gloss even though this made them treacherously slippery. The Australian-built Belize 66 Sedan sliced effortlessly through the cerulean waters of the Whitsundays on a picture-perfect day for cruising. Fresh off the building blocks, the vessel was on its maiden voyage by the proud new owners, the Blaze family.

Michael Blaze had overseen every inch of the 60'4" hull during her construction, much to the annoyance of the construction crew and designers. The bespoke craft offered the finest appointments money could buy, including highly polished teak decking throughout, despite every warning from the ship's builders that it was extremely dangerous, if not technically illegal.

Michael was advised interminably about the need for non-slip decking on the port, starboard and forward decks. In rough seas, anyone attempting to move to the bow sundeck would risk falling overboard. Michael would not be moved on the point. He wanted the uniformity and unblemished appearance of the teak planking throughout.

Spring-loaded, pop-up, highly-polished brass cleats, a lock-up tender garage at the stern, teak swimming platform, a glass bulkhead opening up the area between the cockpit and the saloon to give an impression of greater space: every comfort and high-priced ostentation possible had gone into the construction of the *Blazer*.

Michael Blaze was at the open flybridge helm, replete with peaked captain's cap and all-white outfit. The pleat in his trousers could easily have sliced the smoked salmon they had planned for lunch. They sipped expensive champagne while the plotted course on the auto-pilot guided the ship through the calm waters toward their destination, Hamilton Island, where they intended to stay in their private penthouse suite in a hotel they owned for a week or more.

Life had been good for Michael Blaze and his tech company, Blaze Industries, from about the turn of the century. Y2K, or more specifically, the Y2K bug, was a gift from heaven for the then-fledgling operation. Lucrative contracts for the government and industries relying on computers provided a windfall of unimaginable opportunities and wealth for a computer programmer able to charge exorbitant fees to the ill-informed.

Judicious brick and mortar investments and a wide portfolio saw Michael Blaze become one of the wealthiest men in Australia. Avoiding risky stock market ventures saw his wealth increase when others suffered dramatic fluctuations, often ending in financial hardships they were unable to survive. Michael prospered from their demise more often than not. Like a shining knight come to rescue the flagging companies beset by financial devastation, Michael swooped in to scoop them up for a fraction of their worth. He sent in teams of experts to build them up for a short time, then sold them off at ridiculously inflated sums when the markets revived.

Ruthless in business and personality, Michael Blaze saw himself above most men, and only deigned to acknowledge his trophy wife from time to time under sufferance. She had failed to give him the son and heir he demanded, then refused, ostensibly for medical reasons, to try for another after their daughter, Tara, was born. Michael was thankful he had an iron-clad prenuptial in his possession, which he would use soon when he found a more suitable partner to provide him with an heir on whom to lavish his wealth of business acumen, to prepare him for when he eventually took the helm of the empire.

No longer the computer nerd attracting the derision and bullying he experienced through all his school years and beyond, Michael gave back that and more in his business dealings with competitors, suppliers, underlings and anyone else who had the misfortune to cross him in some manner.

"Michael, dear, tell me again why we're not going to Paris as I asked? Why are we going to that dreary little island with the tiresome tourists?" asked Angela Blaze through the intercom system. She lazed on the sunbed on the bow deck, looking for all the world like a bored model under her enormous, floppy white hat.

Though the day was perfect, the ocean relatively calm and the temperature comfortably warm, Angela Blaze was dressed from neck to ankle in the latest pure white Parisian designer outfit that cost more than some family cars. She was bored out of her brain, if truth be told. Tipsy from champagne, frustrated and upset about her plans being changed so suddenly, she whined at her dreadful husband through the intercom at the side of her white leather lounge.

"Because I know whom you were going there to meet, you dumb bitch," Michael whispered to himself on the bridge, where no one could hear him. Into the intercom, he said, "Once again I have to remind you that I have some business contacts lined up on Hamilton...*dear,*" he sneered, imitating her tone. How he hated that affectation of hers.

"Well, why ever did *I* have to go along? I could have flown over to Paris on my own. You could have caught up with me after your meetings," she moaned.

"Aren't you forgetting something? Or, should I say, someone?" he asked snidely.

"What?"

"No, not what, who?"

"Okay, I'll play your silly game, darling. Who?"

"Remember your broken promise...*darling*? Hmmm?"

"Tara?"

"Yes, surprised you remember her name."

"Very amusing, dear. What about Tara?"

"You do know that she's on holiday from school at the moment? That we're taking a family holiday *with* her?"

"Oh, don't be so melodramatic, dear. You could have had her babysat while you attended your boring meetings, and I certainly didn't have to be here."

"Oh, charming! I hope she isn't around to hear her mother talking about her like that...oops! Too late, there she is, right behind you, listening to every word. That's right, Tara, your mother didn't want to spend your holidays with you. She would much rather have jetted off to Paris to go shopping for yet more useless, ugly clothes, while...Jean-Luc chauffeurs her around."

"Oh, you aren't still jealous over that silly misunderstanding, are you, dear?" she asked, with a little more emphasis than she intended.

"Of course not, *dear.* Whatever gave you that idea? We both know what would happen if I suspected that."

"What are you talking about, Michael?" she asked, sounding more serious and less drunk.

"Don't you remember the little piece of paper you signed, giving up all rights and privileges in the case of infidelity?"

"Proven...infidelity, it cited, if I'm not mistaken," she challenged quietly.

"Well, it could hardly be fair to be just on suspicion, now could it?"

"Michael? You, you haven't...done anything, have you?" Angela asked, with fear creeping into her voice.

"Besides firing Jean-Luc without references after securing a full confession, you mean?"

An empty, poignant silence hung between them despite the thrum of the twin Volvo Penta D13 1350s pushing the sleek white hull through the small waves. Michael had a triumphant smile across his store-bought tan, Angela a look of shocked understanding descending upon her.

"Mummy, Mummy, look," exclaimed the innocent young child, pointing to the starboard bow at a pair of twin geysers erupting from the surface of the ocean.

Then a leviathan of the deep breached not more than a hundred metres from the yacht, breaking the surface in a joyous show of superior strength and agility for an animal of such proportions. A pod of humpback whales appeared in the waters surrounding the vessel.

Michael hauled back on the twin throttle levers to avoid ploughing headlong into one of the many large whales directly in the *Blazer's* path. The *Blazer* had travelled from Shute Harbour on the mainland past the northern tip of Long Island on its path to Hamilton Island. At present, the ship was drifting in reasonably deep water, predominately sheltered by the bulk of Whitsunday Island, located east of their position between them and the open ocean and prevailing winds.

Michael was not too concerned when the engines stalled soon after he decelerated. They were in open waters surrounded by the pod of whales, cavorting and breaching in a magnificent display of nature. The *Blazer* was soon drifting with the strong currents in a north-easterly direction, which would see them approaching Cid Island within an hour at the current rate. Michael judged it sufficient time to restart the engines.

Tara squealed with delight at the antics of the numerous whales rising from the ocean in mighty leaps, with their huge flukes slapping the surface upon re-entry with surprising volume. The little girl raced forward and back in excitement, trying to witness every breach. An alarm sounded suddenly by the ship's automated warning system, indicating shallower water imminent. The *Blazer's* onboard computer satellite navigation system, the best and most expensive in the world, pre-empted the ship's course and speed to calculate well before time the possible obstacles and depths the ship might encounter.

Although Michael was aware that he still had ample time to restart the engines and continue their journey, he believed it was better to err well on the side of caution where nautical alerts were concerned. But the engines would not respond to the turn of the key in the ignition. His brow furrowed as he heard no response at all from his efforts. He knew of a manual starter on each engine below decks, but hoped he would not have to resort to that, as he'd had next to no training on that particular aspect of the ship's operation.

The more often he tried to turn the key with no effect, the more concerned he became, and the more he regretted not having accepted the designer's offer to take them out on a shakedown cruise to familiarise the new owner with all aspects of the modern cruiser. After half an hour Michael was surprised to see islands closer to the ship than he thought possible in the short time they had been adrift. He decided to drop the anchor to gain sufficient time with which to sort out the electrical problems, which he believed the malfunction to be.

"Daddy, where are they?" shouted Tara from below his position.

"Not now, Tara. Ask your mother," said Michael, in a manner approaching panic.

The anchor release refused to activate and he didn't know if there was a manual release option or not. He fumbled about in the overhead compartments looking for a manual, to no avail, as the islands loomed ever closer. Michael took out his binoculars to scan the area carefully, judging the direction they were drifting. He had no physical charts at hand because he was told the navigation system had a stand-by battery should the electrics fail.

From what he could tell, and he was guessing, their ship would drift into the straight between Cid Island and Whitsunday Island, with any luck. He figured that might give him enough time to get below and manually start the engines, if he could find the right way to access that option.

CRACK!

Tara screamed and Michael was so startled he nearly fell to the lower deck. Somewhere from the bow, he heard his wife yell abuse at either him or the weather, whichever had caused her to spill her champagne. When Michael peered skyward he was surprised to see a lack of any clouds heralding a storm. He had checked the forecasts before departure and no warnings had been issued.

Then the sky fell, landing squarely on the *Blazer*, ripping her in half. Michael had no idea what he had just seen. One moment the sky was a brilliant blue, then, out of nowhere, the sun was blotted out by a huge black shape falling from the heavens. Whatever it was had completely cut the ship in two, with Michael clinging desperately to the stern rail as the weight of the two massive engines quickly pulled his half under. He heard a desperate shriek from the bow, where he saw his wife gripping onto the bowsprit with dogged determination and sheer panic. Of Tara, there was no sign.

Within seconds, the water surrounding him turned pink, and more sharks than he had ever seen before converged on the area, attracted by the scent of blood in the water. Just before the stern section of the *Blazer* disappeared beneath the surface, Michael jumped well clear. After surfacing several metres away from the mêlée of shark activity, Michael struck out for the nearest shoreline. What happened to his wife and daughter he didn't know and cared less.

Struggling to regain the surface after being thrown well clear of the sinking vessel, Tara Blaze, confused, scared and unable to determine up from down, managed to break through to open air. Gasping in lungsful of air, desperately kicking beneath the surface of the water with her little legs to stay afloat, she found a piece of floating jetsam onto which she could cling. While the contents of the plastic storage locker onto which Tara clung for dear life were unknown to her, it saved her from drowning.

She watched with bright green eyes as a large dark lump bulged the ocean in front of her as it rose slowly from below. Fiercely attacking the immense lump of black and white were more sharks than Tara could ever imagine, in a feeding, gorging frenzy. Although the leviathan on which they feasted was immense, it was only a fraction of its original size when Tara last saw the beast rearing up out of the ocean to perform its display of playful enjoyment. The remains of the large male humpback whale shivered and shook with the motions of the feeding sharks fighting for their share of the spoils, turning the ocean around them into a frothy pink milkshake.

Tara screamed long and hard as she slowly drifted away from the horrifying scene on the swift, unpredictable currents between the islands. It took some time before the girl was able to cease her panicked screaming, becoming almost hoarse and exhausting herself. When she realised that she had drifted well away from the immediate danger, she started to notice other pieces of debris floating along with her.

When she saw an arm atop a leather cushion, she screamed anew, knowing it to belong to her mother, recognising the diamond rings her mother wore. It was only when she noticed a small movement to indicate that the arm might be attached to a body that she settled once more. Frantically, she began to paddle with all her might toward the cushion. Behind the cushion, she found the rest of her mother, alive, at least for the time being. She had a nasty gash on her forehead, with a large lump developing there.

Tara managed to get hold of her mother, and draped Angela Blaze's arms over the storage container as best she could. Using what little strength she had, Tara gripped her mother's hands in hers as tightly as possible, offering a counter-balance to the container as they hung on either side, drifting inevitably towards land.

Little did Tara know that she and her mother were drifting directly towards the straight between Cid Island and Whitsunday Island. If they remained caught in the current it would carry them through the straight and into the open ocean beyond. Were it not for Tara kicking her legs to try to speed up the process of reaching land, they might never have made it out of that current.

All the time she was afloat, swallowing copious amounts of seawater as she gasped for breath, Tara kept a fearful eye open for sharks. Never loosening her grip on her mother's wrists and hands, she gamely kicked her little legs to painstakingly propel them out of the main current, heading closer to the beach she could just make out in the distance. Hour after hour, nearing total exhaustion, the little girl kicked her aching legs with all her remaining strength.

The land never seemed to be any closer than the last time she looked. She rested for periods when her legs turned to leaden jelly, her hands constantly cramping with the effort it took to keep hold of her precious mother, who had not shown any signs of recovery. Tara made sure to keep her mother's head atop the storage container to prevent her from drowning. Unfortunately, that meant that Tara was lower in the water on the opposite side than she would have liked, making it easier for the seawater to enter her mouth each time she breathed.

Glacially, the sodden pair drifted towards the snow-white sands of the beach, becoming larger and clearer, to Tara's immense relief. Demonstrating bravery and good sense well beyond her eight years, Tara kicked on, over the reef into the calmer lagoon. The water in the bay was crystal clear, with a crushed white coral bottom reflecting the brilliant sunshine, making it seem far shallower than it was in reality. Ever onwards she kicked, until her strength failed and the pair were finally washed ashore on a gentle wave.

Her chest heaving, her arms and legs completely useless, Tara lay at the water's edge gasping, while her mother remained silent, though alive, as far as Tara could tell. It took fully ten minutes before Tara was able to regain movement of her leaden limbs. She was amazed to see part of the wreckage bobbing on the waves beyond the outer edge of the reef. The white exterior paintwork of the once sleek craft bore the scars and stains of its unnatural demise.

Tara could not be sure if the wreckage would make it into the bay or not. Casting her eyes about the beach area and the dunes, though grateful to be in one piece herself, she cried a torrent of pent-up tears. She had a terrible thirst, agitated by the amount of seawater ingested during her ordeal. Her mother had still not moved, but Tara noticed the steady rise and fall of her chest to indicate the presence of life.

The girl had no idea what she should do. It was late in the afternoon, with evening breezes cooling her body enough to make her shiver. She immediately thought about starting a fire. However, she had no clue as to how she might achieve that without matches or a lighter. She had been taught how to make fires and other survival techniques on the many camps she was sent to by her parents while they holidayed overseas. While she lamented the lack of fire-making materials, her clever mind considered how she might go about enacting some of the survival strategies taught her, such as erecting a form of shelter.

With growing interest, she finally decided to open the storage container she had been using for buoyancy since being cast into the ocean. When she spied the emergency floatation vests inside, she quietly groaned. Even her young mind could grasp the irony of the situation. Had she opened the container at first, she could have saved herself a lot of wasted energy and strength by donning a vest and placing her mother in one as well, thereby alleviating the necessity of keeping her draped over the container the entire time they were adrift.

Her keen eyes spied the emergency energy bars under the jackets. She quickly ate a couple, then took a sip of the precious water from one of the dozen plastic bottles stored with the rations. Inside there was also a basic first-aid kit and other provisions to assist survivors of an accident at sea, including...a lighter! Tara's eyes lit up like a Christmas tree the moment she spied the lighter and tin of lighter fluid. With the training she had acquired due to her parents' neglectful nature, Tara knew mostly how to proceed from that point.

With night approaching it would be imperative to have a robust fire going to keep them warm and free from hypo-something-or-other. She couldn't remember the name of it, but she knew it would cause her and her mother to shiver and shake and possibly die if they couldn't get warm. Their clothes needed to be dried out and her mummy needed to be treated with some iodine or something, if it was in the kit. At the very least Tara knew that she had to bandage her mother's head to protect the open sore from infection.

Stepping out of her wet clothes, Tara made her way to the highwater mark, where she collected branches and twigs to start a fire. She dug a shallow pit in the soft sand to protect the fire from the prevailing breezes. She was trained sufficiently to imbue her with the knowledge that the fire needed to be built at or above the highwater mark, to ensure it was safe from the incoming tide. All those resentful hours under the painful tutelage of Mrs Maher and her daughter Amelia at Camp Survivor were paying off handsomely for the young girl who never believed in a million years that she would benefit from their teaching.

Further up the dunes, she spied the desiccated husks of old coconuts littering the ground. She quickly gathered some of the precious material, which she knew would start a fire in no time. She found a nice clearing atop the dune, shielded from the breezes by the natural sand berm covered in low vegetation, protecting the area. Tara quickly decided to change the position of her campfire to the new spot.

She dug another hollow into which she placed the coconut husks, followed by a selection of small, dry twigs. Onto those she placed some medium-sized wood, knowing that ignition temperatures needed to be achieved before she could place heavier night logs onto it. She touched her treasured lighter to the base of the pile, praying it would work. After a nervous flick or two with the new flint needing to be worked in, Tara was relieved when she saw the spark ignite the wick, which set the husks aflame instantly.

Only when the fire was sufficiently alight, with a pair of heavy logs casting embers high into the evening sky, did Tara finally traipse back down to the water's edge to retrieve the container and its contents. Then she steeled herself for the ordeal of dragging her mother up the beach to the fireside, where she would have to remove her mother's clothes as well. Her own shorts, T-shirt, socks, deck shoes and My Little Pony panties were all hanging by the fire on branches to dry.

She shivered in the stiffening breezes as she topped the berm to begin her descent to the water's edge once more. To her immense delight and relief, she noticed her mother sitting up as she approached.

"Mummy, are you okay? Mummy? Mummy?" cried Tara.

Angela Blaze did not acknowledge her daughter, did not bat an eyelid nor show any sign of comprehension when Tara attempted to assist her to her feet. Heaving with all her might, pulling her mother's arms before her, Tara finally forced Angela to stand. Taking her persuasively by the hand she led the beleaguered woman up the sand to the waiting fire. Once there, Tara faced the ominous task of undressing her mother when it became clear that she would not do so herself.

Patiently, Tara removed her mother's soaked clothing, which she hung by the fire as well. The flared pantsuit looked woefully drab compared to the magnificent outfit it had appeared earlier that day. Tara envied her mother the enormous wardrobe of clothes she owned, whereas Tara had only a smattering of school uniforms and the barest essentials in hers. She did not own any pretty frocks like the other girls in her classes and her mother never went shopping with her.

Tara marvelled at the skimpy underwear her mother wore that looked more like a slingshot than knickers. When she removed the underwear she was shocked to see the heart-shaped, closely-cropped coarse hair at her mother's crotch. Tara had no idea what her mother or any grown woman looked like down there. She had only ever seen girls like herself, naked, with no hair at all. Only Julie, who was a year older than Tara, had some short black hairs growing above her vagina. Tara smiled as she recalled the name for the part between her legs her teacher had recited to the class one day.

The other girls all giggled when they heard the name, though Tara couldn't be sure why it was funny. The teacher explained that all girls would eventually bleed from down there. Tara didn't understand how it was possible that every girl managed to injure themselves in the same place or that it was inevitable. She sighed when she thought about that. She knew so little.

Her mother stood statue-still with a vacant stare. Tara gently coaxed her down to the sand in a sitting position atop the life jackets to avoid sandy...parts. The raging fire warmed them both. Tara forced her mother to chew on an energy bar, which she had to push into her mouth. Then she made her drink some water from a bottle. As Tara turned to retrieve another bar for herself, she heard a movement. When she turned again, her mother had fallen on her side into a deep sleep.

Lying back on the life vests, Tara marvelled at the magnificent panoply of stars dotting the black backdrop. She began to hum the tune 'Twinkle, twinkle, little star', before also giving in to heavy eyelids.

EIGHT

Around midnight, with a waxing moon and a stiffening breeze making its way over the sandy berm, appreciably decreasing the ambient temperature, Tara woke with fearful cramps in her legs and aching muscles throughout her body. She tossed and moaned atop her life vests as cramp after cramp assailed her. While she knew it was advisable to massage the cramps as she had seen the camp instructor indicate in such circumstances, she demurred at performing the duty on herself. Biting back on the screams that threatened to escape her lips, in order not to wake her mother, Tara battled on gamely.

An hour later the seizures abated, leaving the girl exhausted and sore. She knew she should get dressed in her dry clothes and build the fire up once more. Though she attempted to resist the common-sense notion, she eventually hauled her aching body to a standing position. She caught a chilly blast of wind once she was standing high enough to escape the protection of the sandy berm, so she carefully shook her clothes free of loose sand and quickly struggled into them.

Tara scoured the immediate area to gather as much firewood as possible to stoke the fire back to life. While she assumed that she would have to get her mother dressed before too long, getting the fire raging was her first priority. Forcing her taut limbs to respond to her commands, she soon had the fire providing comforting heat. She managed, somehow, to rouse her mother from the depths of her slumber to awkwardly dress her in the dry clothes. For a tiny eight-year-old, it was a tiring and cumbersome task.

The only item she did not return to her mother was the slingshot panties. Tara didn't think it was worth the extra effort for so little reward or the discomfort such a useless thing might produce. Tara thought it might come in handy as the slingshot it appeared to be. *If only she knew how to use a slingshot.* Tara settled on her makeshift mattress of life vests once more, snuggling closer to the fire. Her mother had already returned to the deepest slumber, snoring softly.

Wide awake, despite feeling exhausted and leaden from her episode earlier, Tara stared into the mesmerising flames. With only the crackle of the fire and soft wind sloughing through the leaves of the trees a few metres away, the night was eerily quiet. Tara felt alone and scared for the first time since the ordeal began. She hadn't had time to think of loneliness or the dangers she faced. Only a few more energy bars remained before they would be out of food. The bottles of water would not last long. She wondered where her daddy went.

She wept silent tears as she remembered seeing her precious daddy swimming off after he saw her struggling to reach the floating container. He looked right into her eyes, then turned around and began to swim frantically away. Tara thought she might have seen one of the enormous shark fins slicing through the water after him, but she couldn't be sure. There was too much happening for her to remember exactly. She desperately yearned to be back home, or at school, or even with the dreaded Mrs Maher at Camp Survivor. Despite her dislike of the camp teacher, she would have to thank her profusely for everything she had taught Tara, if she managed to survive.

Eking its way through her reveries was a distant sound. Tara didn't think it was associated with the wind, the gentle waves lapping at the shore, or anything else she was familiar with. Sitting up, she strained to hear the sound repeated. When Tara forced herself to stand on top of the dune, looking down towards the waterline, she was surprised to see the ghostly image of the white bow from their ship, with its name visible in glowing letters on the side of the hull.

However, she didn't think that was responsible for the sound she heard. The small noise had an organic feel to it, like something alive. At least, that's the way it sounded to Tara's young mind. She moved away from the glare of the fire to improve her night vision, but was still unable to see anything other than a few objects associated with the wrecked ship, scattered on the shoreline and bobbing in the waves, ready to be washed ashore.

Tara was too scared to go down to the water's edge. She'd seen many shark fins in the bay earlier in the afternoon. She wasn't sure whether they remained in the bay or not. Though all her common sense was assuring her that sharks were unable to come ashore, she did not trust that logic. The briefest movement in her peripheral vision caught her attention. When she concentrated on the area to the south of her position she saw something wet glistening in the moonlight, being pushed farther up the shore with each incoming wave.

Shaking her head in frustration, she resigned herself to make the effort to discover the nature of the indistinct and dark lump, fearful that it might turn out to be her father. Then she remembered that he also wore all-white yesterday, looking so smart and handsome at the wheel of their ship. She longed for the comforting, infrequent embrace of her estranged father. Even the cold and distant inattention of her mother would be welcome at that moment.

Tara shuffled along the squeaky white sand, in no rush to get near the water's edge. She deliberately kept her eyes averted from the lagoon. She had no wish to confirm the presence of the ugly, menacing sharks. She had seen them gorging themselves on the carcass of the humpback whale as it surfaced under her. She had no idea a whale could leap from the water so high that it could smash a ship to smithereens, just like in the movie, Moby Dick. She was enjoying the cavorting whales immensely until one of them fell from the sky. She didn't understand what happened while it was in the air, because only half a whale came back down.

"Oh, you poor thing. Did those horrible sharks hurt you?" asked Tara, as she came across the injured animal.

There was evidence of blood and a deep gash as Tara bent to peer at what she thought might be a penguin. On its 'flipper' she noted a notch that may have been a bite, which was bleeding. She lifted the small creature into her arms to take it back to the camp, where she could administer some first aid. She wasn't sure she had the wherewithal to help the poor penguin or not, but she thought she might try.

Once more by the warm fireside, Tara rummaged through the first-aid kit to retrieve some antibacterial cream with semi-anaesthetic properties she knew to be in there. The cream had been administered to her on many occasions during camp when she suffered minor injuries. The soothing cream helped alleviate the sting of a cut or abrasion.

By the light of the fire, Tara was perplexed by the unique colouring and odd proportions of the penguin. She had never seen anything quite like it on the nature shows or in the zoos she had visited. When the animal made a small sound, as it regained consciousness, Tara broke off a piece of her invaluable energy bar to feed the forlorn creature. It gulped the morsel with relish, so she fed it another piece, then another. Before long it had consumed the entire bar.

"Sorry, I can't give you any more or else I won't have any left for me and Mummy. She's not feeling very well either. She hurt her head," Tara said with a smile, tucking the creature under her arm for comfort while she sat and gazed at the fire.

She woke hours later to the sound of flopping and a spray of water droplets in her face. She shrieked when she opened her eyes to find a decent-sized fish flapping about in front of her. She searched the area quickly, determining that her guest from last night was no longer with her. Instead, it seemed, was a fish.

"Mummy, Mummy, look at the pretty fish," exclaimed Tara excitedly.

Much to Tara's surprise and alarm, the fish then flopped straight onto the embers of the fire, where it reacted swiftly to the intense heat, before succumbing to its inevitable demise. Tara watched in fascination as the beautiful coral trout slowly roasted on the embers, its dashing hues soon turning to the colour of charcoal. The smell of roasting fish had Tara salivating. Instinctively, she used a nearby branch to turn the fish over, ensuring it cooked evenly.

After a time, Tara removed the cooked fish from the glowing embers with two green branches placed carefully beneath it. The head and tail immediately dropped off as she placed the fish on the lid of the container. Using her fingers, which she burned several times, Tara managed to remove the skin from the delicious white flesh beneath. Before she could taste the first bite, however, her mother descended on the repast, frantically picking the flesh off the fish and pushing the meat into her mouth.

"Don't eat the scales, Mummy," she chided, as Angela devoured one complete side of the fish before turning it over to start on the other.

Tara was able to push her mother aside for a moment as she carefully removed the remaining scaly skin. She grabbed a mouthful of flesh before her mother started on the carcass anew. No sooner had her mother eaten every bite and licked her fingers clean, than she collapsed onto her side and fell into a deep sleep once more. Tara was sad and disappointed that her mother did not leave her some, and that she had completely ignored her daughter while swallowing down the entire meal in gluttonous greed.

"You're a piggy, Mummy," she scolded the sleeping woman.

Tara added a few large branches to the fire to get it going once more, then threw the bare fish frame on to it. With the fire stoked, Tara decided to explore the beach in the hope of finding anything useful, as well as poking around the wreckage to gauge its helpfulness. When she topped the dune with the sun rising in the eastern sky above the outline of the island in front of them, Tara assured herself that the sharks no longer occupied the bay, then skipped down to the waterline.

She was amazed at how far up the beach the wreckage had ascended during the morning's high tide. There wasn't much to the remaining piece. When Tara looked closely she made out a small covered area which she and her mother might use if the weather got bad. It was a cramped area at the very bow of the ship, used for storage of ropes, spare anchors and things. If she arranged the life vests in there she could make a nice cubby to sleep in. Tara smiled at her ingenuity. She began to feel more confident about surviving their accident.

Turning to look at the interior of the island, she wondered if she might explore in there to look for help. She thought there might be someone else on the island who might help her. Then she wondered if she might have a better chance of a rescue if someone visited the island with a boat. She nodded her head in agreement. It seemed more logical to her to stay put in the bay. Someone would be looking for them because her daddy was an important man. Maybe when her daddy reached the shore he would alert the authorities to search for them, if he made it.

There was nothing of any use inside the wreckage, nor anywhere near it as far as Tara could tell, just broken pieces of the ship and a few bits of internal cupboards and such. There was nothing useful, like an esky of food or maybe some more clothes. Her dirty clothes were full of sand and made her skin scratchy. With the sun warming the air sufficiently, Tara thought she might rinse off her clothes in the water to get rid of the annoying sand.

Before she could change her mind, she stripped off quickly and ran into the water to thoroughly rinse the lightweight material in the gentle waves. She kept an eye out for the menacing sharks, and remained firmly in the shallows, where she believed it to be relatively safe.

She dipped her naked bottom into the cool water to force out all the grainy sand from her delicate places where it irritated her. She then decided to go all the way and wash her entire body in the refreshing water by scooping handfuls of water over her. She spent more than ten minutes in the water before being satisfied that she was free of all sand on her upper body. Below her knees, she knew it would be impossible to remain sand-free. She rinsed her sodden clothing in the water once more.

Tara returned to the campfire and placed the clothes to dry over branches in the nearby trees. Her mother remained fast asleep. It would soon become too hot for her, exposed in the blazing sun. Tara decided to move their meagre equipment into the shaded area beneath the trees before she and her mother burned their delicate, fair skin. It was again a chore to move Angela, rousing her from her torpor to blunder the few paces to the tree-line, where she collapsed again.

Tara still felt the remnants of aching muscles and tightness from the cramps. Though greatly relieved by movement and the cool water, she still winced every so often if she moved in a particular manner. She sat down in the shade to wait out the hottest part of the day.

Tara sighed as her young mind attempted to cope with their predicament. Although she had made some good decisions based on the little she had learned, she was still just a confused and frightened child. She did not know what else she could do to help her mother, or what options there were for getting off the island. She did not even know on which of the islands she'd washed up. Daddy had told her they were heading to their holiday apartment on Hamilton Island.

She knew and loved the penthouse apartment in the hotel her family owned. She had been there on those rare occasions she holidayed with one of her parents. Tara was very excited to be spending time with both parents: it was rare that she experienced some quality time with both of them together. While she understood that they were not happy about the prospect, especially considering what she overheard moments before the whale fell from the sky, she held out hopes that they would all have a good time together. She didn't understand exactly what was being said, but she was saddened by the tone of the discussion. Judging by the shocked look on her mother's face at the end of the conversation, Tara guessed that her mother had been given some bad news by her father.

Tara Blaze resembled her glamorous mother in many ways and, by rights, should have shared a warm and loving relationship as so many of the other girls at school and their mothers did. She had the blue-black hair that her mother tended to turn blonde from time to time, and the creamy skin that her mother took great pains to maintain and protect. Angela Blaze hardly ever ventured into the sun without full protection from clothes, sunblock, hats or all three. Tara saw that her mother's skin had taken on a reddish tinge from the little time she had spent in the sunlight already.

The day was heating up, though Easter had yet to arrive. Tara had been looking forward to the chocolate treats that the Easter bunny provided. Not that she believed in that particular fantasy creature since she discovered Jose, their gardener in Brisbane, planting chocolate eggs in the garden early one Easter Sunday. Apparently, her parents didn't even enjoy that simple pleasure, employing staff to perform those duties where they applied to their daughter.

Tara recalled that Easter always seemed to herald the cooler weather to that region of Australia. She had been skiing in mountain resorts as part of school events before, so she knew it never got that cold in Queensland. She just remembered that the extreme heat of summer normally abated by the time Easter came around, so the previous night had felt a lot cooler than she would have liked. The day was now heating up outside their shaded patch, but would not reach the high thirties until summer came around again.

Tara reached inside the storage container to retrieve the lip-zinc tube, which she applied to her lips and the tip of her nose, just as she had been shown. She almost succumbed to eating another of the precious energy bars, but demurred. Secretly, she hoped the penguin might return and she hoped to have some energy bar remaining with which to feed it. Tara pondered the odd possibility that the penguin might have provided them with the fish that morning. It seemed a silly notion, but it delighted her to imagine it might be true.

Although she saw it only in the moonlight and then by the firelight, it appeared to have peculiar colours for a penguin. However, Tara was no expert in marine birdlife and therefore had no real basis from which to compare or judge. In her child's mind, she accepted what she saw without questioning it too vigorously. Tara had never known the joy of owning a pet, as had some of the other girls in her class, who spoke about them often. Her heart went out to any dog or cat she came across on the streets in front of their Brisbane home in Brookfield, a lush suburb abutting natural hilly bushland on the north-western outskirts.

She longed for the comfort of holding an animal close to her, as she had with the penguin last night. It provided her with momentary comfort and succour in the terrible loneliness she felt, stranded and alone despite her mother being right next to her. Gentle tears cascaded down her cheeks again as she pondered her situation and how hopeless she felt. She spent the rest of the long day beneath the dappled shade of the scrubby trees, ducking out periodically to throw another limb onto the smouldering fire, to ensure she did not have to start another fire from scratch.

As the afternoon sun began to sink beyond the tree line behind her, Tara crept out from their sheltered camp. For the rest of the afternoon, she busied herself with gathering firewood, dragging the biggest limbs possible up from the highwater line where mountains of driftwood collected. Feeling gritty and itchy from her efforts, she decided to wash before it became too cool in the water.

She had seen the sharks enter the bay earlier, then watched them gradually depart a few hours later. She inspected the water carefully before stripping naked and plunging into the shallows, allowing the waves to wash over her. She was very pedantic about ensuring she removed all the sand from her body again. Somehow, she would have to convince or force her mother to do the same before the sand caused nasty rashes on her delicate skin.

Despite her precarious situation, the great fear of the unknown and whether she would ever be rescued from the island, Tara found herself enjoying the camping experience. She only wished she could have more food to stave off the hunger pangs she felt. Her stomach had been growling and rumbling all day. She'd had only a small nibble of an energy bar since the meagre breakfast morsels her mother had deigned to leave her.

Tara washed her clothes out thoroughly once more, especially her panties, which seemed to attract the sand no matter what she did to avoid it. She walked up the beach with her wet bundle to the side of the fire, where she hung her clothes to dry after doing her best to wring them. Her muscles felt better after taking a cool plunge. The aches and pains were gradually subsiding with the exercise of gathering wood and frolicking in the mild surf.

Her mother had not moved since she relocated her to the fire's side. Tara decided she had better try to make her mother wash.

"Mummy, Mummy, come on, you have to wash. You stink, Mummy."

Eventually, Tara was able to make her mother stand or sit as directed to enable her to remove the clothes she wore. Once more she marvelled at the hairy pudenda her mother sported, styled into a lovely heart shape. Tara determined that she would also have a stylish arrangement like that one day. She led her mother by the hand down the beach toward the water. Angela showed no signs of resistance or fear about entering the water again after their harrowing ordeal that had brought them to the island.

Tara kept up a constant stream of reassuring sentiments as she gently bathed her mother. She felt awkward when she proceeded to wash her intimate parts, thinking her mother might rebuke her harshly at any moment. Instead, Angela's vacant stare caused more concern for Tara than any sharp retort would have done. Tara pushed her mother farther into the water so that she could rinse out her lovely long hair, which had become matted and knotty. Painstakingly, she managed to remove most of the offending tangles by the end of their session. Tara was becoming chilled with her second time in the water, so she urged her mother to get out.

Tara placed her naked mother on the life vests in front of the roaring fire to warm and dry her. She then returned to the water's edge, where she proceeded to wash her mother's clothes just as she had done for herself. The sky was beginning to darken and the breezes were getting fresher, though the pair were well-protected from the worst of the chilling winds in the hollow behind the dune. Tara used the excuse of rearranging the clothes periodically to take her mind off the growing hunger pangs causing her tummy to protest, producing mild cramps. Once everything had been done that she could think of, Tara stood with her back to the fire to warm her bare bottom.

Around midnight, Tara stirred from her deep sleep for some reason. She used the opportunity to dress into her dry clothes again.

Once she had the fire roaring, she dressed her mother, who seemed to be more compliant and easier to manipulate. When her mother was settled, with closed eyes and breathing regularly, Tara sat by the fire, staring into the flames.

Only when the creature snuggled up under her arm did Tara realise the penguin had returned, as she had hoped it might. Though initially startled by the foreign touch, she soon attended to the bird's minor injuries again, dabbing more of the antiseptic ointment onto the damaged area. She then opened her second-last energy bar, half of which she fed to her friend in small bite-sized morsels.

Unable to keep her eyes open for long, she drifted off into a hunger-filled, troubled sleep of mysterious dreams. It was as though her subconscious was advising her about something important, something she should have discovered already, but failed to recognise. Perhaps she did not wish to delve too deeply into whatever aspect it was that troubled her. Whatever caused her uneasy dreams was as lost to her in sleep as it was in her waking moments.

Day three on the island started in the same manner as the previous morning, with a fish slapping the sand close to Tara's face. Tara came alert with a start that soon turned to a smile when she believed she had solved the mystery of the magical fish. The large spangled emperor flopped about in vain as it attempted to get itself back to the water.

Tara grasped the fish firmly, throwing it onto the red-hot coals of the fire. The distinctive aroma of cooking food soon filled her nostrils. Angela Blaze also came awake at the familiar aroma. Tara had to force her mother away from the fire before she burned herself as she tried to get to the cooking fish.

"NO, MUMMY!" Tara demanded with all the bluff she could muster, standing in front of her mother with her fists clenched, and ready to defend her share of the meal. "Now, you sit back down straight away, Mummy, or I won't give you any food at all," she asserted, with her hands planted firmly on her hips.

Angela displayed no signs of acknowledgment or recognition, but she no longer attempted to move past her daughter. Taking her mother firmly by the hand, Tara led her back to her place on the vests. She turned every so often to make sure her mother did not sneak up to the fire while Tara was attending to the delicious-smelling fish.

When the fish was deemed to be cooked through, in Tara's inexperienced eyes, she lifted it onto the lid of the storage container with two forked sticks again. She removed the scaly skin in one neat sheet from the steaming white flesh. Using a clean green twig, Tara then set about removing the flesh from one side of the fish, pushing the mound of meat to one edge of the lid, where she indicated to her mother that she could begin eating.

"Not too fast, Mummy, or you'll be sick," she admonished gently. "And the other side is mine today. I have to eat too, Mummy. I'm so hungry," she admitted.

Angela ignored her daughter as she greedily gorged on the succulent, fresh white meat, shoving stuffed fingers-full into her mouth. Tara quickly repeated the process of removing the skin on her half of the fish so that she could eat her share as soon as possible. She could not let her mother steal her food today. Tara tucked into her meal ravenously, ignoring her own advice of eating slowly.

It wasn't anywhere near enough for either of the females. Angela and Tara were both good eaters at home. Michael often wondered how they managed to eat more than he did. His wife never gained a gram of weight and his daughter was as thin as a rake. Michael was pleased that he didn't often have the chance of dining with his family to watch the vulgar display of gluttony.

Tara tossed the bare fish frame into the fire just as a loud crack shocked them both to the core. A loud splash from the lagoon made Tara run to the top of the dune to find out what caused it. It appeared to be half a whale, possibly the missing half of the whale that had destroyed their ship.

NINE

A high-pitched scream startled the trio out of their brief reflections. Arlon was the first to react, sprinting down the beach. A young, naked girl was backing out of the shallow water as he rounded the wreckage of a ship that obscured the child from their view on the dune. Clarice and Freddy followed close behind. At first, it appeared that the young girl was screaming and backing away from the naked woman sitting quietly in the shallows in front of her. It then became obvious, as they drew near, that the girl was staring at something being pushed towards the shore on the small waves.

Clarice rushed to the girl's side, whereupon she screamed anew at the surprise of strangers surrounding her. Clarice did her best to calm the child with soothing words and a comforting embrace. Arlon waded into the knee-deep water to inspect the object, looking askance at the woman sitting nearby with a vacant stare. When he recognised the identity of the object, he understood the reaction it had received.

The girl whimpered sadly into Clarice's shoulder as she was picked up and carried back up the beach.

"Mummy!" she cried suddenly. "Mummy mustn't see...Have to..."

"There, there, love. We'll take care of your mummy for you. Arlon, is the girl's mother okay?"

"She's naked," uttered Arlon simply.

"I can see that, Arlon. What I asked was, is she okay?"

"I suppose."

"Mr Boggs? Can you kindly look away to give the lady some privacy," warned Clarice in a stern tone, when she spied him ogling the woman.

"He's a bad man," whispered Tara through her tears.

"Who, Mr Boggs?" asked Clarice quietly.

The girl nodded sadly, "He watched us from the bushes, looking at Mummy and me while we were washing."

"You saw him watching you?"

Tara nodded.

"Arlon, can you ask the lady to get dressed while I take care of the girl? What was in the water?"

Arlon shook his head as he picked the object from the water.

"A foot," he shouted back.

"Daddy's foot," whispered Tara with a shiver.

"What happened to your daddy, pet?" asked Clarice gently.

"He...it, fell from the sky like the whale," she explained cryptically.

Clarice shook her head, wondering what the girl's words could possibly mean. "How about we get you dressed, young lady? It'll start getting cool soon when the sun goes down. Were they your clothes up by the fire?"

Tara nodded. Clarice left Arlon to deal with the woman, who was probably the girl's mother. She gave Freddy a fierce glare as she passed him on her way to the top of the beach. Clarice clutched the frightened girl to her ample bosom protectively.

Arlon was somewhat perplexed. He quickly bagged up the severed foot, complete with bloodstained deck shoe, into a plastic bag from his knapsack. Turning his attention to the woman, who sat perfectly still in the water up to her waist, left him feeling awkward and unsure. Her filthy clothes appeared to be in a pile above the water line on the hard sand. He couldn't understand why the woman was acting so calmly, having been intruded upon during her bathing routine.

It was only when he approached her that he saw the faraway look in her eyes. There was no comprehension in them, no indication of awareness at all. Arlon reached down to take her hand. A sudden flicker of the woman's eyelashes indicated recognition of sorts.

"Michael? Oh, Michael, you made it. Thank goodness. I was so worried," she said mysteriously.

Arlon merely nodded his head, not knowing what else to do or say.

He led the woman to her pile of stained clothing that may once have been pure white. While Arlon turned, to offer the woman some privacy, he noted that Freddy had not followed Clarice's instructions to avert his eyes. He was staring at the woman while she struggled to don her clothes.

"Look, Tara, it's Daddy. He made it," announced Angela brightly as they neared the fire.

Tara looked up suddenly at the sound of her mother's voice, the first time she had spoken in almost two weeks. She looked at the strange man wearing the funny outfit, like a jungle explorer from an illustrated Tarzan book she had read once. She couldn't understand why her mother would make such a strange comment. The man looked nothing like her daddy except for the wavy black hair which could hardly be seen underneath the helmet and the fly net. She could also see that the man was equally nonplussed.

"Daddy, Daddy," she squealed, leaping up and running to hug his legs. "Mummy hurt her head," she whispered to Arlon, who nodded sagely.

Clarice watched the exchange with surprise and admiration for Arlon, who seemed to handle the odd circumstances with unusual grace. She tried to diffuse the situation by changing tactics.

"Are you hungry...um...? What's your name, love?"

"Tara, Tara Blaze."

"Hush, Tara. You must let the adults speak. Oh, Michael, I didn't think we would ever see you again. Where have you...? How dare you leave us here alone for all that time!" Angela suddenly admonished.

"Well..." started Arlon.

"I'm hungry," admitted Tara quickly, to save the man from having to explain.

"Good, Arlo...I mean, Michael, has brought plenty of food with him. Haven't you, dear?"

"Who are you?" demanded Angela.

"I'm Clarice Manning, and you are?"

"Angela, Angela Blaze and that is my husband, Michael Blaze. I'd be much obliged if you didn't call him 'dear'."

"I'll try to remember that. Would you like some food?" suggested Clarice, sharing a look with Arlon.

"Of course I would like some food. What a stupid question," she muttered, as she sat on her set of vests awaiting service.

Clarice busied herself preparing a meal for the two from the provisions in Arlon's knapsack.

"Mr Boggs, I thought you said you came across these ladies on the path?" asked Clarice pointedly.

"Well, that might not be altogether correct, miss..."

"The bad man watched us from the bushes," claimed Tara with

growing confidence, while accepting a sandwich from Clarice.

"That, that's not entirely true now, young lady, I..."

"Did, too. Saw you hiding right over there while Mummy and I were having a wash down at the water, like today," Tara accused.

"How is it you two managed to survive here all on your own," asked Arlon, for the dual purpose of gaining information and deflecting the conversation.

"Why don't you tell them, Tara Blaze," insisted Angela.

"Fishing," she answered simply, feigning innocence while indicating the many fish frames littered about the campsite.

Before anyone could make more of the matter, Angela suddenly keeled over. Clarice moved to her side, where she found there was little she could do.

"Mummy's sleeping again," explained Tara, as everyone stared.

"Does she do that often?" asked Clarice.

"She likes to sleep a lot more now. She hurt her head."

"Yes, I saw the contusion there. If I had to guess, I'd say she suffered a severe concussion or even a brain haemorrhage. We need to get her to a hospital as soon as possible for x-rays," stated Arlon quietly.

"Mummy never talked before," added Tara. "Sorry about calling you Daddy before. I know you're not my daddy. He's dead, isn't he?"

"I don't know, Tara. I can't say for sure," admitted Arlon.

"You have the same colour hair as Daddy. That might be why mummy got confused. It was my daddy's foot that fell from the sky, wasn't it?" Tara asked, with her bottom lip beginning to quiver.

"My, you are a brave little girl to have helped your mummy so well and kept yourselves fed. How old are you, Tara?" asked Clarice quickly.

"Nearly nine," she announced proudly, displaying nine fingers. Tara suddenly dropped her chin.

"What, what is it, Tara?" asked Clarice in alarm.

"I didn't catch them," admitted Tara with shame.

"The fish?"

Tara nodded.

"Who did then, Tara?" Clarice asked gently.

"My friend," answered Tara shyly.

"There's someone else here on the island?"

"No," she admitted.

"Who is your friend then?"

"A penguin," said Tara uncertainly.

"Arlon?" Clarice questioned.

"This far north? I don't see it being possible. Far too warm for penguins in these waters. Only find them in cooler southern climes, as far as I know," explained Arlon.

"Why do you say it's a penguin, Tara?" asked Clarice kindly.

"I saw penguins in the zoo one time. My friend looks like that, only..."

"Only what, Tara?" Clarice pushed.

"He's not the same colour as the ones I saw. They had tux-tux-tuxedos on, my teacher called them. Little black and white suits. My friend is blue and green with lots of other colours. The naughty sharks bit him, and I put some cream on him to make it better," she announced.

"So, the...animal was injured and you helped it. Then what?" enquired Arlon.

Tara squinted up at him from her seated position. "He comes in the morning to drop off a fish for me and Mummy."

"You see this, do you?" he asked.

"Not really," Tara admitted.

"Then how could you know it was this animal you helped that provided the fish?"

"'Cause."

"Because you can't think of any other explanation?"

Tara nodded reluctantly.

"Tara, do you think your mummy will wake up soon?"

"She sleeps a loooong time," Tara said.

"Well, I would suggest we stay here the night. It's getting late and there's no way we can move her mother like she is. We have a nice fire to keep us warm and enough food for at least another day."

"Are you going to rescue us?" asked Tara hopefully.

"We sure are, princess," said Clarice, placing a protective arm around the girl's shoulder. "We'll take you back to my sister's house and we will get us all off this island as soon as we have mobile coverage again."

"Perhaps we can go gather some wood, Mr Boggs?" suggested Arlon reasonably.

"Not sure I want ta be helpin' no one what said I was a bad man," mumbled Freddy to no one in particular, as he turned toward the beach. Arlon followed him as far as the highwater mark, then veered off on his own.

Arlon wanted to take a close look at the large skeleton laying half out of the water. It appeared odd to him, almost as though it wasn't complete. At first, he believed the rest of the carcass was in the water. As he drew near, however, he observed only a portion of the whale. Sharks had made short work of its blubber, leaving only shredded flesh on the remaining bones. The vertebrae ended cleanly, with only a few rib bones to indicate the front half of the animal. Arlon was able to see the bones sliced neatly where the animal was bisected.

He shook his head in wonder at the mystery surrounding the island. People and animals were being sliced in pieces by some fantastic tool that defied the scope of current technologies, as far as Arlon was aware. His voracious reading in all things scientific and technological had revealed nothing capable of performing the precision cuts he had witnessed. Strange creatures that defied explanation, fisherman and females were running around lost and hungry. Boats sank or fell foul to other inexplicable forces.

He continued to toss about all the incidents in his mind as he joined Freddy to gather driftwood for the night's fire. He turned his concentration on the mystery animal that the young girl spoke about. He instantly discounted a penguin. Even a wayward bird would not stay around in such warm climates. It wouldn't even seem feasible for a penguin to provide fish of the size he witnessed in the scattered skeletons.

After several trips, they had sufficient wood to sustain a raging fire all night long. Arlon deemed it necessary as they had not brought with them any extra clothing or blankets to keep the chill of the evening at bay. Arlon was impressed by the skills exhibited by the young girl, Tara. She had placed the fire beyond the small berm to protect it from the onshore breezes. She had cleverly procured the container with life vests and survival equipment. She had displayed great maturity in caring for her seriously-injured mother, and perspicacity in identifying Freddy as a peeping Tom.

Arlon felt all along that something had not been copacetic about the fisherman's tale. He didn't trust him from the outset and felt vindicated for his suspicions. He wasn't sure what he might do about that fact, though. Most men coming across the sight of a nude woman, especially one as shapely and attractive as Mrs Blaze, would stop to admire her, if only for a moment. If a man who has been lost and alone for some time stumbles upon a vision of beauty, an enchanting siren to a fisherman's beliefs, he is hardly apt to avert his eyes naturally.

As they sat around the fire, trying their best to avoid the smoke drifting in all directions at the mercy of the swirling breezes, they settled into an awkward silence. Arlon, Clarice and Freddy had each eaten a small meal from the remaining food. Gradually, all but Arlon drifted off. Arlon remained wakeful to keep the fire well fed. He hoped to catch sight of the 'penguin' if it returned, as Tara said it probably would; having returned most nights since they washed ashore.

At the stroke of midnight, according to Arlon's watch, a movement from the direction of the dune caught his eye. From the darkness outside the ring of light provided by the fire, he witnessed a dark shape moving slowly forward, furtive and aware of its surroundings. It stood about sixty centimetres tall and walked with the familiar waddle one associated with penguins. Arlon immediately discounted the popular fairy penguins, as they were far shorter than this midnight guest. As it drew nearer to the fire, ignoring the sleeping mounds, Arlon saw flashes of brilliant colours, depending on its angle in the firelight.

The creature made its way unerringly towards Tara, who slept next to Arlon. He had placed himself purposely by her side to protect her in the event of danger, something he instinctively anticipated. Standing still for a moment in the firelight, Arlon examined it surreptitiously from his peripheral vision, hoping not to alarm the creature by turning his head.

It did have the basic shape of a penguin, with a distinctive feathery fur dispelling droplets of seawater from its oily coating. That was where the similarity ended, however. Arlon could plainly see that its wings were not the same shape, and its feet were not like the webbed penguin foot at all. Tara stirred as it gently nudged her with its...beak? Arlon could not be sure if it was a beak or not. It was dark and multi-hued, like the creature's fur, set beneath what may have been eyes.

Tara came awake slowly, rubbing the sleep from her eyes. She beamed when she saw the creature in front of her. She looked about her at the sleeping adults, then saw that Arlon was awake. He gave the faintest shake of his head to indicate that she should not acknowledge his presence. The creature seemed unaware of the exchange. Tara reached for the morsels of food she had retained from their meal in her shorts' pocket.

Arlon could not quite discern whether the creature ate the proffered pieces or not. It certainly seemed to accept the food into its unlikely beak, but did not swallow as a penguin might, or any animal for that matter. Instead, the creature seemed to store the pieces within its thick fur. It could be said that a bird was capable of storing food in its crop to feed its young, but it didn't look right, in Arlon's opinion.

A small movement from one of the sleepers suddenly alarmed the creature, forcing it to take precautionary steps in reverse. Arlon snapped his fingers to attract Tara's attention and to test the hearing capabilities of the creature.

Observing no reaction from the creature to sound, he said, "Tara, I want you to move over very slowly. Get behind me."

"He's afraid of the others, that's all. He won't hurt me," she explained quietly.

"Tara, I want you to do as I ask right now. If the creature is frightened, we don't know what it will do, do we? We don't want it to hurt your mummy or Clarice, do we?"

Tara shook her head resignedly, inching over toward Arlon, who had not moved a muscle. The creature waited at the edge of the firelight, wanting to gauge if any more movements from the others would be forthcoming, unsure why Tara was edging away. Its fur was rising and falling, bristling with suspicious energy. Once Tara had moved entirely behind Arlon, the creature seemed to become annoyed at the alteration to its routine.

Incredibly, the creature's legs began to unfold right before Arlon's eyes. It rose to nearly double its original height on spindly, knobbly, multi-jointed, grey legs. Arlon continued to gaze in incredulity as the beak and eyes flattened into the surrounding fur as though they had never been there. Then the area rose and tilted backwards to reveal a new head unfurling like a flowering bud. Only the new oblong head displayed hideous red eyes twitching with malice above a wide maw filled with tiny, razor-sharp, needle-like teeth.

Tara screamed. In a flash, the creature leapt forward on its spring-like legs. The spear entered its chest in mid-air, penetrating all the way through. The creature tumbled and folded in on itself into many contorted configurations. It finally found its legs again to retreat at pace, only to reach the end of the tether attached to the spear, which Arlon held firmly. The thing then somersaulted and screeched its indignity in a frenzied display of pain and frustration.

The rest of the party, except Angela, was soon wide awake, staring at the impossible scene with a mixture of revulsion and fear. Tara continued to squeal as she watched her friend roll and squirm in its death throes, attempting desperately to break away from the line holding it fast. Soon its movements slowed and then halted altogether. Clarice moved over to comfort the tearful girl in her arms, while Arlon walked forward to inspect the incredible creature. Freddy joined him.

"Never seen nothin' like that in all me years, nothin'!" he spat. "The devil hisself, I reckon, or its plaything," he added with a shiver.

"I wonder if we can keep religion or superstition out of this for the time being. It isn't helping," suggested Arlon.

"What else could that abomination be?" asked Freddy, crossing himself.

"Well, it wouldn't be dead if it was the devil or a demon, now would it?" asked Arlon reasonably.

"Comin' out at the midnight hour-n-all," remarked Freddy, in a reverent tone.

"Yeah, disguising itself as a penguin to get into the good graces of an eight-year-old girl. Does that sound like a demon to you, Mr Boggs? Heard tales of such things, have you? Care to regale us with your fascinating knowledge of all things mystical, Mr Boggs?"

"Don't like ya tone, I don't," said Freddy, with an air of superiority. Ya don't know everythin'," he added.

"Like you would?" said Clarice with disdain. "Are you all right, pet?" she asked Tara, who was weeping.

"Michael?"

They all turned to see Angela sitting up with a confused look.

"Okay, I think we should all get going now. If we hurry, we could be back at the house by early morning. With any luck, we'll have mobile reception back again and we can get off this island and get your mum seen to, little one," suggested Arlon, as Tara turned to face him, with grief straining her young features.

Tara nodded her understanding bravely.

"Michael?" asked Angela again in confusion, as Tara took her hand after being lowered to the sand.

"It's all right...Angela, we're going home," Arlon deliberately lied for perhaps the first time in his life.

Clarice was filled with such admiration and love she thought her heart might burst. The tears were already forming at the corners of her eyes as he led the way with a makeshift flaming torch he'd made by wrapping cloth around a branch, which he lit from the fire.

Before they had moved more than a kilometre the ground began to shake and the air was rent with the sounds of a cataclysm in the making. The sky immediately above their position lit up momentarily with a blinding, shimmering halo of intense white and blue light. Shadows caused by several falling objects swept over the huddled group. Everything lasted only a split second, yet seemed like an eternity to the frightened humans, shielding their eyes from the harsh glare.

"I have to go back and retrieve the spear," announced Arlon when the silence returned.

"Why?" asked Clarice with grave concern.

"It's the only one I found to go with the speargun," he admitted with a shrug.

"Arlon, you can't possibly be thinking of touching that...thing back there?"

"How else do you suppose I'll get back the spear?"

"Arlon!"

"Well, I don't like the idea either. I would have been quite content to leave the spear back there in that animal."

"Why are you convinced we need it now, when you were set to leave it behind before?"

"Um..."

Arlon was reluctant to discuss his reasons in front of the others, especially the child.

"Michael, why are you even listening to this lady who is calling you strange names?" asked Angela in confusion. "Where are we, Michael? What happened to the yacht?"

"All good questions, Angela. You'll have to wait for answers, though. For the moment...Actually, let's all go back to the fire. I think it might offer us some protection and better light."

"Protection from what, Mr Arlon? Why are yiz headin' back ta the fire?" asked Freddy pointedly.

"I'm...okay, this will sound odd, but I think we may experience...further confrontations similar to the one earlier," he admitted.

"Is the penguin coming back, mister?" asked Tara fearfully.

"Maybe. Maybe worse," he added ominously.

"That's enough for me to go back," announced Freddy, leading the way through the pitch-black night, only to stumble on a tree root several metres away.

"Either take the torch or let me lead, Mr Boggs. Which is it to be?" asked Arlon hastily.

"In a hurry to leave women and children on their own again, Mr Boggs?" Clarice asked as they passed Freddy.

"I wasn't..." Freddy's voice trailed off as they walked away, following Arlon. He quickly rose and trudged after them.

When they arrived back at the campsite, the fire had burned down considerably. Arlon more or less forced Freddy to accompany him onto the beach to look for suitable logs.

"We need to build the fire up substantially," Arlon almost whispered.

"Eh? What was that? Speak up, can't hardly hear nothin' in me old age," Freddy barked.

"I was trying to keep my voice down and I would advise you to do the same," explained Arlon.

"Whaffor?"

"To avoid our visitors, if possible, at least until daybreak."

"What bloody visitors? Ya talkin' rubbish, mate. No one here but us," Freddy said uncertainly.

"Then why were you in such a hurry to return to the fire, Mr Boggs?"

Freddy couldn't answer him with any confidence. He remained silent as they gathered armfuls of driftwood, carting them back to the camp, then repeating the exercise several times before Arlon was satisfied. The group watched in perplexed curiosity as Arlon extended the fire, originally started by Tara, by creating a second large ring encompassing them. In the shallow trench he dug out, he placed several burning branches from the fire, then placed more and more wood onto it until they were completely encircled by a ring of fire, with the original site at the centre like a bullseye.

Though Arlon was not entirely satisfied that he had gathered enough wood, he had effectively eliminated the possibility of collecting more.

"I'm scared," whispered Tara into Clarice's ear as she clung tightly to the woman.

"It's okay to be scared, sweetie. Arlon will protect us, don't worry. He will, won't he?" she asked Arlon quietly, after releasing the girl to care for her mother. Angela appeared to be going to sleep once more.

When Arlon did not immediately answer her, Clarice became worried. Arlon held the speargun at the ready after having retrieved the spear from the bloody corpse of the strange animal. He slowly rotated his body to inspect all points of the compass as best he could through the roaring flames. It was impossible to see beyond the flames into the night.

"We have about three hours before dawn. Except for Angela and her daughter, I want you to be vigilant. I want each of you to face a different direction. Between the three of us, we can cover the whole circle. Don't bother trying to look beyond your section. Leave it to the others. Understand?"

"No, Arlon, I don't understand. Can you please stop scaring us and tell me what it is we're worried about," asked Clarice in exasperation.

"Keep your voice down, Miss Manning," Arlon warned.

Clarice was jarred by his use of the formal title he had used only in the office since their engagement. It was either a clear indication of the danger he believed they faced or an unintended slip of an impending relationship split.

"Folks," began Arlon in a lower than normal voice, even for him. "I can't tell you exactly what's happening here. I don't know. I don't like not knowing, but that doesn't mean I'm any wiser or can be forced to tell you something to allay your fears. There are a few things we do know, and we can address each of them at another time. For the moment, I have reason to believe that we can expect more...'penguins' to be lurking about out there. I'm hoping the fire will keep them away from us, unless the girl can tell us that fire doesn't affect them?" Arlon asked, looking directly at Tara, who was now seated next to her sleeping mother atop the life vests.

"He didn't like the fire much, mister. Whenever I tried to move closer, he wouldn't come with me," said Tara.

"That's what I was hoping you'd say. Thank you, Tara. You should try to get some sleep now. We'll stay up and keep an eye out for you and your mummy."

"Arlon? Can you tell us anything, even a guess?" asked Clarice, once she had settled the girl into a sleeping position with her mother.

"Face outwards again and concentrate on your third," Arlon instructed.

Clarice and Freddy obeyed.

"Well, you sure had it right when you called our agency bizarre and mysterious because I have never come across anything quite as strange as this, even though our last assignment stretched the bounds of normalcy. What you've seen so far is what I've seen and I don't have proper explanations for any of this. We felt the earth move before. Was that a precursor to a big one, or an eruption? Still a possibility in my mind. But that's me and my logic trying to make sense of it, rather than fact.

"Something immense and possibly catastrophic is about to occur here. I'm convinced about that much at least. The weather may be affected by that. We might be experiencing atmospheric alterations because of it. It's not impossible to imagine changes in magnetic forces, or electrical discharges resulting from tectonic plate movements on a grand scale. Localised temperature fluctuations in the water from undersea volcanic activity could conceivably produce any number of weather anomalies.

"I'm not a meteorologist, I'm not a volcanologist and I don't have qualifications in any of the sciences, so everything I say can be taken with a grain of salt. Okay?"

"Keep going, Arlon. Even the sound of your voice is enough to make me feel better," begged Clarice.

"Me, too," added Tara sleepily.

"Hey, you, you're supposed to be asleep," chided Clarice with a warm smile.

"It don't explain them animals, though, Mr Arlon," said Freddy in a hushed tone.

"No, it doesn't accurately explain that particular phenomenon. I suggested an undersea fissure opening to release or force unknown specimens to the surface for the first time, to explain that thing we saw on the beach. That couldn't adequately explain a land-based animal. Although the 'penguin' wasn't necessarily land-based, was it? Semi-aquatic, I would have described it, or perhaps amphibian."

"Mister Arlon? How did the whale fall out of the sky on our boat?" asked Tara.

"I have to admit, little one, that has me stumped if it's true. Are you sure it fell from the sky and didn't simply swamp your boat when it breached?"

"Don't know what that means. It fell, I saw it."

"Okay, if you say so. I didn't mean to make it sound like I doubted you. I'm just trying to figure some things out in my head and I say the first thing I think of sometimes. I'm a bit strange, you see? I don't have any feelings like normal people and, even though I don't ever mean to be rude, I say the rudest things, even to my lovely fiancée. People don't like me much after they meet me and talk to me. I can't help it. I don't get scared, or sad, or angry, but I can't experience love, laughter or friendship, either."

"So sad," whispered Tara as she finally succumbed to sleep.

"Yes, I suppose it is. Only I can never feel that," said Arlon, mainly to himself.

Rushing from the darkness came a shadow, then a piercing screech of insensate anger, a galloping, and a snout thrusting through the wall of flames. Fierce, menacing, gnashing teeth of unbelievable length, snapping, howling, then yelping alarmingly as the animal suddenly realised it was in pain. The girl and Clarice screamed, adding to the confusion. Arlon stood to aim the spear at it. It withdrew swiftly beyond the barrier of flame, where it mewled pathetically before retreating into the night.

"I am never going to doubt you again, Arlon," admitted Clarice, after a moment of silence. "What was that?"

"Not another 'penguin', that's for sure," muttered Freddy.

"Make sure there aren't any breaks in that ring of fire, folks. It's the only thing saving us at the moment, unless they decide it's worth the pain to get at us," asserted Arlon quietly. "And keep your voices as low as possible."

"Arlon, you make it sound as though those things are

intelligent," said Clarice, shaken by the harrowing experience. Tara had rushed to her side, where she remained.

"Any animal has intelligence, Clarice. It may be only an instinctive urge to feed, defend, attack or breed, but it's a basic intelligence, nonetheless. I'm hoping it can't see beyond these flames or hear us. It might not be tempted to repeat the painful exercise it just experienced if it doesn't know there is something worthwhile behind it. That's not to say another one might not try it."

"Another one?" asked Clarice.

"Several, if I'm not mistaken," announced Arlon, worryingly.

"How can you know that?" sneered Freddy.

"By remaining observant when others are too ignorant to perform that simple function, Mr Boggs. While you were cowering and shielding your eyes earlier, I was being watchful and I heard several thumps to indicate something landing nearby. I calculated or guessed that they might be larger than and different to the penguin, from the sounds they made upon hitting the earth."

"I would have thought that you might have more respect for Arlon by now, Freddy. It appears I was wrong, about you, and about my husband-to-be as well. Arlon, I am so very proud of you and I love you, from the bottom of my heart, I love you. I wanted you to know that."

"I know that, Clarice. Somehow I managed to upset you before but, for the life of me, I don't know how I did it. I won't apologise because I can't mean it. If you let me know what it was at some point, then I can at least remember not to repeat the mistake."

"You got it, mister."

"Mister Arlon?"

"Yes, Tara?"

"I like you," she whispered, with a big tired smile.

Arlon peered back at her briefly as she reposed comfortably in Clarice's arms. It was the first time in his life he had experienced an unconditional declaration of friendship from anyone. While it did not evoke in him an immediate sensation, it did manage to touch something deep inside the man. It was like throwing a stone into a seemingly bottomless well, only to have it reach the surface way below with a muted splash. That small, insignificant stone caused the slightest ripple in the pool of sentiments that Arlon firmly believed to be non-existent within him.

Clarice beamed at him, knowing for certain that he would make a perfect father for any children they brought forth during their marriage. Instantly any doubts she once harboured vanished. Whatever he lacked where emotions were concerned, he made up for with strength of character, loyalty, dependability and so many other more worthwhile qualities. It dawned on her suddenly that romance was not necessarily the be-all and end-all it was made out to be. She finally released some of those ingrained, false sentiments from the myriad of romance novels she'd consumed over the years.

Clarice was astounded at the mini revelation within her. She'd been beside herself with worries about how her life with Arlon could hope to succeed with his condition, when all along it was her angst that seemed to cause the most consternation.

Arlon wasn't and couldn't be worried about his condition. He had accepted it long ago. Clarice saw how it was she who was unable to accept his disadvantage. She was repeating the mistakes made by Arlon's parents, who had hoped one day to break through to him, to finally gain the love and affection they believed they deserved. They had hoped to change him, and Clarice understood at once that she was guilty of the same irrational notions.

Arlon could certainly drive a person to distraction at times, barely able to withhold his acerbic comments. Otherwise, he was an ideal man. He had unlimited patience, spoke quietly, for the most part, never raising his voice in anger and Clarice knew he defended the little man always, having been on the receiving end often enough himself. She could trust that Arlon would never raise a hand to her, or verbally abuse her. She also understood that he would stand by her through thick and thin, as he had demonstrated already.

It surprised her to see him acting so wonderfully and tactfully with the young girl, and it delighted her to hear Tara say something touching to him. She even imagined that the comment by Tara had reached him somehow. Not that anyone but Clarice would have identified the infinitesimal reaction he exhibited upon hearing he was liked for maybe the first time in his life. It warmed her heart and forced her to reassess her beliefs.

Arlon and Freddy fed the fire throughout the remaining hours of the early morning. Several times the group started as the snuffling, snarling sounds of something foreign and fierce skulked about the perimeter of the fire. However, they did not experience a repeat of the earlier incident, much to everyone's relief.

"Not long now, and we will try to make a break for it along the beach. I don't trust using the inland trail. We only used that to avoid the hazardous rock area at the point of the bay. I'd prefer to face that than venture inland, where we can't see what's coming," said Arlon.

When no one answered, he turned. Everyone was fast asleep. Clarice, still with Tara in her arms, was curled up on a pair of vests. Freddy, slumped sideways, was oblivious to the world. The first signs of dawn lit the distant horizon with a faint glow. Arlon could no longer hear any creatures nearby, and the flames were being allowed to burn down. Although Arlon preferred to keep the fire going until the last possible moment, they were trapped unless it died down. He couldn't risk any of his party getting badly burnt because they had to cross the fire.

He didn't like the idea of being in the open. Didn't like it one bit. Bearing only a small spear gun with limited range to defend them, Arlon was not confident of reaching the house safely. He hoped, and it was a long shot, that the creatures had sought better hunting grounds inland or farther along the beach. Arlon was under no illusion that they would survive an attack by the beasts. Judging by the head that had struck through the flames, the rest of the animal had to be as large as a bear.

TEN

When the sky was light enough for the group to make their way, Arlon stepped over the smouldering ashes in the ring around their camp to scout the surrounds. While he admitted that he was by no means an expert tracker, he could make little sense of the signs around the camp. The confusing array of imprints that had trampled the leafy vegetation atop the dunes gave no clue as to the proportions of the animal that harassed them, and Arlon concluded that more than one animal had stalked their camp.

He turned to the group watching his every move and signalled them to follow him quietly. Angela had woken earlier in her previous fugue, and remained silent and vacant. She followed her daughter obediently as the rest made their way down the beach to join Arlon. They began to walk slowly toward the next bay. The rocky promontory sat at the farthest point, about three kilometres away. According to Freddy Boggs, that rocky outcrop went on for many hundreds of metres, with no room between the boulders to walk on the sand, requiring them to traverse along the tops of them.

Arlon worried how the girl and her mother would fare with that task. One slip could spell the end for either of them if they sliced themselves open on the treacherous barnacles and oysters festooning the low-water portions of the rocks. It was the sole reason they had chosen the inland route to search for the woman and child.

Clarice stepped close to Arlon, out of earshot of the rest, or so she hoped.

"Arlon, this doesn't make sense. No way could we have creatures just dropping from the sky because of some geological event: creatures that have no place being here."

"I agree."

"Well?"

"You expect me to explain?"

"Speculate, Arlon. I know you have a theory or two rattling around up there in that beautiful head of yours."

"I don't know that it would do any good to speculate or guess."

"Humour me," she suggested nicely, placing a loving arm around his waist, feeling the firm muscles there.

"I'm not sure I'm willing to share where my mind is going with this. It's so far-fetched and improbable that I risk sounding crazy. I've read a lot of science journals and magazines, Clarice. I know of every new development around the globe and every experiment underway. I've read tons of well-founded theories and all of the arguments about some outlandish ideas, some complete balderdash, in my opinion. This comes close to one of those theories that I wrote off as complete and utter bunkum, science fiction or fantasy rather than having a basis in fact."

"But you think it comes close to explaining our situation, if it's true?" she asked.

"Maybe."

"Let's have it, balls and all."

"Pardon?"

"Don't hold back. Just tell it to me plain. I won't hold you to any of it and I won't scoff," she said with a smile.

"Oh, you wouldn't scoff. You get off on this garbage. You practically live for this rubbish."

"Stop trying to whet my appetite, lover. Tell me," she demanded.

"Portal."

"Come again?" she asked, not quite knowing if she had heard correctly.

"A portal, a fissure, an opening," he explained simply.

"A space portal?"

"We aren't in space, Clarice."

"So, not some portal to other planets, then?"

"I don't think so."

"Then?"

"Interdimensional."

"You have to be kidding?"

"I think it was a chap by the name of Vallée, Jacques Vallée, a ufologist, who may have been the first to propose the hypothesis of interdimensional travel to explain the sudden appearances and disappearances of UFOs. As I said, it's an extreme theory that I instantly dismissed when I read about it," admitted Arlon.

"So what makes you think it is less than extreme right now?"

"I don't. You asked me to reveal my thoughts, so I did."

"Explain this dimension-thingy?"

"The theory is that we live in one of an infinite number of dimensions all coexisting within the same timeframe. Pure and utter hogwash!"

"Then why are you thinking about it?"

"Because it is the only theory that encapsulates most of the phenomena we have encountered. It shouldn't, but it does. I still go with my geological event hypothesis. Unfortunately, that may also tie in with the interdimensional portal."

"How?"

"Well, we have to ask ourselves why this is suddenly happening. If such a thing as a portal exists, why is it functioning now? It can't have been happening before the year your brother-in-law died under such strange circumstances. It would have been noted, been investigated by scientists, if these events had been occurring. This is recent and it may well have been activated by undersea activity."

"So it was released somehow by the eruption or quake or whatever?"

"If we accept its existence, then that may explain its sudden appearance, or, at least, its sudden activation."

"How does it explain the death of my sister's husband?"

"Once again, I urge you to accept that it's all an absurd notion, and probably so far from the truth that I'm ashamed to mention it."

"You can't be ashamed, so get on with it."

"Imagine, if you will, a portal suddenly appearing in front of you as you are walking along. It stays open only a microsecond, not enough time for you to physically react. Not enough time for you to back up, say. The portal opens and you are halfway through when it closes."

"Your other half is still on the other side of the portal?"

"Ostensibly."

"Why is it only open for such a short time?"

"It may be that it requires time to stabilise."

"You said it's escalating, right?"

"Something is escalating in frequency and duration, yes."

"The creatures..."

"Are coming through as the portal remains open for longer periods."

"Why aren't they like normal animals?"

"Why would you assume that other dimensions are identical to ours? An infinite number of dimensions spells an infinite number of possibilities. That penguin sure didn't look like anything from...here. That head we saw poking through the flames last night wasn't anything I've ever seen."

"Why are they falling from the sky?"

"Let's assume it is a portal and that some form of disturbance is activating it, what's to say it has to be earthbound?"

"So how could one of our creatures, the whale, for instance, come falling out of the sky to smash their boat?" asked Clarice, pointing toward mother and daughter a few paces ahead.

"Half a whale."

"All right, half a whale. What? Are you saying we might be seeing the other half of my brother-in-law dropping from the sky? The half that entered the portal before it closed?"

"Shush, Clarice. It's just an impossible theory at the moment. It would explain the sudden appearance of her father's foot, though."

"Jesus!"

"I don't like my explanation, Clarice. I don't believe my theory, so don't let it get to you, okay? Spitballing is what they call it, I think."

"Lotta spit there and some King Kong-sized balls."

"What I don't understand is why there aren't scientists swarming all over this place at the moment. The sort of activity we're experiencing must be attracting all sorts of attention on the mainland."

"Unless they've been warned to stay away because of imminent danger from an underwater eruption."

"Wouldn't have thought that would stop them."

"A resulting tsunami would. The authorities may have ordered an evacuation of the area pending a possible Thailand-size tsunami swamping the islands and mainland. We must have learned something from the one that killed all those people in Thailand and the one in Japan"

"Good point, Clarice. I didn't think about that."

"Wow! I thought of something for once."

"You have a very acute mind, Clarice. I would never have agreed to marry you, otherwise."

"Arlon! Are you saying you would never have accepted my

marriage proposal if I was dumb?"

"Absolutely!"

"I think there's something politically incorrect about that. Not sure how I should feel."

"Knowing that I consider you to be intelligent is worrying?"

"No, saying that you wouldn't marry me if I wasn't."

"Would you accept a proposal from someone you loathed?"

"Of course not."

"Same thing. While I can't like or loathe someone, I could certainly not tolerate someone if I believed they were not worth the effort of knowing."

"Arlon, I don't come close to matching your knowledge."

"No, you don't."

"Arlon!"

"Well, it's true. That doesn't mean you aren't intelligent."

"I think you'd better stop before you spoil it all for me. It was just getting to be quite wonderful," said Clarice.

The tired little party trudged along the beach while the sun rose majestically in the eastern sky. Within a few hours they reached the rocks. Large volcanic boulders blocked the path from the waterline to the dense scrub at the dunes. Arlon rubbed his stubbly chin as he thought about the ordeal ahead. The way across the boulders seemed treacherous at best, while the inland route held any number of disadvantages.

"Wait here a moment, folks. I want to get up onto these rocks and take a look. Here," he said to Freddy, handing him the speargun.

"What ya want me ta do with this?" he asked unnecessarily.

Arlon simply angled his head.

"What the f...heck do you think he wants you to do with it, dummy?" accused Clarice.

"Not much good against that lot we saw," complained Freddy.

"Then throw it away and use your multitude of other killing skills against them, Mr Boggs," said Arlon, as he disappeared behind the first boulder.

"Weren't no need ta be like that," mumbled Freddy.

"If any of you like oysters, now might be a good time to eat a few while you're waiting," suggested Arlon suddenly from above. "I assume you have a knife in that sheath on your belt, Mr Boggs?"

"Course I do. Wouldn't be much of a fisherman without one,"

he stated proudly.

"A half-decent fisherman would not abandon his precious vessel upon seeing a mythical monster, Mr Boggs."

"Weren't nothing mythical about that monster we saw last night," came the retort.

"No, just as well we weren't in a boat with you in charge, eh?"

"Now just wait a mo..." began Freddy, to vacant air once Arlon disappeared. "Don't much like that bloke," he muttered more to himself than anyone else.

"I'm fairly sure the feeling would be mutual if Arlon was capable of feelings, Mr Boggs," stated Clarice.

"No call for that, miss. No call at all. If ya want some oysters I suggest ya be nice ta me," argued Freddy.

"I'm fine, thank you. Never did get a taste for the slimy things."

Arlon paused on the boulder he'd jumped upon. For several hundred metres, there was a sea of grey and black boulders before him. It would be tough going, particularly for the young girl and her mother. Arlon leapt from one rock to the next in easy, sure-footed bounds. On the top of the boulders that were not subjective to daily tidewaters, the surfaces were dry and safe for footing. Only lower down the beach did they become slippery and he was able to discern the darker shades to indicate moisture or seaweed growth.

"Okay, here's what I think we should do," announced Arlon when he returned to appear at the top of a boulder. "Clarice, I want you to take charge of Mrs Blaze. Freddy, I'd like you to lead them over the rocks, sticking to the high side where it's mainly dry. You'll probably have to get down many times and get back up where you can. Can't be helped unless we take the inland route or if anyone has any better ideas? No? All right then, get going and don't go so fast as to cause an accident, but don't go too slowly either."

"What are *you* going to do, Arlon?" asked Clarice.

"Tara and I are going to defend your rear while you get going. Then this brave little girl is going to get on my back when I follow you lot. I'll catch up to you before you make it to the other side."

"No way, Mr Arlon. I seen that bunch-o-rocks and ya not gonna catch us if ya give us a head start," pronounced Freddy with confidence.

"Well, for once you're showing some confidence and some hutzpah! Good for you. Get them to the other side as safely and quickly as you can," Arlon ordered.

"Arlon, why are we suddenly in a hurry?"

"Something you said makes a lot of sense. I haven't reacted quickly enough to it and I'm worried now. No time to explain, though. Go, and take care."

Arlon hopped down out of sight and walked round the first boulder as he had done moments ago. He knelt in front of Tara to be at eye level with her.

"Tara, I have to ask you to trust me. You don't know me but I'm much stronger than I look. I've been exercising and honing my body for a long, long time, and it can pretty much do most things I ask it to do. I have to construct a makeshift sling for you out of my knapsack and a couple of ropes I have in there. I am going to ask you to get on my back, where I have to secure you so you don't have to hold on to my neck and you can't fall. This is the scary bit where I need to know if you'll trust me.

"I have to run and jump over those rocks with you on my back because you are too small to do it on your own. It's not that you don't have the agility or the courage to try, it's just that you don't have the strength and the height advantage it requires."

"Mr Arlon, have you done it before?" asked Tara timidly.

"On my own, many times as a teenager. I used to bounce around from rock to rock like a mountain goat when my family took me to the waterfall where there was just a big jumble of rocks and boulders lining the course of the river."

"Did you ever fall?"

"Never," said Arlon, with complete honesty and confidence. "The trick is to accurately calculate the next jump each time knowing your strengths and judging the distances instantly. It's almost instinctual, because you don't have time to test each jump. For some reason that I was never able to explain, I found I could concentrate hard, find a route and simply go. The thing is, Tara, if you agree, you'll have to trust me unconditionally all the way and not make a sound to break my concentration after we start. I can't hold you because I'll need my arms for balance and landings. You'll have the straps over my shoulders to hang onto and I'll make sure you're fully supported. The rest is up to you."

"You promise you won't drop me?" asked Tara with uncertainty.

"All I can promise is to do my best, Miss Blaze. I won't lie to you, there is an element of danger."

"Can't we walk around?"

"Yes, we could. If that's what you decide, then that's what we'll have to do. I just worry that we might come across one or more of those animals you saw coming through the fire. In the scrub, we don't stand much of a chance: too confining. Out here in the open, we have room to move, run, take aim with the speargun or hide in the rocks."

"Don't have a choice then, do I?"

"When did you get so smart, young lady?"

"I learned on my own and at survival camp."

"I know that feeling well. I learned a lot on my own as well. What do you say, Miss Tara Blaze, ready to take a chance on me?"

Tara nodded her head bravely, though her eyes gave away the fear and uncertainty she felt. Arlon worked quickly to jury-rig the knapsack into a semblance of a boatswain's chair, commonly used on sailing ships for hoisting a man into the rigging for repairs and maintenance. Attempting to keep the girl from becoming concerned, Arlon ignored the sounds he heard emanating from the interior, indicating the proximity of their unfriendly visitors.

He finished with a few last knots and loops and quickly guided Tara into the makeshift apparatus whereby he would carry the girl in a larger version of a baby sling. He explained carefully how he wanted her to hold onto the straps that would go over his shoulders, and not grip his neck as she might be inclined to do naturally.

"Once I have you on my back, I'm going to have to tie your legs around my waist so that they don't flop about. Not so much for upsetting my balance as for limiting the friction for you. Do you know what that is, friction?"

Tara shook her head.

"That's when things rub together. We don't want you to develop a rash or worse, do we?"

"Nope," she said brightly, with an infectious smile.

"Good girl. You ready?"

Tara nodded. Arlon scooped her up easily, placing his arms through the shoulder straps supporting the girl's weight. He threaded his belt through some loops in a rope to secure the chair around his waist. Gently placing padded loops around the girl's ankles, he wrapped her pliant legs around his midriff as securely as comfort allowed.

"Now, grab those straps like I showed you. Ready? No point in nodding, Tara, I can't see you anymore. You have to speak up if I ask you a question. Ready?"

"Yep," she replied.

"Good. If I slow down or stop for a moment, use that time to ask me something or for me to make an adjustment if you're uncomfortable. Otherwise, nice and quiet, okay?"

"Okeydokey," answered Tara with a grin.

Noting movements from the scrub immediately to their right, Arlon wasted no time in walking around the boulder to clamber up a small one behind it which gave him access to the top. Arlon carefully scanned the field of grey, searching for the quasi-route he had selected earlier. Once he had that etched into his mind he peered into the distance, dismayed to find the others had proceeded only a short distance in the time he had taken, perhaps only a hundred metres of the kilometre or more they must traverse.

Arlon made a first tentative leap to an adjoining rock to test the weight and balance of the load. He made a couple of minor adjustments before taking a more confident leap to the next. Within moments he was leaping and bounding with the grace of a gazelle from one to the next. Tara was almost dizzy with the speed at which he ran and jumped, landing on spring-like legs as he absorbed the shock.

Arlon knew it did not pay to dither about his selections. He forced himself into a zone where he 'saw' the route he must take, 'saw' the next surface or edge where his feet must land with unerring accuracy. The dangerous gaps between the enormous boulders threatened to swallow them at times, when Arlon landed on a lower rock, only to bound up and higher again in the blink of an eye. Tara was scared witless and felt exhilarated simultaneously. The man beneath her was slowly becoming some sort of superhero in her eyes.

Arlon managed to keep up the intense pace while Tara could only look on in astonishment. She felt her thighs and arms rubbing on their restraints painfully, but didn't utter a sound of complaint for fear of causing him to make a mistake. She bit down on the small amount of pain and continued to gape at the spectacle of being airborne so often between gargantuan boulders. She understood immediately what the man had meant about her not being able to negotiate the route on her own. She wasn't strong enough or big enough to make the jumps from one rock to the next.

Clarice couldn't believe her eyes when she looked up suddenly to see Arlon standing above her, while she was helping to get Angela up the next rock. Tara, seated behind him, had the biggest smile on her face when she leaned out to see why they had stopped.

"Mr Arlon?"

"Yeah, little one?" Arlon said, breathing hard.

"Can I give my legs and arms a rest from the...fitchen?"

"Friction? Are your legs and arms rubbing?"

"Uh-huh," she admitted.

"You should have said something," admonished Arlon gently.

"Couldn't..."

"I guess I didn't stop or slow down, did I?"

"Nuh-uh," she agreed.

"All right, how about we all have a short break here?"

"Sounds good to me," Clarice agreed, as she clambered up the rock behind Angela.

"Mr Boggs, how are you faring?" asked Arlon.

"Right as rain, right as rain."

"We can't take too long. We don't want to be caught out here if..." Arlon trailed off into silence.

"If what?" begged Clarice, catching her breath as she sat atop the boulder.

Arlon lowered Tara to enable her to stretch her legs and arms. He peered about him. There was a disturbing lack of sound. He heard only the lazy splash of the water slapping gently against the rocks about thirty metres down the shore from them. Nothing else moved as far as he could tell, not even crabs scurrying around the rocks, normally disturbed by a human's passing.

"If what?" Clarice repeated.

"Hmm?" Arlon feigned ignorance.

"Oh, okay, I get it," Clarice accepted. She understood that Arlon did not want to frighten the girl by discussing what the problem might be in front of her.

Freddy, however, *did* want to know and was opening his mouth when he spied Clarice shaking her head insistently. He closed his mouth. Angela sat with them without making a sound or giving any indication she knew what was happening around her. Clarice worried, knowing that hospitalisation for her was crucial. She watched the woman's daughter standing next to Arlon with a smile you couldn't hope to remove. As harrowing as their ordeal had been for the young mite, she never wavered in her stoicism and courage for one so young.

Clarice also noted a glow about her man that she'd not noticed before, a glow that was not entirely explainable as exertion alone. If she didn't think otherwise, she might be tricked into believing it was some form of paternal pride she'd observed. It may have even been an indication of something deeper than that. He stood next to Tara with a protective hand resting on the girl's shoulder and she did not attempt to move away from the gesture. Anyone without a good knowledge of Arlon Grey would speculate that a bond had formed between the pair.

Clarice dismissed the absurd notion immediately. She knew Arlon couldn't form any sort of relationship based on emotions. Yet he had a sparkle in his eyes she could not disregard altogether. The girl, too, had something shining through her. Clarice gathered that Tara's parents were not entirely enamoured with the delightful child. How that could be escaped her. Tara could melt hearts and showed infinite signs of high intelligence. Clarice sighed inwardly, imagining the pure joy of raising a child like Tara, showering her with unlimited love and affection.

Clarice had debated the inclusion of children with Arlon in her mind a hundred times or more. She had not yet discussed that notion with him, nor did she assume it would be a natural progression in their lives, married or not. Everything about Arlon defied the tropes of a 'normal' marriage. It would not be easy, but she was prepared for it and invited it with all her heart and soul. He was a good man. He would make an excellent father one day, if only in the sense that he would be a marvellous protector. Until only a moment ago, she had permanently dismissed any idea that he might display some kind of love or affection for a child...or her.

"Clarice, if you've caught your breath, I'd like you to keep going with Mrs Blaze. Push on as fast as you dare without endangering yourselves. Mr Boggs, I know you have no reason to want to help, but would you mind giving them a hand to make it across as quickly as possible?"

"No need to think I'm not grateful for ya help, Mr Arlon. I'll do what I can..."

"Hey, mister? How come you watched us?" accused Tara, without realising how cross she sounded.

Freddy cleared his throat in embarrassment, "Thought yiz were beautiful mermaids at first and it was the loveliest sight I ever seen. Couldn't take me eyes offa yiz, I couldn't. Lost me missus ten years ago and never set eyes on another woman since, 'til I saw yiz havin' that swim. Never had no children and I...A man gets lonely sometimes when he's at sea mosta the time, miss. When ya caught me starin' I got ashamed and left quick. I didn't mean no harm and I's sorry for leavin' ya like that, I am. I wouldn'ta done it again if I had the chance," explained a remorseful Freddy.

"Sorry for calling you a bad man," Tara confessed.

"Yiz was right ta call me that. I shoulda stopped ta ask if yiz needed help. Didn't think straight at the time. Sorry 'bout that," Freddy said.

"I don't want to sound like the party-pooper here, but can we save this for another time?" asked Arlon. "We need to get back as soon as we can. Mr Boggs? Once I'm through, I'm going to push on to get Miss Blaze up to the house, then come back to the beach. When you lot get there I'd like you to help me pull the tender up to the house while Clarice takes Mrs Blaze to join Tara."

"Yiz wanna pull the tender up ta the house?"

"Correct."

"Why?"

"Because I think we'll need it," Arlon answered simply.

"At the house?" he asked incredulously.

"Yes."

"Ya gonna fill it with sand for the girl ta play in, like?"

"I think we already have an abundance of sand for a child to play in, Mr Boggs, don't you?"

"But..."

"Come on Freddy, I'll explain something as we go," urged Clarice.

She led a bewildered Freddy Boggs to the next gap between the boulders. Gently guiding Angela across the gap, the pair of them moved forward, with Clarice whispering to Freddy as they went.

"I'm not scared any more, Mister Arlon," admitted Tara after the others had departed.

"I never thought you were. You've shown remarkable courage and tenacity, young lady. Your parents would be very proud."

"No, no, not my mummy and daddy. They don't like me much."

"Parents are not always very smart and don't always know what's good for them or their children. My parents loved me so much that they ended up pushing me away when they saw I couldn't return that love. Or maybe they didn't love me in a real sense, otherwise they would have loved me unconditionally. That's what a parents' love should be, all-forgiving, everlasting and blind to imperfections, or perhaps stronger because of those imperfections.

"If I am ever fortunate enough to have a child like you I will move heaven and earth to find a way to express myself meaningfully. I couldn't allow such a treasure as you to go unnoticed or unwanted," said Arlon quietly, poignantly, almost sorrowfully.

Tara tugged his sleeve, urging Arlon to come down to her level, where she hugged him tightly about the neck, holding back tears as best she could. She had never experienced such deep respect and warmth from a grown-up before. Ironically, that experience came from a man devoid of all emotions; or so he said.

"Thank you," she said, as they pulled apart after a short time.

"Have you recovered enough to continue?"

Tara nodded enthusiastically. Arlon padded the areas where he thought her legs and arms had been chafing with the padding from his pith helmet. He threw the item away once he finished, as it would no longer fit comfortably on his head, nor stay in place.

"You look better without that silly hat, Mister Arlon. You have beautiful hair."

"Hmm, not sure a man is supposed to have 'beautiful' hair, but I'll take it as the intended compliment. Thank you," he said, as he rose with Tara firmly on his back once more.

"Ready, Miss Blaze?"

"Ready, Mister Arlon."

Arlon took off lithely, once more bounding from one rock to the next with the certainty of an accomplished athlete who knows his anatomy and strengths intimately. They caught and passed the struggling group ahead of them quickly. Clarice waved to Tara as they passed. Tara did not move her hand to wave back in the fear that she might cause an imbalance. Instead, she smiled as widely as she could and continued to smile while Arlon exhibited his mastery of the art of rock-hopping.

Not once did either Tara or Arlon feel less than one hundred per cent confident during the trek over the treacherous terrain. Arlon would leap from one boulder, landing like a cat onto the next, even occasionally on the side of a boulder, where he managed to cling to the surface with uncanny dexterity, speeding up and over before gravity had a chance to take effect. For Tara, it was unlike anything in her memories, more exhilarating than a carnival ride.

Arlon ran across the surface of a large, flat rock to leap a gap of a couple of metres with consummate ease, despite the burden of extra weight. His sinewy, slim, muscled frame gave him the agility required to deal with the irregular landscape, while his mind calculated each leap with instant precision. The trek to the other side of the rocks took next to no time at all for the pair, landing softly on the pure white sand with the last jump.

Arlon did not wait to catch his breath, suspecting that time was of the essence. He raced toward the centre of the bay, where the track would lead them to the house. Sitting on the shore at the highwater mark was the small tender he had secured fast to a palm tree on their first day on the island. The pitiful little boat hardly seemed capable of the task for which it was designed, let alone for what Arlon perceived as its next assignment.

Keeping a watchful eye on the surrounding scrub, Arlon raced at his top speed for the house at the end of the sandy path. Tara was jostled about more than ever as he ran, but she kept quiet as she had been ordered, despite the irritation caused by the rubbing. She was becoming concerned with the man's need to keep running flat out. She could not believe how strong and fast he was. She never knew it could be possible for a human being to do what he had done for the last half-hour. That she adored and admired the man was a given for her.

"Tara, I am going to leave you in the house on your own for a while," said Arlon, as they exited the path into a clearing. "I have to go back and get the small boat we passed."

"You think we are going to get a tootsie-nami."

"Well, aren't you a clever girl? I was trying so hard not to worry you by talking about it and you knew all along. Yes, Miss Blaze, I'm worried about a tsu-na-mi," he replied, pronouncing the word correctly and carefully for her edification. "I just need to get my breath back and get you safely inside. We don't want any unwelcome visitors dropping by to carry you off while I'm gone, do we?"

"I don't think the penguin would have hurt me, Mister Arlon," explained Tara, as she was being ushered through the front door of the house.

"I'm so sorry if that's true, Miss Blaze. I couldn't take the chance, though. I hope you can understand that and can forgive me?"

"That's okay. He did look scary when he changed," admitted Tara.

"Look, there's some cold water and food in that esky next to the fridge. The ice would have kept everything reasonably cool when we had to turn the generator off. I want you to eat something, drink and rest while I wait for the others and get the boat up to the house. Okay?" Tara nodded while heading for the esky. "I'm going to lock the door after I leave. Don't open any windows, no matter what," he warned.

Tara nodded her understanding gravely while she reached eagerly for some chicken wings from the esky. Arlon nodded his head to acknowledge that the girl would be hungry for any food that was not marine-based after her ordeal. Arlon removed his sweat-soaked, long-sleeved shirt, then stretched his fatigued muscles as Tara watched in fascination. Although he was slightly paler underneath his shirt, he reminded Tara of pictures she'd seen depicting the artist's impression of Greek gods.

Arlon locked Tara within the house, then glanced upwards towards the roof before sprinting off down the path to the beach, his hi-tensile legs pumping like engine pistons beneath him. When he reached the top of the dunes, he paused momentarily to view the ocean. The large island between Cid Island and the open ocean would take the brunt of any tidal assault, but they would still be vulnerable to a destructive surge.

Looking back towards the rocks from which he and Tara had emerged a short time ago, he thought he could see the shapes of the other three still struggling with the extreme landscape. Arlon sighed, believing he might have to make the supreme effort of catching up with them to transport the Blaze woman over the rocks in the same manner as the child...if he could convince her to cling onto him. He wasn't confident of doing so.

He was exhausted by the strenuous activity already, even though he was not entirely depleted. The mouthful of water and the half sandwich he had consumed before leaving the house had revitalised him to a degree. The start of a stitch in his side warned him that eating so soon after vigorous exercise was not optimal. Without wasting more time in contemplation, Arlon sprinted down the beach toward the far northern point of the bay. His fresh white singlet was soon drenched as well.

He was breathing hard when he arrived at the group, who had perhaps a hundred metres to go, looking as exhausted as he felt. He'd decided he would not be able to piggyback the woman over the rocks. It would be too difficult to make her hold on with her arms and legs and he didn't like his chances. Arlon opted to assist her, while he urged Clarice and Freddy to move ahead. They both readily agreed to the suggestion, being tired of boosting and pulling the woman over the rocks.

Arlon saw that they made far better progress once they were on their own. Arlon then turned his attention to the woman, standing as still as a statue with expressionless eyes. The concavity in her head where she'd hurt herself was evident in the full sunshine. It was obvious to Arlon that the woman would get no better until the pressure on her brain was relieved. That required surgery by a neurologist, someone they did not have at hand.

He'd read an account of an emergency operation performed on a person using a cordless drill to pierce the cranium and release the built-up blood therein. He certainly hoped that he would not be asked to perform such a risky procedure on the woman. Reading skills he had in abundance. Knowledge from that erstwhile pursuit he had in spades. Surgical skills he did not possess, nor wished to. While he wasn't squeamish about the thought of drilling into a human brain, he wasn't confident of either his diagnosis or the prognosis. He had no way of knowing what to test for to produce a reliable and accurate diagnosis. He was guessing, and that just wasn't good enough to cause possible further injury through ignorance.

While Arlon was mulling over those thoughts he had been gently guiding the woman before him, coaxing her up the incline of the next rock. She offered very little to assist herself or Arlon during the procedure, and Arlon instantly understood why the others had taken so long to get anywhere with her in tow.

When they finally reached the top of the first boulder in their path, Arlon shook his head in dismay. Two people assisting the woman was slow, but not impossibly slow. With only one person assisting her, it would take an age, an age that Arlon predicted they did not have. With resignation, he moved swiftly to place the woman on his shoulders in a fireman's lift. She did not protest, did not baulk or make any sounds at all. She hung limp and lifeless, like a rag doll.

Arlon turned to face the remaining sea of rocks before him, attempting to find a route that would enable him to navigate the labyrinth without removing the woman from his shoulders. Before he could change his mind he leapt onto the adjoining rock, then the next, feeling and testing the weight and balance before he attempted to set off at full speed. He was very strong, toned and tuned to a high degree of efficiency. He was a superb athlete in the martial arts. His daily exercise routine would see an Olympian gasping for breath.

However, Arlon had already strained himself considerably with the effort of transporting the child all the way. The effort of that, combined with running flat out to the house and returning to the group, had taken its toll. He was flagging after only a few short hops. Angela Blaze was no fatty, but neither was she an anorexic model. Her weight atop Arlon's shoulders taxed his every move within the dangerous boulder field. Blowing hard and straining every muscle, Arlon continued doggedly.

When Arlon finally made the beach he was spent. His legs and shoulder muscles had turned to leaden jelly. He breathed as though his lungs were on fire. Indeed, he felt as though he were breathing pure flames. He sat down heavily after dumping Angela to the sand in an undignified heap. He spied Freddy along the beach, standing next to the tender, waiting for him. He closed his eyes to concentrate on his breathing, on his internal organs, on his limbs and all the muscles, a mental exercise he went through after all of his most rigorous training regimes.

The sign of a first-rate athlete is their ability to recover quickly, to resume normal breathing and to continue moving after sustained physical duress. Within moments Arlon's breathing had returned to normal, his pulse rate was regular and his muscles had regained life.

He assisted Angela to her feet by taking her hand. He then walked her along the beach to where Freddy waited. Clarice had been resting in the shade not far from the tender.

"I would never have believed that was possible had I not seen it with my own eyes, Arlon Grey," declared Clarice, as she stepped out into the sunshine.

Arlon looked at the golden ringlets falling about her dimpled cheeks and felt a warmth cascade through him. She was the only person in his life who produced those sorts of physical reactions in him. She was the first woman with whom he'd experienced sexual relations. He had not known if he could perform the act of procreation, since he had understood it required emotions.

Desire was an emotion, a stimulus derived from a mutual attraction. He conceded that there were the physical elements of pheromones and such that science journals referenced when describing the mating habits of animals. That might play a part in human interactions, for all he knew, and might explain his ability to engage in carnal delights with a woman. However, Clarice was the only female to ever lure him into the act, for which he was undeniably thankful.

She aroused him without needing to do much at all, such as standing there in the sunlight with a glow of pride and pure love emanating from her in pulsating waves. Rubenesque could be the best way to describe her voluptuous body, once undressed. She had grown up fairly tomboyish, according to her stories, her father's pride and joy among a throng of sons and one other daughter. She was not a delicate flower, nor thin. She called herself big-boned, never truly appreciating her wholesome attractiveness. When she spoke she also glowed with an inner kindness and genuine concern that endeared her to everyone she met.

Arlon counted himself lucky for having the opportunity to explore her many facets and to spend his life doing so...if she didn't get sick of him...or if he didn't open his mouth too often. Arlon often neglected to curb his tactless tongue when it came to...*anyone*. It just affected him more if he managed to blurt out something inappropriate to Clarice. He didn't want to hurt her, yet he managed to do so with monotonous frequency.

"Arlon? Are you okay?" asked Clarice with growing concern.

Arlon snapped out of his reverie. "Yeah, sure. Wouldn't have believed what?"

"You, anyone, capable of running and jumping around on rocks with a woman on their shoulders. Especially after you just did the same thing with a child on your back. Are you okay?"

"Exhausted. Not sure how much more I can do today. I may have stuffed myself for important things coming up. Clarice, can you take Mrs Blaze up to the house and then get everything edible into an esky without the ice taking up space. Pack that single-burner gas stove and some basic utensils, along with coffee, mugs, etcetera, into a bag."

"We going somewhere?"

"No," he replied cryptically. "Mr Boggs, a hand with the boat, please?"

Clarice bit her tongue rather than ask more questions which Arlon seemed reluctant to answer. It was unusual because she assumed he didn't want to talk about whatever it was they should be worried about when Tara had been present, like she's explained to Freddy along the way. Without the girl with them, she hoped Arlon would be more forthcoming. She grabbed Angela by the hand, only to have the woman whip it away fiercely.

"What the hell do you think you're doing? Michael, why is she touching me?" asked Angela with unsubdued rage.

"She...she needs to take you home, dear," said Arlon.

"I...Michael?"

"Yes...Angela?"

"Where, where are we?"

"On the island."

"Hamilton?"

"Yes, Hamilton Island. Now just let Clarice here take you back to the house, okay?" asked Arlon urgently.

"But, but we live in our hotel, Michael, not a house," said Angela, in a state of total confusion.

"Well, Clarice is the new concierge and she'll take you to our room, okay? Sorry I called it a house. Didn't mean to confuse you."

Clarice took Angela's hand to steer her towards the path. Angela peered backwards, hoping to gain some insight from Arlon, who kept insisting it was all right to go with Clarice.

"In a bad way, she is," said Freddy, after they were gone.

"Yeah, I don't like her chances of surviving this if we can't get her some serious medical attention. Come on, we have to get this boat up to the house pronto."

"Not until yiz tell me why?" said Freddy stubbornly.

"Tootsie-nami!" explained Arlon.

"Come again?" asked Freddy, in a rising inflection while scratching his head.

"Never mind, no time. Haul arse, Frederick Boggs!" commanded Arlon in his loudest, sternest voice.

"Jeez! All right, all right, keep ya knickers on," replied Freddy with exasperation.

After placing the three-pronged sand anchor and its painter into the tender, the two men each grabbed hold of a lifeline drooped either side of the small vessel's bow to begin hauling the lightweight lifeboat up the sandy path behind the ladies. Gripping onto the seine floats attached to the lifelines, the men were saved the pain associated with hauling on the lines for too long. The fibreglass boat was quite light, however, dragging it a long way on the sand was never going to be easy on the hands.

When they reached the house in the relative shade of the surrounding scrub, Freddy and Arlon sat heavily on the gunwales to rest and catch their breath. Arlon especially was feeling the physical fatigue of overexertion.

"Mr Boggs, I have to go inside to check on their progress. Can you try to locate a sturdy stepladder capable of getting us all onto the roof safely?"

"Ya want us ta get on the roof?" asked Freddy incredulously.

"Precisely. Then I want you to remove the anchor from the painter, leaving the other end attached to the boat. Make sure it's long enough to tie up the tender to the finial up there, I think I saw a spare painter in a pouch on the underside of the bow. No, no more questions if you want to stay alive," advised Arlon, when he saw Freddy opening his mouth to protest or ask more questions.

Arlon marched inside the house to supervise the preparations. He saw Angela sitting stiffly on the cane lounge while Clarice and Tara filled the esky with foodstuffs after emptying the ice into the kitchen sink.

"Blankets, spare clothes, some pillows, and anything else you think we might need to survive a couple of days doing it rough, Clarice. Any signal on the mobile?"

"Nope, not a single bar. Why are we going to 'do it rough', Arlon?"

"Tell her, Miss Blaze," instructed Arlon.

"Tootsie-nami," responded Tara confidently, believing she had corrected her earlier mispronunciation of the word.

Clarice smiled, "Oh, that's just adorable. But did she say what I think she just said? Tsunami?" she asked Arlon.

"His name is Michael," blurted Angela from the lounge, before subsiding again into whichever realm she existed of late.

"Hurry, Clarice, we may not have much time," urged Arlon.

"You really think we might be smashed to bits by a tidal wave? I wasn't being very serious when I thought about that before," she admitted.

"For every action, there is a reaction. If we had a massive underwater movement causing the island to suffer a quake, it's only natural to assume we could be subjected to a tidal surge as a result. I don't think it will be a theatrical showstopper of epic proportions because the island in front of us creates a barrier, a buffer, but it will be a sufficient surge of water to inundate this island. I hope I'm wrong, Clarice," he admitted with a shrug.

"You're never bloody wrong. Go, Tara, get some blankets from the cupboard down the hall. I'll finish up in here."

"I don't think I'm wrong, either, Clarice. Did you notice that no birds were singing out there, not a sound?"

"Ooh, that doesn't bode well. I didn't notice it, no. Nothing out there?"

"Nothing. Still as a graveyard. Which is a pretty stupid expression, because a grave..."

"Okay, okay, we can do without the lesson. So you want us to get into that tiny boat with all these provisions and wait?"

"No, I want us to wait it out on the roof."

"You can't be serious?"

"Think of a better plan, then," said Arlon.

"What if the water rises higher than the roof, or the house gets swept away?"

"Then we have the tender as a last resort."

"Not going to be very comfortable on the roof," she warned.

"The roof of the house has a fairly low pitch, but the skillion veranda roof is probably the best bet. We'll ascend higher as the water rises, if it does. As I said, we'll only use the tender as a last resort, as it's far too small to accommodate all of us for long. Emergency use only. We can also cover it with a plastic tarp to keep everything dry."

"How long do we have?" asked Clarice quietly.

"We may have an hour or a day, no way to be sure. We need to plan for the worst. So move it."

Arlon walked over to Angela Blaze, who was sitting on the sofa with a blank stare. Arlon feared she was getting worse. Her periods of lucidity, confused as they were, lasted less and less, and he felt sure that did not bode well for her. He took her hand gently to lead her outside, but changed his mind before getting there.

"Clarice, maybe you or Tara could take Mrs Blaze to...attend to her ablutions? It may be a while before she can do so again with any degree of privacy. The same goes for you and the girl. Take the opportunity while you can. Try to move your bowels if you're able."

"Oh, charming. Not sure I can simply perform on command like that." Sighing, she took hold of Angela's hand. "Come on, Angela, time to make wee-wee and poo-poo," said Clarice, in a patronising manner which surprised Arlon.

Clarice did not like Tara's mother and made no bones about it. The behaviour she displayed toward her daughter during her 'lucid' moments left no doubt in Clarice's mind that she was a terrible mother who did not deserve such a blessing. However, she took the woman's hand and led her to the bathroom, showing patience and consideration for her condition. Tara returned from the hallway with a huge bundle she was barely able to carry in her outstretched arms.

"Here, let me take some of that from you," suggested Arlon.

He relieved Tara of most of the items she carried, including face washers and hand towels.

"I don't think we'll take these, Miss Blaze," he said, discarding the unnecessary towelling items. "I think one towel each is all we need. With any luck, we won't need any of this."

"What about the tootsie-nami?" asked Tara.

"I'm hoping I'm wrong about it, Miss Blaze. Hoping for the best, but preparing for the worst. Won't do us much good to be trapped inside this house if it does come. So, how about we go and put these in the tender?"

"What's a tender?" she asked innocently.

"It's the little boat used to get ashore in conjunction with a larger vessel moored in deep water. It may have gotten its name from being used to tender to a ship's maintenance and provisioning. It's also used as a lifeboat in many cases."

"Oh," said Tara, looking more confused than before.

As they exited the house with their burdens, Freddy came from the rear, carrying a step ladder.

"Is that the longest one there is?" Arlon asked, as he passed him on his way to unburden himself.

"*Only* one there is," answered Freddy.

"It will have to do, in that case. Set it up at the corner of the veranda there. Get yourself up on the roof so I can bring up Mrs Blaze when she's ready. I'll need you to give us a hand from above while I assist from below. Tara, I want you to scoot up the ladder and onto the roof as soon as you put those down."

"Okeydokey," said Tara happily.

"Mr Boggs, see that Tara is up safely while I go back and get the esky with our food and anything else I can think of that we might need," Arlon said.

"Aye-aye, cap'n," said Freddy in a sarcastic tone.

"Sarcasm is completely wasted on me, Mr Boggs. Now, up you go, young lady. Take very good care of her, Mr Boggs. Protect her as though your life depends on it...because it does," Arlon warned.

He returned to the kitchen, closed the esky, and carried it through to the exterior. Tara had ascended the ladder and was sitting comfortably on the edge of the veranda roof. Freddy was still mumbling under his breath as Arlon pushed the laden esky up to him.

While it was true that he could have left the esky in the tender below, Arlon thought it best to have food and water where they could be reached easily. A long and arduous afternoon and night could be ahead of them. He also did not want them to have to descend to the ground too often, possibly leaving someone stranded if anything happened quickly. Blankets and other non-essential items he would leave in the small vessel.

Clarice appeared with Angela in tow. Arlon managed to escort her up the ladder and onto the roof with Freddy's help and her daughter urging her on. He then told Clarice to ascend.

"Mr Boggs? I suggest you use the opportunity to relieve

yourself while you can. It may be a while before you next get a chance."

"Relieve meself?"

"Go to the toilet?"

"Oh! Once in the mornin' and once in the evenin'. Regular as clockwork, I is."

"Been this morning, have you?"

"Well...um..."

"No, you haven't. Unless you took a dump while you were out in the boulders?" asked Arlon tactlessly.

"Well..."

"Hey, no skin off my nose if you did or didn't. I'm just saying it might be best to do what you can while you can. I am. Right now, as a matter of fact. The rest of you stay up there. Look after each other."

"Arlon?"

"Yes?"

"Hurry," urged Clarice.

"I'll be as quick as I can..."

"Look, look," cried Tara suddenly.

"What is it, Clarice, what can she see?" asked Arlon.

"Looks like a pack-o-dogs ta me," replied Freddy.

Arlon scaled the ladder with haste, retrieving it once he was aloft. He peered in the direction everyone was pointing. He became immediately concerned when he spied the movement.

"All right, everyone, I want you to sit down and remain quiet. No movement, no sounds. Speak in whispers only," Arlon warned. "I assume you're colour blind, Mr Boggs?" he asked softly, sidling up to the man.

"How the heck..."

"Quietly, Mr Boggs, quietly," advised Arlon. "I assumed so because I doubt that you would ever have seen a pack of purple dogs with black legs in your lifetime."

Arlon turned to watch the unlikely parade of three purple animals, about as large as medium-sized dogs, sauntering up the sandy path from the direction of the beach.

They had an ungainly manner, stilted and jerky movements without any fluidity. The heads were bobbing up and down with the erratic actions. The bodies appeared to be almost segmented like an insect's into three distinct sections. Arlon presumed them to be the head, thorax and abdomen. The creatures continued forward until they reached the perimeter fence. They regarded one another in silent communication to ascertain an agreement on the nature of the boundary and the safety of their passage through the object in front of them.

The heads of the creatures looked quite reptilian, with a prominent nose sniffing the air for signs of danger. The long narrow snout led Arlon to deduce that they might not be predators. When a long tubular tongue extended from the snout to taste the air, Arlon decided that they might eat the equivalent of ants wherever they came from.

Detecting nothing of a dangerous nature in their path, the threesome negotiated their passage through the small gate. Arlon watched in fascination as the creatures came closer. The four black, hairless legs of each animal ended in nothing more than a stump, while the entire bodies were covered in a thick mat of outrageously purple hair that would make any punk rocker green with envy.

The trio halted a few metres from the house which was blocking their path. Heads bobbed and tongues protruded in a display of confused testing as they determined the nature of the enormous structure before them. They remained in their position for many moments, seemingly fearful to advance any farther.

The silence was oppressive as the group of humans sat upon the roof in full sunshine while the strange animals stood a short distance away on the sandy soil. Arlon knew that the low paling fence surrounded the house, so the animals had only one entrance and one exit. If they decided to explore the rest of the yard they would eventually return. They looked nothing like the fierce head that poked its way through the fire during the darkness of the previous evening.

Clatter, clatter, roll, roll, clump, thump, went the plastic bottle that Freddy discarded after drinking the water. It cleared the roof and went sailing into mid-air, dropping directly in front of the three startled animals. They went berserk. In the blink of an eye the snapping, snarling, gnashing, toothy beast from the previous evening returned, multiplied by three.

Arlon had to replay the transformation in slow motion in his head to understand how it took place...

The plastic bottle landed on the ground in front of the creatures. Incredulously, the creatures' front legs split into two, giving them each four forward legs. Those legs then unfolded in a disjointed impossible manner, lifting the body to a vertical position. Then the legs unfolded once more, lifting and stretching back over the body to turn each into an inverted and reverse position. The legs that were once in the rear now repeated the process to form four more spindly, hairless, black legs in the front.

From the abdomen, that was then facing forward, appeared the snarling head that Arlon recognised immediately, on a long neck in a disturbing display of fierce aggression. Turning every which way to locate the source of the danger, the creatures eventually all settled on the plastic bottle. From their abdomen-heads shot a stream of hissing, frothing, pungent liquid that hit the bottle with unerring accuracy, melting it into a gooey, stinking mess.

The trio of animals formed a tri-pointed star with their abdomen heads facing outwards as they rotated in unison on their multitude of legs to form a solid defensive circle. After several tension-filled moments, while the witnesses held their collective breath, the creatures slowly ratcheted down their alert status, finally coming to a standstill. Each of the animals transformed slowly into its original form.

Then one of them imploded!

The creature seemed to crumple inwards before ejecting out in a spray of bluey-red droplets that covered the entire front yard and wall of the house. The two remaining creatures went straight back into their defensive display, one shooting its stream of toxic or acidic liquid in every direction. They turned every which way, getting their thin legs in a tangle, unable to discern the direction of the new threat.

Then one peered upwards with its real head.

It spied the humans sitting on the roof of the veranda, spattered in the blood and guts of their kind. With a form of communication not obvious to the humans, the creatures then unfolded more leg segments to rise higher than before on impossibly thin limbs. They angled their abdomen-heads in the direction of the group.

Tara screamed loudest, with Clarice a close second and Freddy not far behind. Arlon moved swiftly to stand in front of the group, to shield the girl and Clarice as best he could. The sudden movement only made matters worse, as the creatures angled their weird abdomen-heads toward them. Arlon knew that they were about to be sprayed with the lethal ejecta they had witnessed earlier.

A new movement attracted everyone's attention. After an initial push, the laden esky was making its way down the slight decline of the veranda roof. The bright red esky immediately attracted the full brunt of the explosive liquid emanating from the abdomen-head of one creature. The esky dissolved in mid-air after sliding off the roof, landing on the ground with a wet and syrupy whump. The creature let loose with yet more of the substance to eliminate any possible threat residing within the red casing, bubbling and oozing away.

Before the creatures could return their attention to the humans, a loud crack sent shockwaves through the air and under the house. The ground shook and the house abruptly yawed as an undulation rippled outwards from the direction of the rear yard, sending the occupants of the roof sprawling precipitously close to the edge. The creatures remained stable on their outspread limbs, though they were confused by the dramatic events occurring around them.

Arlon lurched sideways milliseconds before Angela Blaze slipped off the edge of the roof. A corner post holding up the section of roof nearest her had collapsed, causing her to roll and slip awkwardly towards that end. Arlon managed to get a hand on her arm before she fell. However, the dead weight of the unhelpful woman soon told on his aching muscles. Thankfully, she was not panicking or kicking, which would have made matters far worse. Instead, she hung there like a dead sausage, gradually reducing Arlon's ability to maintain a hold of her sweaty arm.

Tara was crying out for her mummy and Clarice was begging Arlon to let the woman go. Freddy was throwing full water bottles at the creatures to divert their attention away from the dangling woman. Loud, watery, slurping sounds could be heard out in the bay, where some sort of commotion was happening. Arlon strained to keep a grip on Angela while trying to regain his feet. His muscles rippled beneath the unblemished smooth olive skin, screaming at him to cease the punishment they were receiving.

He finally let go. He was at the end of his physical limits.

The creature stopped shooting at the plastic bottles with the sound of Angela thumping to the ground only a metre from their position. They turned their abdomen-heads to face the woman lying on the ground, moaning. Only the dull sound of rushing water in the distance prevented Angela from becoming a victim of the lethal ejecta. All heads turned towards the ominous sound.

Unable to see from their position atop the roof, Arlon urged Tara to hop on his shoulders in the hope of discovering the source of the new danger.

"Tell me what you see, Tara," instructed Arlon urgently, forgetting about everything else for a moment despite the imminent danger from below.

"All the water is gone and the whales and fish are all flapping around," she replied.

"Look farther out, past the bay. What do you see?"

"A wall," she stated.

"A wall?"

"Water," she declared. "That's where all the water went. It's a tootsie-nami, Mister Arlon."

"I was afraid you'd say that. Come on down."

"Can you please help my mummy?" she cried, the moment she was in front of Arlon.

"I'm going to do my best, little one. Don't give up on me just yet."

"Arlon, you can't possibly be thinking of going down there?"

"It's not in me to do nothing, Clarice," answered Arlon, as he applied himself to the first priority as he saw it. "You three, get farther up the roof and hold onto those finials with all your might. This house may not remain grounded and it'll feel like riding a bucking brumby. Clarice, hold on to Tara while Mr Boggs goes to the opposite side. You can't all hang off one."

"Arlon, please don't do anything foolish, After all, she..."

"Whether she makes it or not in her condition doesn't mean I shouldn't do everything I can, Clarice. Tara needs her mother more than ever with her father out of the picture."

Arlon turned his attention to the scene below once more. Clarice took Tara by the hand to make their way reluctantly up the roof to the gable peak. Below, the creatures were still confused by the sounds in the bay and possibly the smells emanating from there as well. Angela remained slumped on the ground, unaware of her predicament, staring blankly about and moaning softly. Arlon leapt from the roof to land on his feet by her side. The creatures, towering over them on their spindly legs, still peered seaward with their real heads.

Arlon looked about him, quickly searching for anything he could use as a weapon or shield against the animals. As yet, they remained unaware of the new presence. Arlon used the opportunity of their distraction to drag Angela away from the direct firing line of their abdomen-heads. He was unsure where to go or what to do, and how long he might have to do it.

The animals turned toward the sound of the new disturbance. Then another imploded, showering the area once more in a foul matter. With the demise of its second companion, the last creature seemed to decide that the danger was too extreme to bother with the humans. It quickly folded in on itself to recreate the innocent creature they first saw, then scurried off in the direction of the back yard.

Arlon could hear the first sounds of trees in the distance cracking under the strain of the wall of water advancing inexorably across the island. His options were greatly diminished by the tide descending upon them. His eyes settled on the small tender only a metre from him. Without pausing for thought he dragged his human cargo over to the pitifully small dinghy to take refuge there. He simply couldn't think of anything else. He didn't believe he had enough time to get the woman back onto the roof.

He heard Clarice yelling for him to come to her, pleading with all her heart. He faced the prospect of his imminent demise with his usual stoicism, turning to smile at her confidently. Tara was also waving at him frantically as she clutched the finial, begging him to save her mummy. Freddy was showing the horror of what they faced as he peered at the oncoming avalanche of water and debris crushing everything in its path.

Arlon expected the sound of a dozen freight trains to descend on them from the wall of water. Instead, all he heard was the terrible tearing, cracking and crashing sounds of trees being immolated by the liquid juggernaut that tore through the diminutive scrubland without check.

When Arlon detected another movement from the periphery of the rear yard, he recognised the creature returning. With nowhere to run unless it vaulted the back fence, it returned to the front yard, where it became mesmerised by the sight of the water.

To Arlon's utter astonishment, it then leapt towards him in a single bound, landing between him and Angela, who was cowering in the bow. It immediately slumped to the deck of the small boat, where it curled up into a tight little ball just as the water arrived. The impact of the water left Arlon unbalanced and windmilling his arms to retain his position in the small vessel.

The boat was picked up by the unforgiving voluminous mass, which took it swiftly past the house and its screaming occupants on the roof. Arlon managed to seat himself on the stern bench. Careful to keep his body well away from the purple ball in the centre of the boat, he watched as the tender came to the end of the painter. He braced himself for the inevitable. The rope pulled impossibly taut as the boat, gripped by the pull of the water, swung around, perilously close to capsizing.

Arlon did not believe the mere stick on the roof gable or the insignificant rope would be able to sustain the combined weight of the boat, its occupants and the immense strain of the surging water. Incredibly, Arlon saw two distinctive, dark shapes heading directly for them. He recognised them immediately and felt sure the predictable collision would see them finally succumb to the fates. If by any quirk of fortune they avoided a head-on assault by the oceanic leviathans, the slightest touch would snap the rope instantly. It seemed impossible that they could survive, yet survive they did as the two whales passed harmlessly to either side of the shuddering, swinging boat.

"Well, there's something you don't see every day," Arlon muttered, as he absently noted that the African elephant had just had its title as earth's largest land mammal usurped.

The rope twanged and sprayed moisture as it quivered with the impossible tension.

All about them flotsam and jetsam of driftwood and broken boughs amid a host of other litter scraped by their boat without managing to catch on and break them free. Arlon became worried that whiplash from the snapping rope would ultimately be responsible for Angela's death as she sat in the bow fully exposed to the possibility. He could do nothing about it. He wasn't about to risk awakening the inert creature between them by moving to the bow, even if he was able.

The surging water was not like the devastating wave he had pictured, although it was a ponderous and dangerous force just the same. The relentless tide continued to wage its war against any obstacle in its path, causing the house to groan and creak like a gigantic animal in pain. Disbelievingly, Arlon saw the house bend and sway in the torrent, threatening to rip free from its foundations. Clarice and Tara showed the abject fear they felt on their faces. Clarice kept a tight hold on Tara and the finial as the house groaned beneath them, planking tearing from the walls with a rending that set their teeth on edge.

Incredibly, with everything occurring around them, Angela seemed to come out of her torpor to peer about her with clear vision. She spied her daughter on the roof of the house, crying out for her. Angela lifted her arm towards her child.

"Tara," she cried. At that moment her arm disappeared in a spray of blood.

Arlon saw the fin slicing through the water seconds before the animal struck. The enormous white pointer rose through the surface to rip the woman's arm free with consummate ease before descending back into the flow beneath their boat. Angela, momentarily stunned by the incident, gaped at the spray of blood erupting from her ruined arm socket with a look of incomprehension. She managed somehow to stand in the rocking, swaying bow of the boat, then tumbled overboard and disappeared below the water and debris.

ELEVEN

The devastation left by the tsunami was evident for many hundreds of metres inland, with nary a single tree or shrub escaping its wrath. Denuded of limbs and leaves, the remaining tree trunks gave the impression of having experienced a massive bomb blast. All the vegetation acquired a distinctive inland lean, despite the eventual reversal of the flood.

The fence surrounding the house had vanished along with the shed. The earth was a sandy, boggy quagmire, resembling quicksand. The house remained in a semi-state of erection, albeit grossly skewed, with Clarice, Tara and Freddy sitting on the rooftop in pure exhaustion and disbelief. Tara clung close to Clarice, inconsolable in her grief, sobbing heavily.

Arlon managed to get a hold of the trailing painter only when the tide had begun reversing its direction. Until that happened, he did not dare step over the purple ball residing in the middle of the small vessel. Once he had a grip on the rope, he hauled himself and the tender up to the house. Before the tide receded too far, he stepped from the boat. The veranda roof, leaning precariously to one side where the corner post had given way, threatened to tear away from the main roof at the slightest suggestion.

When Arlon joined his motley crew they appeared beaten into submission by the unrelenting events besieging them. Arlon also felt physically exhausted by the ordeal. He was quietly thankful that he was unable to feel the emotional low being experienced by the others. Tara looked up as he approached, with tears streaming down her cheeks. She peered into Arlon's eyes with the most pitiful and heart-breaking appeal.

Slowly, she unfolded herself from Clarice's grasp to walk over to Arlon. He knelt on the roof to accept whatever punishment the girl meant to impart for failing to keep her mother safe. He felt no guilt because of his condition, but he accepted his incompetent failure. He was ready for his comeuppance at the hands of the distraught girl.

"My mummy and my daddy are gone," said Tara through the

sobs, sniffing and wiping her nose with the back of her hand.

"I know," Arlon said in his soft tone.

"I don't have anyone left," stated Tara.

"No one? Aunties, uncles, grandparents?" asked Arlon.

"No one," she said, her heart breaking in two.

Tara wrapped her arms around Arlon's neck to weep on his shoulder. Clarice observed the interaction with a nod of approval and affection for her man and the little girl. Arlon picked her up in his arms and carried her over to Clarice. When he sat down next to her, she placed an arm around them both, starting to weep as well.

"Um, ya might wanna see this," said Freddy urgently.

Creeping onto the roof as Arlon turned toward Freddy, the creature gradually stepped clear of the tender on its elongated legs. Freddy clung for dear life to one end of the gable, while Clarice, Arlon and Tara sat at the other end, with the creature unfolding between them.

"I want everyone to remain perfectly still. This thing does not like any sudden movements. I'd like to believe that it'll share our safe, dry place up here peaceably, just like it did in the boat, if we make no moves that it could consider aggressive. I want everyone to relax. It seems to instinctually sense fear or aggression. If we wait it out until the water is all gone, it may leave on its own," said Arlon, speaking in a tone that was considerably softer and blander than normal.

The creature turned a full circle to take in all the residents of the roof. It had not done the inversion and abdomen-head extension thing. Arlon understood that it was assessing the danger, testing the air to find traces of heightened energy from any of them. He worried about the grief Tara was experiencing and whether that might trigger the creature's defence mechanisms. He needn't have been concerned. As always, Tara was showing how much courage she possessed for one so young, feeling safe in the arms of the strange man.

Eventually, the creature slowly resumed its initial form of a weird-looking purple dog with stumpy, black legs. It lowered itself to the roof, where it rested, completely flat, like a rug. It was impossible to see eyes through the thick mat of fur covering the creature. Arlon wondered whether it possessed any. The markings on the abdomen-head were intended to represent eyes, he supposed. He didn't want to test the theory. The snarling, gnashing, vicious-looking teeth were probably also a fake defensive disguise the creature used when faced with an enemy.

"Whadda we do now?" asked Freddy.

"We wait," answered Arlon.

"For what?"

"For the water to fully recede. With any luck, this thing will be on its way when that happens, or it may blow up like the others."

"Arlon, what the heck is happening here, and how or why do these things just blow up?" asked Clarice.

"Clarice, anything I say is pure guesswork. I'm not a scientist and this falls way outside my educational parameters."

"I'm happy with a guess," suggested Clarice.

Arlon looked from her to Tara, who also nodded, then to Freddy, who agreed.

"Okay, if we take my previous hypothesis for granted..."

"What was that?" asked Freddy, looking confused.

"I suggested to Clarice earlier that there may be a portal of some description occurring here as a result of seismic activity. Anything or anyone caught in the opening of this portal when it collapses is either cut in half or remains on the other side if they make it through in time."

"Make it through ta where?"

"To another dimension," said Arlon, sighing with the impossibility of it all.

"And ya call me out on my 'superstitions'?" remarked Freddy with relish.

"I guess I deserve that. I can't offer anything else," admitted Arlon.

"Let him finish, Mr Boggs, unless you have a better theory," said Clarice. "Go on, Arlon," she continued, when no other explanation was forthcoming from the old fisherman.

"Something is creating a disturbance here, we know that for certain. I postulated that underwater seismic activity released the...energy to allow that to occur. In theory, an infinite number of dimensions occupy the universe simultaneously..."

"Huh?"

"At the same time, Mr Boggs. Normally we remain separated by dimensional barriers, whatever they may be. I couldn't begin to know or understand the complexities or the physics of such a thing.

If we take what I say to be true for the moment, and I am not saying it is, then there are portals to one of these other dimensions opening and closing hereabouts. Every so often, one is open long enough to allow something through from the other side, just as something from this side either makes it through or gets caught halfway."

"Like my daddy?" asked Tara.

Arlon peered solemnly at Tara. "Possibly," agreed Arlon.

"Doesn't explain why these things blow up, Arlon," queried Clarice.

"Think about the two dimensions as being diametrically opposed to one another, opposites, like positive and negative. When one of those interdimensional creatures happens into our world it's exposed to that opposite energy and needs to retreat from that exposure on a cellular level. So much so that it practically implodes. A bit like the theory of matter meeting anti-matter."

"Why hasn't this thing done that?" asked Freddy reasonably.

"I don't know. In my opinion, it's just a matter of time before it succumbs to the laws of nature."

"How did you know it wouldn't hurt us?" asked Clarice.

"A guess. It displayed fear when it curled up into a ball while we were 'all in the same boat'?"

"Very funny," said Clarice.

"Well, we were, actually. We all faced the same danger, so it did not need to make matters worse by trying to wage war with us at the same time."

"You're saying it's intelligent?"

"It has a certain animalistic intelligence, certainly. Much like any animal. Hmm..." Arlon paused suddenly as a thought struck him.

"What?"

"Suppose it didn't shoot that stuff down there like the other two? Did either of you see this particular one do that?"

"Wouldn't have a clue," admitted Clarice with a shrug. "Pretty hard to tell them apart and it looked like all three were shooting that acidy goop."

"What if this one couldn't? What if, say, it's a different gender to the others and didn't have the same capabilities? If it isn't exposed internally to our atmosphere, maybe it isn't affected as quickly."

"Sounds like a load of bullshit ta me," spat Freddy. "Ya still got that knife on ya belt. Why don't ya kill the rotten thing?"

"It isn't hurting anyone," explained Arlon.

"Yet."

"Don't you think it would have if it wanted to?" asked Clarice. "So, Arlon, you think it exposes itself by releasing the stream of...stuff?"

"For want of a better explanation, yeah."

"But you believe this one will eventually go like the others?"

"Yeah, I do. It's just a matter of time before the two elements from different realms clash. Maybe the epidermis or the shagpile of fur gives them temporary protection, but it can't continue for long. Remember the strange insect we saw? It just blew up without doing anything. I just don't think anything can survive out of its natural realm indefinitely. I'm surprised it can breathe our air."

Everyone settled into an uneasy silence as they digested this information. Below them, the waters were slowly retreating. Interestingly, every so often they saw the creature lift its head minimally to inspect the scene before dropping down flat again.

Within a few hours, the water receded far enough to entice Arlon into thinking they might take the chance to move from their uncomfortable position. The sky was taking on an afternoon glow, heralding the coming of nightfall. They were exhausted and miserable. The purple rug remained dormant but for the rare occasions it momentarily scanned the scene below. Arlon was unable to predict how the creature would react to movement.

Tara had fallen into a troubled sleep in his arms. Freddy hung to the opposite finial, barely able to keep his eyes open. Clarice nestled close to Arlon and the girl, smiling at him every so often. He could not understand why she did that. Arlon knew they would be hungry, thirsty and, soon, cold. While the interior of the house might have escaped the full brunt of the flood, it was sure to be a muddy mess.

In the pantry, however, he knew there was an assortment of canned goods that would provide them with nourishment. There were at least three packs of two dozen water bottles. He was not fearful of dehydration or starvation if they managed to get off the roof and back inside the house. Finding somewhere dry to sleep might present problems, though he had an idea about that as well. Arlon was nothing if not efficient in exploring his surroundings wherever he found himself, often searching every nook and cranny without specific permission to do so. He remembered seeing a couple of boxes stored in a linen cupboard that might come in handy. They should have been high enough to escape the water, in his estimation.

Firstly, though, they needed to get off the roof. They had the ladder with them, so getting down was not a concern. The biggest problem they faced was the creature's reaction and whether it possessed the same lethal capabilities as its fallen comrades. They couldn't remain aloft much longer, so Arlon decided that they would have to attempt a move. He gently handed Tara to Clarice, making as little noise and movement as possible.

He succeeded in neither. When he turned, the creature had risen to its full height on eight legs, looking like a weird purple spider. Thankfully, the abdomen-head had not appeared, nor was the creature showing signs of aggression. Arlon did not try to stand. He believed it would be smarter to remain in a lower, submissive stance to avoid the creature's defence mechanisms from activating. He slid on his backside towards the veranda roof, where the ladder remained.

Without turning, he sensed the hairs on the back of his neck rise as the creature followed close behind. He imagined he could feel its breath blowing ever so slightly on his bare shoulders. Remaining alert but calm, Arlon opened the step ladder and proceeded to edge it over the lip of the roof. Ensuring that the metal made no contact with the roof during the process, Arlon was able to set the ladder on the muddy ground beneath the veranda. The unstable skillion roof threatened to give way at any moment. It leaned precariously toward the end where Angela had fallen off in what seemed like a lifetime ago.

In fact, Arlon and the rest of them could probably walk down to that end of the veranda roof and jump the small distance to the ground. However, he didn't think it would hold them, and if it collapsed entirely, that might be all the impetus the creature needed to unleash its demonic abdomen-head. Arlon chanced a glimpse under his arm. The creature had advanced so closely to Arlon, scrutinising him so carefully, that he could almost taste the tension emanating from it in nauseating waves.

Two bloodshot red eyes peered at him from within the purple

shag; piercing, threatening, questioning every movement. Arlon was cornered by it. He had no option other than to continue with his original plan. Through the creature's legs, Arlon could see the others gaping at the spectacle, horrified, expectant, ready to scream. Arlon looked straight at Clarice with a look of warning she did not fail to understand. Tara had woken and clutched Clarice tightly. Freddy watched in dreaded fascination. Arlon fell off the roof.

He landed on his feet exactly as he had planned. Leaping from the roof on its multi-jointed legs, the creature landed directly behind him, into the middle of a large pool of water. Instantly, the creature crumpled in on itself until it was a mere speck before exploding outwards in a spray of foul goo that coated Arlon from head to toe. A deafening clap of thunder rocked the still air. Unaware of the pregnant clouds building in the skies above, the group were startled by the sudden deluge. Arlon ushered them down from the roof.

Fortunately, Clarice's sister had not opted for carpet in their island home, choosing practical, polished concrete floors in most parts of the house except the living room. While they were a muddy, slippery affair, they did not constitute the malodorous and unhygienic catastrophe of sodden carpet. Only the seagrass matting in the living room required removal. Not that the house could be rescued in Arlon's opinion. He doubted it could be straightened with any degree of success. For the time being, it could be cleaned up sufficiently for shelter and warmth.

The solid shutters and doors had prevented the flood from inundating the interior of the house, but did not exclude all moisture. The furniture had been saturated and moved into untidy heaps against the stained walls. Thankfully, the gas stove remained upright and connected, as far as Arlon could tell. That meant they had a means of heating or cooking food. Arlon instructed Clarice to gather what canned goods she could from the pantry, to assemble a meal for them all after cleaning themselves. He advised against anything requiring heating for the time being. He wanted to inspect all the gas pipes before they utilised the stove.

After he'd showered all the foulness from his body, Arlon retrieved the boxes he remembered in the hallway linen cupboard. The brightly-coloured hammocks were meant for exterior use as day beds, he assumed. He would find a way to string them up in various parts of the house to accommodate their little party. There were only three hammocks, so two of them would have to share. He assumed Clarice would share one with Tara.

He found a couple of rechargeable lanterns and candles which he soon had illuminating the house effectively. Righting and cleaning the teak table from the dining room gave them a relatively clean surface from which to eat their meagre meal. He removed the sodden cushions from the rattan dining chairs, giving everyone a dry seat.

Together with a hammer, he found a number of nails in a glass jar under the kitchen sink. He made the others sit for their meal while he banged about the main and spare bedrooms to erect the hammocks: one in the second bedroom for Freddy and two in the main bedroom for the remaining three. He tested them for strength by jumping into each one and swinging roughly. The rain was still beating heavily on the corrugated iron roof as he returned to the dining room to eat his meal of baked beans and tinned ham.

"Get them up okay?" asked Clarice, attempting to stifle a yawn.

"Yeah. I don't think your sister's going to be too happy about me hammering nails into her timber panelling, though."

"I doubt it will bother her when she sees the state of the house overall. It's still crooked, Arlon."

"Yep. Can't be fixed, either, as far as I can tell."

"I think we'd better get you cleaned up and off to bed, young lady. You look like you're about to fall asleep at the table," said Clarice.

Tara nodded wearily.

Arlon watched the pair, wrapped in towels, exit the dining room.

"She's been through the wars," declared Freddy, out of the blue. He had been very quiet since leaving the roof.

"That she has. She faces an even tougher road when and if we get off this island," stated Arlon.

"If? Ya think there's a chance we won't?"

"Good chance that all the tourist islands around here got evacuated before the tsunami hit. If it smashed the mainland around Shute Harbour and the coastal towns, then there's every chance they're not going to be bothered checking this island out any time soon. They probably won't be repairing the communications tower on Hamilton for a while, either. That leaves us with no way of calling the mainland or getting ourselves off here with only a small lifeboat at our disposal," declared Arlon, with an air of finality.

"So, ya just gonna give up?"

"Who said anything about giving up? I never give up, Mr Boggs. That little girl and that beautiful woman in there are relying on me to see that they leave this island alive. I don't intend to let them down. Not while I have a single breath in this old body."

"Hah! Old, schmold! Ya still a spring chicken next ta me. I'm practically a fossil. But I want ta get outta this alive as well. Don't plan on curlin' the toes up jest yet. Yer all right, Mr Arlon. I give ya a hard time and ya didn't deserve it. Ya done right by us all, I reckon, and I don't think I'd be around if ya hadn't. Thanks."

"That's okay, Mr Boggs. Still plan on fishing for a living after this?"

"No bloody way! Had enough-o-the water for two lifetimes and then some. Reckon I might stay a landlubber for good now. If we're gettin' more-o-them land critters and sea critters through that there portal thing, I don't want nuffin' ta do with it. Purple dog-spiders and angry bloody penguins. Not ta mention that kraken I saw. Scare a body to a quiverin' mess, it would."

"Hmm, you're right."

"Huh?"

"Well, I was thinking about getting us off the island as quickly as possible. That was wrong. I shouldn't be thinking so selfishly or irresponsibly."

"Come again? After what we been through? What more do ya want ta happen fore we git?" asked Freddy incredulously.

"You're right. I don't want anything more to happen to any of you. We'll see about getting you three off the island."

"Ya not comin'?"

"No. Someone has to get to the bottom of this thing before we have a major disaster that affects more than just this little corner of the world."

"What can ya do against an underwater earthquake?"

"Good point. If that's what it is," replied Arlon cryptically.

"That's what ya said it was."

"I speculated and theorised about a lot of things. Doesn't mean I'm one hundred per cent right or wrong. I was paid handsomely to find out what happened to Clarice's brother-in-law and I aim to honour my contract. Something happened here a year ago that took his life, and I plan to keep investigating until I find some definitive answers. At the moment, everything is pure guesswork, and that is not how I work. I don't want to be right about my hypothesis. I don't believe in that sort of stuff."

"Ya seen them things! Nothin' like that on planet earth, mate, NOTHIN'! No other explanation for that shit."

"Just because we can't think of any other explanation doesn't mean there isn't one. You might be right about krakens and mermaids, for all I know."

"Now ya makin' fun-o-me," said Freddy.

"Nope! Not at all. It was wrong for me to belittle your beliefs, Mr Boggs. You were brought up with sea tales by your folks and I shouldn't have berated you for it. I'm hoping that I'm completely wrong about my theory. I'm hoping there's a perfectly reasonable and logical cause for everything that's happening here. If it turns out to be krakens and mermaids, then I'll be the first to eat some humble pie, even though I won't *feel* humbled."

"Don't like yiz explanation much but I don't got another. Weird shit, that's for sure. Tales of krakens and mermaids is just tales and never seen. I seen *them* things. We all did. Don't know about them portals or nothin', but seems like ya mighta hit the nail on the head," said Freddy, with a big yawn.

"I've set up a hammock in the second bedroom for you. An old salt like you should find it comfortable enough."

"Yiz'd think so, wouldn't yiz? Never slept in one, though. Don't reckon it's gonna be all that comfy for me old bones. Probably clear a space and sleep on the floor."

"I wouldn't do that if I were you," advised Arlon.

"Oh, and why's that?"

"Bound to be cool tonight and the rising damp won't do you much good."

"Well, if it's all the same, I'll sleep where I wants."

Freddy wiped his mouth with a paper napkin before rising from the table to saunter off to his room. Arlon decided to make himself a cup of coffee. It had been some time since his last and he thought he might need the stimulant to stay awake through the night. While he believed earlier that he should grab some well-earned rest with the others, he changed his mind. He did not want to be caught totally by surprise if anything else should occur during the night. Arlon was one of those rare people who could function normally on very little sleep. A power nap for ten minutes was all he required for days on end.

Arlon took a chance on the gas stove. Just as the water boiled and the whistle blew on the old tin kettle, Tara walked in, rubbing her eyes.

"Where's Clarice?" Arlon asked quickly.

"She's asleep," said Tara dreamily.

"As you should be. How come you're awake?"

"I'm...sad. I keep thinking of my mummy and daddy, but I can't be with them anymore."

"If I can find some, how would you like a hot chocolate drink?"

Tara nodded. Arlon went to the walk-in pantry to see if he could locate the beverage.

"Tara, do me a favour?"

"Sure," she replied.

"I want you to close your eyes and think of your mummy, daddy and yourself at a time when you were happiest," said Arlon, as he emerged from the pantry with a container of drinking chocolate.

"Do you see them?"

"Yep," said Tara, brightening a little.

"Well, then, doesn't that prove that you can be with them any time you want? They still exist in your heart and your mind, little one, and no one will ever be able to remove them. Keep them safe there and you'll never be lonely."

"They didn't really want me..." she said, with great sadness.

"They weren't good parents, if that's true. They were also very stupid," said Arlon, leaning in towards Tara as she sat at the dining table. "I tell you what," he said, as he went to the kitchen to prepare the chocolate milk for Tara, "I know a person in the government who deals with family matters. Once we get out of here, would you like me to ask him if you could stay with us, maybe permanently?"

"You and Clarice?"

"I haven't discussed it with my fiancée yet, but I have a feeling she'd agree very quickly."

"Why?"

"You mean you don't think we've known you long enough to make that sort of offer?"

Arlon saw Tara dropping her head slightly and guessed what might be troubling her.

"Tara, you have probably never been told this by anyone before, but you are a remarkable girl. Extraordinary, actually. It would be a great honour to be your guardian, to help you in your education and growth. Unfortunately, I probably wouldn't be of much help in the love department: you'd have to rely on Clarice for that. I have a condition that prevents me from loving someone in the usual sense. It also means that I can never be angry or mean to you. I would never raise a hand to you, and I would not send you away to boarding school or camp or any other place unless you specifically told me you wanted to go.

"I think you are probably the smartest, bravest little girl I have ever had the privilege to know."

When Arlon turned around from the stove, Tara's tears were falling freely down her cheeks. Arlon went to her and picked her up into his powerful arms. She hugged him tightly. He carried her back to the stove to finish pouring the chocolate milk. He then carried it and Tara back to the table and sat down with her on his lap. The rain had decreased in intensity and was pattering softly overhead. Candlelight flickered, casting dancing shadows on the walls.

"I found a marshmallow, which I plonked into your drink," said Arlon, once Tara had recovered sufficiently to try it. "If you drink it quickly you'll find it and get a mouthful of gooey, sweet, chocolaty goodness."

When Tara turned to face him, she had a large chocolate moustache, which made Arlon smile. He wiped her mouth clean with a napkin.

"Do you really want to be my new daddy?"

"I would very much like to be your new friend and guardian, if you'll let me. If you say you'd like to, I'll do everything in my power to make it happen, and I know a lot of people who can help me. I don't know if I'll be ever worthy of the title 'Daddy', Tara. I think you have to have the capacity for love to qualify as a daddy, and that's something I'll never have."

"Would it be all right if I loved you?" asked Tara.

"I doubt you'll find that's possible, but it's perfectly fine by me if you do."

"I do already, Mr Arlon," said Tara, in a shy voice.

"Now it's my turn to ask why, Tara?"

"You saved me. You helped me and Mummy. You were nice to me, and talked to me, and..."

"And?"

"Didn't laugh at me if I said something childish," said Tara, mimicking her mother's tone.

"That's because I don't laugh at anything. I get what you mean, though. I still think I'm just giving you the respect and consideration you so fully deserve, young lady. It was you who saved your mummy's life. It was my fault that she...didn't make it."

"No, Mr Arlon. It was that awful shark. I hate sharks."

"It was only doing what comes naturally to them. They only know to eat, live, breed and swim. They have no other purpose than that; there's nothing personal in anything they do. That's nature, Miss Blaze."

"See?"

"See what?"

"No one talks to me like that," said Tara.

"You mean like an adult?"

"Yep."

"Adults have enough difficulty talking to each other without causing problems. I think what you're trying to say is that adults generally talk down to children. You have to understand that someone your age hasn't gone through most of the experiences that adults have to deal with as they age."

"Like being left alone? Like no one caring? Like losing someone?"

Arlon was caught out by the truth of her questions. Momentarily silenced by her unique astuteness, he could only smile and nod his head.

"What do you think, then?"

"Do you promise not to send me away every holiday?"

"You only go where you want to go, I promise. I will always ask your permission to do something on your behalf and talk to you as an equal, a partner. I don't want to replace your daddy. I would much rather be someone on whom you can rely and turn to for support and understanding. There will be times when you are not allowed to do things you might want, but that's part of being responsible. If we let you stay up all night eating and drinking all the sweets and chocolate milk you wanted, you wouldn't learn anything at school and you'd most likely become sick and very fat. Then I would have to roll you to bed each night."

Tara giggled. Clarice, standing just out of view, listening closely to the entire exchange between them and peering around the corner now and then, could not prevent happy tears from flowing. In her time with Arlon Grey, she had never heard him so much as attempt sensitivity or compassion, let alone come within a kilometre of joking. It was pure bliss listening to him, her man, showing signs of true humanity for the very first time. How she yearned for him to show her those same signs. She loved him with every ounce of her being, but still longed for those simple touches and endearments that demonstrably signalled love.

Clarice remonstrated with herself sharply for thinking that way. She was once again allowing her misguided indoctrination by romanticists to interfere with her peace of mind. Here was clear evidence that Arlon was perfectly capable of far deeper sentiments than any other man she had known, and still she hoped for more. She berated herself for thinking like that. His parents had alienated themselves from their son for wanting that exact thing. She could not fall into the same trap.

Seeing the two of them sitting there so peacefully and talking like old friends warmed her heart and gave her promise of a wonderful future with them both. While she secretly desired children of her own someday, she had become very fond of Tara. She'd had no idea that Arlon was also becoming attached to her. It didn't seem possible.

She had almost relegated herself to being childless with Arlon because he admitted he was unable to express or know love. Clarice considered that essential to rearing children. She could not imagine bringing a child into this world without being able to lavish all the love from both parents upon the child. Although Clarice was the teensiest bit upset about her fiancé making major plans like adoption without consulting her, she forced that thought to the back of her mind in the light of the revelations she heard and saw.

"I'd like it if you and Clarice could be my new mummy and daddy," said Tara shyly.

"In that case, I'll call my contact the moment we get off this island. Thank you."

"Huh?"

"Thank you for allowing me the opportunity to share in your remarkable life. It will be my honour and my pleasure to help you become all that you can be. If you've finished your drink, I think you should be off to bed. Tomorrow will be another big day for us, with no solutions to our problems yet."

"At least we have a roof tonight."

"That's the way to see it. Do you need me to tuck you in?"

"I'm not a baby."

"Of course not. Tucking you in would be more for my benefit than yours. I've never done it before and I have a lot to learn."

"Maybe after?"

"Sure. Good night."

"Good night," said Tara, moving to stand next to him. She reached up to peck him on the cheek. She skipped off toward the bedroom happily, passing Clarice in the hallway, who held a finger to her lips to indicate she should remain quiet. She took Tara's hand and led her back to the bedroom.

TWELVE

"Can't we do something for them?" asked Clarice, with a look of desperation.

The heartbreaking scene was discovered by Arlon as soon as dawn broke. Passing the non-existent shed with only the generator left in place, Arlon walked towards the boundary where the rear fence once stood. The tide had left a wide swathe of destruction on its inland route. He had noted a few fish and other marine species scattered about it, but this had not prepared him for the sight of the two humpback whales in a flattened clearing.

He heard their anguished calls first and the sound of their laboured breathing while they battled gravity. In the near weightlessness of their watery environment, they seldom had the pressure on their internal organs they now experienced on dry land. The calf was very close to death, while the mother struggled gamely by her infant's side. Arlon could think of nothing he might try to save the lives of one or both. The small tractor belonging to the property would not be capable of hauling the leviathans to the beach, always supposing he could get it started, which seemed most doubtful.

"Aside from finding where to stab them in the heart, there's nothing I can do, Clarice. Maybe Mr Boggs could tell me where the entry point might be, but I doubt it. He's not a whaler, just a fisherman. As upsetting and distressing as it may be, there's bugger-all we can do to ease their suffering or relocate them. Better make sure Miss Blaze doesn't get to see this," Arlon suggested thoughtfully. "By the way, Clarice, I think I have something to confess to you, and I hope you won't be angry."

"I won't be," said Clarice, with more conviction than Arlon thought she should have.

"You can't say that until you know what it..."

"I already know, Arlon."

"She told you?"

"She isn't awake yet, poor little thing. No, Arlon, I heard you two talking last night."

"Eavesdropping?"

"Yes, I admit I was eavesdropping. I didn't have the heart to interrupt. It was so, so lovely and...right."

"You don't mind?"

"A little, at first. Not because of any doubts where Tara is concerned. I have fallen completely under that young lady's spell. No, I was just a tiny bit upset that you didn't discuss it with me first, that's all. Wait," said Clarice, holding her hand up. "I realised it was an impulsive move on your part and that you assumed I was asleep at the time."

"It wasn't an impulsive move. I'm immune to impulsiveness."

"Really? You could have fooled me."

"You don't mind?"

"Oh, Arlon, what I saw and heard last night made me one of the happiest women alive. It was all I could do to stop myself from ravishing you there and then."

"You agree, then?"

"Can we discuss this someplace else? I can't stay here listening to these poor creatures dying a slow and agonising death."

Arlon led Clarice back towards the house.

"Oh, sis is going to be so unhappy when she sees her lovely pathway completely ruined. They worked on finding all those bits and pieces for nearly a year before they had it finished. They made a contest of it to see who could find the perfect item to fit the next space. It's all gone now, even the solar lights."

"Except for those two big rocks at the entrance to the shed," said Arlon, pointing towards the white-painted boulders.

"Hmm, Gail told me they had a hard time with those, the last ones in place. She said they found them on opposite points of the bay and had to haul them back behind the tractor. She told me it took them an age to finally wrestle them into place."

"Yeah, all the other rocks and tree trunks were washed away with the surge. I tried to move one before. Couldn't budge it. No wonder they're still in place. Odd shapes," he remarked absently.

"Don't go changing the subject on me, Mr Grey."

"Well, certainly not, Miss Manning," Arlon complied.

"It'll have to be Mrs Grey before long if we hope to adopt that adorable young girl," suggested Clarice.

"Yes, I suppose it'll help our chances, won't it?"

"Unless your contact is a miracle maker."

"He's a cabinet minister and he owes me big time. Does it make such a big difference in these modern, enlightened times if we aren't actually married yet?"

"Wouldn't like our chances."

"Do you still want to marry me, Clarice?"

"What a question!"

"I just thought some time with me might've changed your mind, that's all. I know my limitations and I know your expectations."

"Well, my expectations have changed dramatically in the last few months, Arlon. I'd even given up on the idea of having children until I saw you last night. You're an old softy, Mr Arlon Grey."

"Not so old," he protested mildly.

"There! You've even started joking. I could hardly believe my ears when I heard you telling Tara a little joke about rolling her around. What's happened to you?"

"Good question. I'm as confused and surprised by my behaviour as you are."

"So you admit that you aren't behaving in your usual manner?"

"A slight deviation from the norm, I would say," he admitted without conviction.

"Well, no, you aren't breaking down and weeping or anything as dramatic as that. I am seeing differences, though, especially where Tara is concerned. It's almost like you have a real affection for her, which makes me a bit jealous."

"I think you're exaggerating now. I am impressed by her and I have great respect for her. She is quite remarkable for someone of her age, to have looked after her mother so well in times of catastrophe. No one her age should have to endure such hardships."

"I don't think her parents treated her all that well."

"That's an understatement. Mr Blaze is lucky I wasn't around to witness the neglect he imposed on the girl. They didn't deserve a miracle like her."

"Miracle?"

"Nothing short of it, in my opinion. How that girl managed to develop into the wonder she is escapes me."

"Wow, high praise coming from you."

"Totally deserved. Now, I'm hungry. How about we wrestle up some breaky?"

"You don't think we need to discuss this more?"

"No point in getting into the nitty-gritty of it until we know we have more than just a chance of succeeding."

"Very pragmatic of you."

"I am nothing if not pragmatic in everything I do, Clarice."

Something made Arlon stop mid-stride as they were about to head back to the house. Arlon turned sharply, expecting to see something behind them. There was nothing.

"Arlon, what is it?"

Arlon said nothing for a time. He stood perfectly still, urging Clarice to do the same with a look. Only his eyes moved back and forth, inspecting the area with a practised eye. He placed a tentative step forward. Before him stretched the littered path to the concrete slab of the iron shed that had been removed by the tide. Only the large diesel generator remained atop the platform. Everything else had been flattened and swept away.

Some debris had returned on the receding tide, littering the entire area around them. Nothing moved, not a breath of wind stirred, yet something intangible had attracted Arlon's senses.

"Arlon, you're scaring me. What is it?" asked Clarice nervously.

"Can't you feel that?"

"Shit! Feel what? No."

"I detect a pulsation, a wave of some sort, emanating from somewhere around here."

"You mean like that pressure thing?"

"Yes and no. There is a little of that same alteration in pressure, but there's something else."

"Arlon, there's nothing here. If there was anything before, it can't be here now because it all got washed inland."

Arlon took another step forward, then another. He walked slowly up to the edge of the concrete slab. He scanned the entire area, not knowing what he was hoping to find. He rotated on the spot for a moment.

"Can you feel the temperature difference right here?" he asked Clarice.

"No, sorry."

"It's slight, I'll grant you that, but it's there. Warmer by a degree or two," said Arlon, in a soft, ominous tone.

"Coming from the dead generator?"

"No, of course not."

"You make that sound like I said something crazy. You're the one talking about a temperature difference coming from nothing. There aren't even any trees left standing here...nothing. The sun's coming up," ventured Clarice, as another possibility.

"It was just inside the shed, only a metre away from here where your brother-in-law was found. If we say that was the first occurrence of anything odd happening here, then we can assume that we're at ground zero. If the portal theory is correct, then here is where it first appeared over a year ago."

"You said a movement under the ocean, those plates, caused the phenomenon."

"I postulated one possibility. If that happened then there should have been geologists all over this island, seismologists and a host of other -ologists swarming over the area to conduct experiments, tests and measurements. That didn't happen."

"You just killed your own theory."

"Something every good scientist or investigator should do. If you can't prove your theory, you should at least try to disprove it."

"Have you?"

"Not necessarily."

"I'm confused," admitted Clarice.

"It may have been totally localised and too insignificant to trigger seismographs on the mainland. Or..."

"Ooh, I don't like the sound of that. Or, what?"

"Or it didn't happen," said Arlon after a moment, while walking slowly around the perimeter of the concrete slab.

"Arlon, you aren't making any sense. Of course it happened. The police conducted a major investigation here after Gail...you know...?"

"I didn't say the death didn't happen. We know that for a fact. I've seen the crime scene photographs."

"You didn't tell me that. How did you manage to see the police photos?"

"I was in the force once, remember?"

"Yeah, I remember. I also remember that you told me they cheered when you were unceremoniously booted out of the force. That would lead me to believe you had no friends on the force. Ergo, no access to crime photos."

"I have connections, Clarice. You don't get to have a crime

solve rate like mine without impressing a few of the victims' family. Some of those family members have gone on to politics and other areas of advantage to a washed-up detective. Some of them still owe me a favour or two."

"Whoa, slow down there, bucko. Okay, I get that, all right? What I want to know is what you mean by saying it 'didn't happen'. What didn't happen?"

Arlon stopped walking to face Clarice. "The event that triggered the phenomenon."

"The earthquake, volcano eruption, or whatever?"

"Yes. What if we are looking at this the wrong way? What if the phenomenon was causing the other stuff?"

"I don't follow."

"It would take energy to create this fracture between dimensions, correct?"

"I...suppose?"

"Think about it, Clarice. It takes an imploding star to create a black hole in space, a wormhole or portal, whichever way you want to describe it. What if a minor energy source were creating a fracture between dimensions here and that was causing the other anomalies we are experiencing?"

"Here? On Cid Island in the calm and idyllic Whitsunday Islands? Where thousands of tourists flock every year for sunshine, swimming, tanning and all that stuff?"

"Damn, you're right about that. Someone would have noticed something. So what do we deduce from that?"

"That you are off your rocker, mate. Sorry to be the bearer of sad tidings. Want me to measure you up for the form-fitting white coat now?"

"Don't you see?"

"No."

"It hasn't been happening all along. It began a little over a year ago here, ground zero. Your brother-in-law was the first victim of the anomaly, as far as we know. Before then, all the years your sister and her husband came here for holidays, and his parents before them, nothing happened other than his father's accident. Then, suddenly, he is found chopped in half by some, as yet unknown, method. Since then, there has been a steady escalation of events, which we have seen for ourselves during our short stay. Who knows what was happening for the year this place was taped off as a possible murder scene. If no one is here to experience the event, there's no way of knowing it occurred. There weren't any cataclysmic events. We know that because no one was sent here to investigate. There was no mention of anything in the media. I checked."

"Have a look around you, Arlon. There were trees here before the tsunami, and a shed housing the only energy source around here. Nothing else! I don't see any imploding stars, you know?"

"Of course not. We aren't in space."

"Well?"

"A fracture between dimensions may not require the amount of energy derived from an imploding star. The fractures may have been infinitesimal at first, lasting only fractions of a second, allowing only insect-sized objects to enter our dimension. They developed in size and frequency until we get what we are experiencing now, big enough and long enough to swallow a pod of migrating whales.

"The Blaze family were happily boating on the ocean, watching a pod of whales, when, beneath the water, a portal forms to swallow some or all members of the pod as they swim through the opening. One or two unlucky animals were caught as it closed, severing them in the same manner as your sister's husband. When the portal opened again somewhere above the Blaze's ship, it rained one of the whale pieces onto their craft. Another part of a whale landed here in our bay. You saw the bones there.

"Mr Boggs' kraken may have been a creature attempting to breach the portal into our dimension. He may have seen that window appearing before his boat, with the creature on the other side, clear as day. His boat may have continued into that dimension after he abandoned it. The opening closed before he regained the surface of the water. That could be why he didn't see where his boat went."

"Wow, is this the same Arlon Grey who didn't believe in any of this guff? The same Arlon Grey who poo-poohed the idea of the Bizarre and Mysterious Detective Agency?"

"I admit that I'm unable to explain this away in conventional terms. That's not to say I fully accept my theory yet. I have still to prove or disprove anything, and I am keeping an open mind. You can't ask more than that of me."

"No, Arlon, I can't. What I want from you at the moment is for you to find a way to get us off this bloody island before it's too late. I don't want to see anything happen to that little girl...or us. She needs us as much as we seem to need her."

"In that case, the boat I found will probably come in handy if..."

"Boat? What boat?"

"If I had to guess, I'd say it was Mr Boggs' boat."

"What? Where?"

"Washed up near the path to the house. Not sure if it's much good to us, though."

"Why not?"

"Looks like the outboard got swamped and there's a hole in the hull."

"Can we fix it?"

"Sure. I'll just whip out my instant hull-fixing materials and patch that hole in no time flat."

"That's the first time I've ever heard you use sarcasm. I hope it's the last."

"Just a small quip rather than dripping sarcasm, Clarice. I thought you would be astute enough to realise that I can't simply produce boat-fixing materials from thin air. Everything that may have been of assistance was in the shed. Unfortunately, we seem to be missing a few shelves and cupboards."

"Comedy again, huh? You should be on stage; the first one out of town."

Arlon rewarded Clarice with a rare smile. Her heart soared briefly. When Arlon smiled his whole persona changed instantly. She had experienced that smile only during their most intimate moments. His perfect teeth and swashbuckling, movie-star good looks almost caused Clarice to swoon...if she knew how.

It was the image she carried of him in her heart and memory, always. It was only when he opened his mouth that the image was generally washed away in bitter disappointment. Except lately: something odd was altering her man's customary demeanour. It was almost as if...as if he were experiencing an emotion or two, and she knew that just wasn't possible.

Arlon led her along the ruined path towards the beach. They each remained in their thoughts as they strolled companionably along. Arlon shocked Clarice to the core by holding her hand. It was the only time he had ever voluntarily displayed an affectionate gesture resembling romance. While it warmed her aching heart, it troubled Clarice. It was unnatural for Arlon Grey and, compounded with the evidence of the previous night, when he displayed super sensitivity towards Tara, it became a concern in her mind.

Arlon had explained that he experienced certain emanations or variances in the atmosphere and even a temperature difference around the area of the shed. Clarice wondered if those emanations were altering his mentality in some way. Subtle though they were, she detected the small variations nonetheless, as only someone who knew their partner intimately might. While wholly grateful for their presence, making her deepest wishes and dreams come true, she was disturbed in a profound and ironic sense.

If some strange energy force affected her man, she was not willing to accept that as a wish answered. She refused to see anything detrimental to his wellbeing as a godsend. And it had to be detrimental if it was fundamentally altering him on a molecular level. The proof of the pudding was in her hand. Arlon did not hold hands. He did not need to hold hands and certainly saw no point in doing so to please another. It was yet another increasingly odd turn of events on an island fraught with unnatural occurrences. Her thoughts were interrupted as they came to the vessel Arlon had mentioned.

"Bondy, come back ta me," said a voice from somewhere behind the boat.

"So, it is your boat then, Mr Boggs?" asked Arlon, as Freddy rose from below the gunwales.

"What's left of her," he said. "All me fishin' gear, gone. Motor's flooded, and she's been scuppered," said Freddy sadly.

"No hope of repairing her?" asked Clarice hopefully.

"On the mainland, sure. Patch up the ole girl good as new. Not *here*, and no way ta get *there*."

"What about the outboard, Mr Boggs?"

"Gotta be taken apart, down ta the bones. Re-oiled and greased after wipin' down every single bit. Not gonna happen, is it? No tools, even."

"What about the radio, an EPIRB, anything?"

"Radio's buggered and everythin' else-o-use is washed away, 'cept a few tethers and such. Least me darlin's back, though. Never find another bondy like her. Love this boat better-n-a woman, and that's a fact."

"What if we found some way of applying a temporary patch and some tools to take the motor apart?" asked Arlon.

"Where ya gonna find that?"

"I suggest we go inland to find what we can of the shed's remains and all the tools, etcetera. They have to be somewhere along the path the tide took. I can't see metal tools and such being carried back with the water when it receded. Not enough force. I think everything that got washed away will be somewhere inland of us. Maybe only half a kilometre."

"Ya dreamin', mate," suggested Freddy.

"Do you have a better idea for getting off this island?"

"None of us is gettin' off here. We're all gonna..."

"Knock it off, Boggs. We don't need negativity and pessimism. If you don't want to help us look for some of what we need, fine. Remain behind. I intend to keep doing everything I can to help us stay alive and to get off this island."

"It ain't pessimism. It's reality, mate. Ya not gonna fix it."

"If the choice is to do nothing and suffer whatever awaits us, or make an effort and possibly find a way, I choose to do something, no matter how far-fetched it may seem. I saw some galvanised flat sheeting in that shed, as well as a tin of paintable bitumen. There are a hammer and some nails in the house. That might constitute some very basic waterproofing repairs if we manage to find those other items."

"Ya saw them in the shed?"

"I wouldn't say so otherwise."

"That tin-o-goop mighta floated back ta the ocean."

"Might have. Never know if we don't look. You can keep coming up with a hundred reasons why we might fail, Boggs, and I will come up with a thousand reasons why we should at least try. To do nothing is certain to fail. We will be at the mercy of whatever it is that's causing the disturbances here. If it gets any worse, we probably won't survive. That's almost a given. This island, this part of Australia, is in for one hell of a beating very soon, because it's getting worse, and who knows what other creatures we may face. I'm not overly impressed by the ones we've seen so far. They may be the *friendliest* versions the other dimension has to offer."

"Ya still stuck on that dimension thing, are ya?"

"Until a better explanation presents itself, yes."

"Well, I think we should discuss our plans over something to eat, don't you?" asked Clarice.

THIRTEEN

"Did you really see that stuff in the shed?" asked Clarice, once they had finished their meagre cold breakfast of stale cereal and warm long-life milk.

Arlon and Clarice were in their bedroom talking, while Tara was in the bathroom out of earshot.

"Yes and no," replied Arlon.

Clarice smiled, "What's that supposed to mean?"

"Well, I did see galvanised sheet metal, only it was hanging on the walls."

"Arlon, the whole shed was clad in corrugated iron."

"I know, I just said that."

"Not exactly what you intimated to Mr Boggs."

"I had to tell him something of a positive nature to get him to accompany me and stop him fretting over his boat."

"You don't think it can be fixed?"

"Unlikely, but not impossible. I'm willing to concede that we may find a means to patch the hole. That's the least of our concerns. The motor is another story. Fuel for the motor is probably the most important factor and I haven't seen any of that around here. The generator ran on diesel and I'm fairly certain that outboard motors don't take that type of fuel."

"I thought I saw a small can of mower fuel in the laundry cupboard under the washbasin."

"Why would they keep a container of fuel in the laundry?"

"There's a small portable generator in another utility cupboard."

"So, your sister has solar power, I saw the panels on the roof of the shed, a diesel generator backup and a backup petrol generator for the backup diesel generator?"

"I guess so," said Clarice, with a shrug.

"Why didn't you tell me about the generator before now? I could have had it up and running for us last night."

"We didn't need it, Arlon. The stove runs off bottled gas, and we had plenty of candles and battery lanterns."

"Fair enough. If seawater didn't get into the can, and we manage to get the outboard apart and cleaned, that may solve the problem of fuel. I want you to stay here with Tara, Clarice. I don't want that little girl subjected to any more death, and the sight of those dead or dying whales may upset her."

"Is it safe here?"

"Is it safe anywhere on this island?"

"That isn't very comforting."

"Keep the shutters closed and the doors locked while I'm gone. Stay indoors."

"I wasn't planning on a beach picnic, that's for sure."

"I think it'd be a good time to wash Tara's clothes. Nothing of yours will fit her and what she's wearing stinks to high heaven."

"You plan on getting that generator going?"

"No, why?"

"The washing machine?"

"Hmm, you've obviously never heard of a time before washing machines were around. Clarice, there's a washing tub in the laundry and soap powder. Go old school."

"Gee, ta."

"Get used to it, mother!"

The word 'mother' shocked Clarice. It had not sunk in until that moment that she had agreed to be a mother. Their lives would forever be prioritised around a dependant. She'd managed to provide her nagging mother with a grandchild at long last *before* she was married! Her older sister and mother had told her many times that her biological clock was winding down and she had better get a move on in the man department before the opportunity was gone.

Well, Gail had failed miserably in the baby department when it was found that she couldn't have children, and none of her brothers were getting married any time soon. From that moment, Clarice had been the target of her mother's push for a grandchild. She had even gone so far as to suggest a sperm donor in the absence of a suitor. Clarice was thoroughly disgusted by the thought. She did not want to bring up a child as a single mother, no matter how acceptable it seemed these days.

A mother!

Clarice suddenly glowed from within. While she had taken to the girl and cared for her since their acquaintance, it was always with the mother present or the notion that Tara would be passed onto the relevant authorities the moment they returned to the mainland. She had not immediately taken it for granted that Arlon was capable of achieving the adoption, but it was wrong to underestimate him. He usually achieved everything he set out to do...unless it depended on his 'charming personality'.

Arlon had donned another khaki safari suit, sans pith helmet. Clarice had commented on it, declaring the outfit ridiculous for their present circumstances. He told her didn't care, as usual. He had no time for what any other person thought of his attire. It didn't bother him one iota. Arlon now left Clarice to her thoughts and stepped through the hallway to the rear of the house, where he met up with Freddy, waiting outside. Freddy gave him a look of pure astonishment, but said nothing as Arlon walked past him.

Then Arlon stopped so suddenly that Freddy almost bounced into him. As before, something pricked at Arlon's senses. Whether it was pressure or temperature variance, he couldn't say. There was practically nothing in the area to produce any such occurrence. Arlon was baffled by the phenomena. He peered about the back yard, strewn with debris left by the receding waters. Again he stepped closer to the bare concrete platform where the shed once stood. As far as he could tell, there was nothing of any consequence, nothing that he could observe to explain the strange emanations.

The morning had grown unnaturally silent, though that could be due to the lack of standing trees. Normally he would hear bird and insect sounds coming from the scrub. Arlon shook his head in consternation, knowing he was missing something. He inspected the entire area with his full concentration, while Freddy tutted and muttered impatiently beside him.

"We goin', or what? Daylight's wastin'," declared Freddy.

Arlon ignored Freddy and stepped off the sodden sandy path to walk the perimeter of the concrete patch. Freddy watched him with growing impatience and anger. Slitting his eyes to shut out all distractions, Arlon slowly walked around the shed's boundaries until he returned near to where he began. Beside one of the large barnacle-encrusted rocks, Arlon knelt with an outstretched hand. He moved his hand over and around the rock with his eyes closed tightly.

He stood suddenly. Spying the rock on the opposite edge of the path, he went to kneel beside the second one, while Freddy rolled his eyes at the man's strange behaviour. Arlon tested the air above and around the second rock, drawing the same conclusions he formed about the first.

"There's heat coming from these rocks," Arlon stated after a short time.

"Ya think? Could be that big old yellow ball up there in the sky might be warming the rocks, maybe?" Freddy responded sarcastically.

"When I stand between them I feel an energy, a surge of sorts. Almost like I become a conduit between the two."

"Yeah, right. Like a pair-o-rocks can do that?"

"You mean that you doubt a rock can contain any form of energy?"

"Course," he replied caustically.

"So, you've never heard of a lodestone?"

"What's that?"

"A naturally magnetised piece of the mineral magnetite. A magnet, in other words. A geological formation capable of attracting iron particles. One would call that a form of energy, Mr Boggs. Or are you disputing that concept as well?"

"Pair of rocks are maybe magnetised, so bloody what?"

"I didn't say they were magnetised. I said I felt heat coming from them and an energy passing between them if I stood in the middle."

"Still just a pair-o-rocks, mate. Not worth wastin' time over. Ya gonna look for somethin' ta patch me boat, or what? Seems like that was what ya said we was gonna do."

"Why don't you scout the area ahead of here to see if you can find something? You'd have a better idea of what was required in any case."

"Probably know a damn sight more about boats than anyone here, that's for sure."

"Well, then?"

"By meself?"

"I don't know that here is any safer than out there, Mr Boggs, and I certainly don't know if I can protect you against whatever comes our way. You survived before, didn't you?"

"Whattaya gonna do?"

"I don't know yet. I want to have a closer look at these rocks if I can. Maybe chip away some of the marine buildup. Get a better look at the underlying surface of them."

"Why?"

"I can't answer that. Call it a hunch."

"Bigger fish ta fry than lookin' at them silly rocks, don't ya think? Priority should be about getting off this haunted island. Only way ta do that is in me boat if we can fix it."

"Probably right, Mr Boggs, and I think you're the perfect person to pursue that avenue. It doesn't take two of us to have a look around for something to help us in that regard and you would know best what to look for. I'll give you whatever help you need if you find something and need to get it back here, or a hand with the fixing. Just let me know. Did you take a bottle of water?"

"Yeah."

"Well, go ahead then and give me a shout if you need a hand."

"S'pose," muttered Freddy.

He moved off, shaking his head. Arlon turned his attention to the unusual rocks again. He stood between them to ascertain the truth of his statement about feeling an emanation. Though it was slight, it was apparent. The rocks were placed too far apart for him to touch both simultaneously. He sat between them, adopting the lotus yoga position he often used to meditate. He emptied his mind of all extraneous thought to freely experience the phenomenon.

Soft and insistent pulsating waves became noticeable once he was receptive to them. It was difficult for him to describe the ambiences. The only physical sensation he could identify was heating. Whatever else the waves of energy consisted of was unknown. It was not an uncomfortable experience.

Arlon removed himself from between the rocks. He stood back to inspect each of the oddly-shaped rocks from different angles. His clear and analytical mind soon detected a possibility, but he was not willing to immediately accept his conclusion. He set off to scour the house and the area around it for the tools he required to complete a task he had set for himself.

"Arlon? I thought you went to look for something to fix the boat."

"I sent Mr Boggs off on his own to do that," explained Arlon, as he continued searching through cupboards under the kitchen sink.

"Why? And what are you looking for?" asked Clarice, as Tara joined her, wearing one of Arlon's T-shirts, to follow him around the house.

"I..."

"Arlon, stop!"

"What?"

"You're sweating from head to toe. Have you been exercising in that ridiculous outfit?"

"No."

"Then why are you sweating as though you just ran a marathon? What are you looking for? Why are you acting so strangely?"

Arlon stopped to stare at Clarice.

"Arlon, what is it? You look as though you've seen a ghost all of a sudden."

"Am I?"

"Are you what?"

"Acting strangely?"

"Well, for you, maybe not. Tell me what you're looking for."

"A coal chisel."

"Ask a stupid question... Okay, let's back it up a bit. What is a coal chisel and why do you need it?"

"I want the chisel and a hammer to chip away the marine coatings on the rocks."

"What rocks?"

"The ones on the path."

"You mean the ones in front of the non-existent shed?"

"Yes."

"Why?"

"Do we have to go into this right now? I'd rather go about my task and explain later. At dinner, maybe?"

"Are you feeling all right, Arlon?"

"Fine."

"You don't look fine at all. Is it really hot outside already? Is that why you're sweating like a pig?"

"That should correctly be 'sweating like pig'."

"That doesn't sound grammatically correct at all."

"The term sweating like a pig comes from smelted pig iron as it cools, not sweaty hogs. So, it should be sweating like pig or pig iron."

"Gee, that is so...totally boring and irrelevant! Arlon, you're avoiding my questions."

"Unsuccessfully."

"So you admit you are deliberately trying to avoid my questions?"

"Yes, I have a task I want to perform and you are stopping me with unnecessary questions at the moment."

"Mister Arlon?"

"Yes?"

"You stink. Pee-yew!" said Tara waving her hand in front of her face.

"Oh, one bubble bath with perfumed soap and you think you're above us dirty folks already, huh?" said Arlon, folding his arms in mock indignation.

Tara giggled, "You're funny."

"You, too? Clarice thought I could maybe give up my normal job and start up as a comedian as well."

"I was being sarcastic, Arlon. The day you take up comedy is the day the world loses its laughter."

"Harsh," suggested Arlon with a touch of a smile.

"I'm worried about you, Arlon. You aren't yourself. You don't joke about things. You don't..."

"I don't what?"

"Never mind. Go take a shower and put some fresh, *light* clothes on. If you aren't going traipsing through the scrub then you don't need your Livingstone outfit. Shorts, T-shirt and thongs for you, go!" Clarice demanded.

"Is he going to die, too?" asked Tara seriously, once Arlon had exited.

"Good grief, no! Why would you ask such a thing, pumpkin?"

"Everything dies around me," she said sadly.

"Oh, I know it must seem that way, honey, but you mustn't think that. Arlon and I are going to do everything we can to get us off this island so that we can all live together as a family. It may not look like it at the moment, but that man is practically a genius. If anyone can work something out, it's him," explained Clarice, with an edge of doubt creeping into her words.

"Do you love Mr Arlon?"

"With all my heart, little one, with all my heart. I've never met anyone quite like him and I don't think I ever will again. He's one of a kind. It isn't easy to love a man like him. Sometimes, it's all I can do not to pull my hair out in frustration. I shouldn't be talking to you like this, princess, should I?"

"I like the way you and Mr Arlon speak to me. Nobody else talks to me like that."

"Like what, sweetie?"

"Like a person," she said simply.

"You mean they speak down to you?"

"They talk to me like I'm a baby," she said crossly.

"Hmm, I suppose I shouldn't make the same mistake by calling you all these pet names, huh?"

"I don't mind. You say it kindly."

"How about we get that lovely hair of yours dry now that it's all clean and shiny? Go get me another towel from the linen cupboard, would you?"

"Miss Clarice?"

"Yeah, sugar...sorry, Tara?"

"Do you want me to stay with you?"

"Very much so," Clarice admitted, after a moment's reflection. "It took me by surprise when I overheard you two talking last night, and it didn't sink in until today. It would be my honour to be your guardian when this is all over. I can't promise that I'll be very good at it, though. I've never been a mother or a carer so it will be a huge learning curve for me. I *can* promise to learn and keep learning. I can also promise to listen to you and be there for you if you need me. I'm already smitten by you. You have to know that, surely? It's very, very hard not to fall in love with you after only a short time."

"Honest?"

"Cross my heart."

"And hope to die?"

"Cross my heart and hope to die," Clarice affirmed with all sincerity.

Tara skipped down the hall with a contented smile. Arlon appeared from the bathroom in a towel. Clarice studied him as he approached. Something about him sparked her curiosity. His olive complexion practically glowed within the dimness of the unlit house's interior. His jaunty air confused her as he brushed past her without a word. She watched him as he dressed in a pair of khaki shorts and a white T-shirt. She sighed with lust and longing for her perfect specimen of manhood.

Their dream island excursion had turned into a nightmare. Clarice knew they had travelled there for a work assignment, a serious undertaking considering the grisly death of Ben Sandringham. She had hoped they might explore themselves and their relationship further while ensconced in an idyllic island setting. The sex was great, though infrequent, but she had longed for the romantic intimacy of being alone in paradise.

Meanwhile, paradise had turned into a hell, and she suddenly found herself with a complete family and no time for anything of a romantic or carnal nature. As she watched the man of her dreams don a sensible pair of sandals while sitting on the damaged cane armchair in the corner of the room, she sighed deeply.

"Can you please try to explain why a couple of rocks are suddenly so important to you, Arlon?"

"Not really," he answered in a hushed voice.

"Try," she pleaded.

"I can feel something when I'm near them. Especially between them."

"So? You can't possibly think that a pair of rocks has anything to do with what's happening here, can you?"

"My head tells me that it's impossible, yes."

"Good, because you don't rely on any other organ to assess anything," Clarice insisted.

"Not entirely accurate, Clarice."

"Come again? Arlon, you can't tell me that your heart tells you something that disagrees with your head?"

"No, I can't tell you that."

"What, then?"

"Call it instinct if you want. Call it anything you like. I have a hunch, and I can't shake it. Eliminate everything possible, logical and acceptable, and you are left with only the impossible to consider. My instincts have served me well in the past, Clarice, though I would never admit that to anyone but you. Most of what I do is a process of calculation and elimination, a precise sequence of facts and conclusions based on the evidence. When there is an overwhelming amount of evidence based on an abrogation of the common laws of physics, it's time to step outside the realms of common or specific knowledge. I have to follow the same set of rules for my personal involvement and development. I can't simply disregard facts if they fall outside my sphere of knowledge or belief."

"What does all that mean?" she asked in confusion.

Tara had returned with a second towel, before heading back out of the room. Clarice barely registered her presence before she scrutinised Arlon carefully, unsure what to make of the latest revelations.

"What it means is that I have to explore every possibility, no matter how absurd I once believed such notions to be. This concept of interdimensional reality is a difficult pill for me to swallow, even though I came up with it. It goes against every grain in my body, against every practical, logical, and scientific premise I've studied. You must know how impossible it is for me to even consider such far-fetched theories?"

"And yet you have?"

"And yet I have...do," he admitted reluctantly.

"So, you subscribe to the theory that we are experiencing a fracture between dimensions here?"

"Not entirely. I'm coming close to considering the possibility. I've tried everything I know to disprove it in my mind. We aren't in space and a wormhole theory just isn't possible, as far as I can tell. Nothing else seems to explain what's happening here. None of it makes any sense in a normal world. But then, Birrani Nullah Bone didn't make much sense either, did he? He defied common sense and logical deduction. In the end, we had to accept his existence, didn't we?"

"He wasn't unnatural, Arlon. He was flesh and bone, albeit in a vastly altered state. He was a combination of the human genome gone awry, accidental manipulation of physical properties and human nurture making him a monster. He *was* of this planet, though, however bizarre he may have turned out."

"I understand that," Arlon admitted after a moment. "What do *you* make of the creatures we saw? You can't possibly think they're of this planet, this...reality?"

"Honestly? I don't know what to make of them. I've tried to shut them out of my mind because I find it hard to make any sense of this."

"Doing an ostrich won't change the circumstances. Sooner or later we have to face the facts as they present themselves. Denying their existence keeps us ignorant and allows the events to continue unchecked. Eliminating everything else means that, however improbable, only the truth will remain."

"How does a pair of rocks factor into this, though?"

"I don't know yet. I may never know. We may never find concrete answers for what's happening here. The illustrious Bizarre and Mysterious Detective Agency may have met its match with this particular beast. Hell, we may not even survive to tell the tale. It may all be a moot point and a meaningless conversation."

"It's never meaningless if it brings us closer together, Arlon. It can never be worth nothing if we are talking like this. I love you, Arlon Grey and I'm worried about you. I don't want to lose you and neither does that little girl. We're depending on you. We need you, mister."

Clarice sat on his knee and wrapped her arms around him. Tara appeared at the door. Clarice crooked a finger at her, beckoning her in. Tara ran forward and jumped up on Clarice's knee with pure exuberance, squealing with joy. She flung her tiny arms about them both.

FOURTEEN

Freddy Boggs was working feverishly on his boat after lunch. Tara was forced to take a nap, while Clarice cleared away the crumbs from their meagre fare. They were running low on edible food. Most of the canned goods were hardly consumable. Clarice drew the line at canned Spam, declaring it unfit for human consumption. Unfortunately, they would soon be left with little choice if they wanted some form of protein.

Arlon was unable to provide seafood for dinner, as the rods and reels had gone with the shed; somewhere inland. Freddy had returned from his scouting mission with several items he deemed useful for the enterprise of boat repair. He required very little encouragement to pursue the course. Arlon remained outside for the entire morning. Clarice conceded that she would have to bring some food out to him.

She saw him chipping away at a rock, though she heard only muffled taps, even as she drew near. She saw immediately that he was once again soaked through. The straw hat he wore appeared limp and dispirited in the rising heat of midday.

"Hey, Arlon, time for a break," she announced.

When he ignored her, she tapped him on the shoulder. Arlon swung round suddenly, a grimace of pure disgust twisting his features. Clarice stumbled back in fright. Dark circles had formed under his eyes, sweat poured from him. Clarice saw no recognition in his haunted eyes.

"Arlon, Arlon, what's wrong?"

Slowly, a gleam of recognition entered his eyes as he looked up.

"Sorry, Clarice. You startled me. What, what is it?"

"You didn't come in for lunch even after I called. I thought I'd better bring it out to you. Looks like you could use it, especially the water. Are you feeling all right, Arlon? You look terrible."

"Gee, thanks," said Arlon, accepting the proffered bottle,

"Hey, you said you can't be insulted, right? Just the same, you know what I meant," explained Clarice, as she settled on the path beside him.

She watched as Arlon upended the litre bottle and drained the contents in one long gulp.

"Wow, I'm not surprised you're thirsty, sweating like that, but you should take it easy. You might upset your tummy. Here, have a sandwich."

"You baked bread?"

"Just a damper in the cast-iron pot."

Clarice inspected the rock Arlon had been working on ever since finding the coal chisel. She saw only a very small area where the barnacles and other marine coatings had been chipped away.

"All that time and you only managed that little spot?"

"Critiquing my work? Not up to your exacting standards?"

"Silly," she said, smiling while not entirely certain it was humorous. "Arlon, is this safe, what you're doing?"

"How do you mean?"

"I'm not sure. I don't suppose anywhere is all that safe at the moment, but I wonder about these rocks and your sudden manic interest in them."

"Manic? Hardly manic, Clarice."

"You haven't exactly been blasé about them."

"What's your point?"

"I don't mean to be critical or judgmental, Arlon. I just want to understand your interest in a pair of rocks that seem to affect you physically and mentally. Look at yourself, sweating from head to toe. I've seen you go through the most gruelling exercise regimes and training schedules and you never sweat like this."

"And...?" he asked, seeing her hesitate.

"And you aren't behaving like your usual self. It's almost as though you're reacting emotionally all of a sudden. When I tapped you on the shoulder you looked as though you wanted to strangle me for interrupting you."

"You're exaggerating."

"No, no, I'm not. Ever since you started on this rock idea you've changed. You aren't even helping Freddy to fix his boat so we can get off this island. Don't you..."

"Care what happens to you?"

"No. That's not what I was about to say. That wouldn't be fair for me to ask. No, I was going to ask if you still want to get off the island. It sure doesn't look that way at the moment."

"I think there's a lot more at stake here than just us, Clarice."

"What is it?"

"Can't you feel the urgency of this thing? It's building, getting longer and more intense each time it happens."

"All the more reason for us to get ourselves and those other two out of here, especially that adorable little girl who has lost her whole world."

"Might not be a world left if we don't solve this."

"Arlon? You can't mean that? You mean you think we have no chance of adopting her after all?"

"I'm not talking about our little corner of the world in an emotional sense, Clarice. I'm talking about *the* world, earth, our planet. I'm talking Armageddon on a scale that would make it impossible for this world to recover."

"What? You can't be bloody serious? What could make you think that?"

"When opposites meet without the possibility of separation, a calamity waits to be unleashed."

"This is ridiculous, Arlon. What could cause that to happen here on this little, innocent island?"

"Remember what happened when the creatures were exposed to our atmosphere too long? Bam! Even the one that shared our roof for a time. The moment it hit that pool of water and finally made proper contact with its opposite element, it imploded. The two dimensions, realities, whatever term you prefer, cannot occupy the same physical plane. If a large enough portal is created here, and it remains open long enough to be subjected to its opposite reality, there will probably be a cataclysmic explosion the likes of which we have never seen before, nor will again."

"Probably?"

"You're asking me for certainty when I can't give it. I can't even be 100% positive that I know what I'm talking about," he confessed, as he chewed at his sandwich. "Yuck, is this Spam?"

"Arlon, you don't care what food tastes like, remember? See what I mean? You're changing. You're feeling stuff."

"That's what you wanted, wasn't it? So the first sign of any emotion in me and you're saying what? Don't like it?"

"No. Just that it isn't natural. I've come to terms with your condition and I don't want to change you. I love you for who you are, not what you could be."

"That's a change. Oh, not for you. No, I'm talking about..."

"Your parents?"

"Mmm, hmm."

"Okay, Mr Doom and Gloom, let's say for a moment you're right and the apocalypse is coming. How the heck are you going to do anything about it? How can anyone do anything about it?"

"Good questions."

"I'm waiting for the equally good answers, bucko," said Clarice in her tomboy's voice.

"You haven't used that voice on me for a while."

"High time I did, then. If the world as we know it is coming to an end, there is no point in us staying here, is there? Nothing we mere humans can do will avert the apocalypse."

"You could be right. In which case it doesn't matter where we are when it happens, does it? Better to be at ground zero and get it over with quickly and painlessly, don't you think?"

"Are we at ground zero, though?"

"I believe so. It started here and I think it'll end here."

"If it's a fait accompli, why are you sitting out here with these stupid rocks? Why aren't we inside making wild and abandoned love?"

"Because I don't think it's ultimately inevitable."

"Arlon Grey, saviour of the world? Would look great on the brochure if you can swing it. Not your usual detective agency that can put that boast on the literature."

"Your confidence in me is remarkable."

"Hmm, sarcasm again. Not sure I like this new you. I never had to worry about sarcasm before. Any more surprises you'd care to tell me about?"

"I don't think I accept what you say now, let alone that I may gain further...embellishments to my character?"

"Okay, tell me how you plan to stop the end of the world."

"I can't."

"You can't stop the end of the world? Shocker, that!"

"No, Clarice. I simply can't explain how I can stop it at this stage. I don't even fully understand the concept, its implications or its contrivances."

"In that case, I'll leave you to your...whatever, while I go practise being a mother."

"I think you make a great mother and I wouldn't discount a natural one if I were you. If we make it out of here we should try for the pigeon pair, shouldn't we?"

"Sounds like a..."

A rending crack directly above their heads startled the pair out of their wits. In the sky, heavy, pendulous clouds gathered swiftly in a roiling, swirling mass. Lightning streaked out in every direction, filling the air with the aroma of ozone. The slight breeze that Arlon had been feeling before quickly mounted in strength and velocity until it bore all the hallmarks of a cyclone forming.

Normally, cyclones formed over warm water, utilising the earth's rotation to gain their momentum, only travelling across shore in the latter stages to expend their energy before degenerating into a rain depression. Arlon needn't have bothered dredging up all the information he knew about cyclones. It was no cyclone. Nor was it any common or natural weather formation known to any earth-bound meteorologist. If Arlon had been capable of seeing the island from a bird's eye view, he would have found it to be dead centre of a colossal vortex. They were surrounded by a thickening wall of swirling, angry, wind-driven clouds.

"I suggest you get yourself inside the house before this thing lets loose, Clarice," he shouted above the roar of the building wind.

"A storm?"

"Worse."

"How much worse?"

"Feel that wind? That's probably nothing like what we're in for."

"What about you?"

"I'll stay a bit longer."

Clarice turned to see Freddy loping up the path towards the house.

"I don't know, Arlon. It doesn't sound like a good idea for you to be out here in this. What about lightning?"

"Go, Clarice. I'll try not to be too long. Okay?"

Clarice nodded, despite every ounce of her common sense advising her to drag Arlon back to the house. Unfortunately, if what Arlon said was true, and he had some idea about how to prevent it, she couldn't very well ask him to forget it. Clarice was finding it increasingly difficult to accept Arlon's dire predictions, despite all evidence pointing in that direction. It seemed so impossible. That sort of thing didn't happen in Australia. All the disaster models she'd ever read about centred on or around America or Europe, not a small backwater like Australia. Nothing of great importance could ever be ascribed to her country of birth.

Seeing Arlon return his attention to his previous task, Clarice began focusing on her newfound role as a mother. She found herself prioritising her mind around her newfound, first and foremost, responsibility; protecting her child. It wasn't a conscious decision. It was a natural, maternal instinct. Watching Freddy enter the house only increased her urgency to be with Tara. Nothing else seemed to matter as much as it did even a day ago. The light switch in her mind had been triggered to illuminate a part of the brain reserved for that time of most women's lives when they attained the status of motherhood.

Clarice ran for the door. She didn't take in the worsening surroundings. Had she done so, she might have given more credence to the doomsday scenario Arlon had presented. The increasingly turbulent atmosphere resembled the innards of a mighty tornado, without the characteristic of everything it touched being hurled up into the sky until it reached the famed and magical land of Oz. Clarice smiled because she surmised that being in Australia already qualified as being in the land of Oz. Lightning cracked and thunder rolled in long, tremulous drumrolls.

Clarice struggled to open the door at the rear of the house against the surging winds. Thankfully, they had not been tempted to open all the timber shutters obscuring the windows. If the storm became as bad as Arlon predicted all the glass panes were in danger of exploding inwards, showering the inhabitants with lethal shards. Tara ran into her arms the moment she entered.

Clarice battled to restrain the young girl from bolting out of the door to be with Arlon. Tara screamed hysterically for him. Clarice wrapped the girl tightly in her arms, using all her strength to close the door against the fearsome force opposing her. The house shook and moaned as it stood in the path of the mighty gales assaulting it.

Wiping away her tears, Clarice peered into the sorrowful eyes of the bereft girl as she kneeled before her.

"It's too dangerous for you to go out there, Tara."

"I want Mr Arlon," she cried disconsolately.

Clarice wasn't prepared for the depth of the girl's emotions towards her fiancé. It didn't seem possible that anyone could form such a strong bond with another in such a short time, let alone with Arlon Grey. She wondered if she had missed something about him. Could a child see beyond the unemotional facade he presented to everyone else? Were adults so entrenched and indoctrinated with emotional expectations that they could no longer see the forest for the trees? Weren't emotions the stuff of real life? Without those weren't we all in danger of becoming automatons?

The evidence of that question stared at Clarice. The harrowed look on the girl's face showed her grief at being apart from the man. The man without emotions; or so Clarice had been led to believe. Had Tara managed to plumb the depths of those feelings deep within the man she admired and loved? Was it possible that a child's pure and unconditional love could break through where everyone else had failed for so long, including herself? Clarice racked her brain to come up with a reasonable explanation for the behaviour she witnessed in Tara.

She questioned her actions and reactions with Tara, comparing them to what she'd witnessed of the interactions between Arlon and the girl. Tara's bitter tears left no doubt about the deep affection she held for the man, as impossible as that notion seemed to Clarice. Then she caught herself. She suddenly realised she was envious.

From the moment she had met Arlon Grey, she had become enthralled by the man, until he opened his mouth. She struggled to come to terms with the extreme contradiction in him. The incongruent pairing of the charismatic, movie-star looks and the unemotional, dead-fish persona clashed, horribly, making most persons dislike Arlon immediately.

It had disarmed Clarice during her job interview. It continued to do so during her first year of employment. While falling deeply and desperately in love with one half of the man, she wished with all her might that he would someday conquer the wall separating him from his emotions, so she could love the other half equally. He was a wonderful man in every other respect, gentle, kind, generous and loyal. He was also strong and fit with a brilliant mind. In other words, he was everything a woman could wish for. He was even remarkable in the bedroom when it finally happened at her instigation.

She'd come to accept that one shortcoming in him, treating it as the artifice it should have been. She thought she'd convinced herself that she could live with the situation, but secretly she still yearned to be told she was pretty, wanted, loved. Wasn't that what every woman wanted? Clarice knew it was not a possibility with Arlon. Knowing that had previously altered her desires to have children with him.

She could live with the fact that she was in love with a soulless man who was unable to return her love in a traditional sense. Subjecting an innocent child to that, however, would be cruel. Every child deserved to be loved, nurtured and pampered, just as Clarice had been in her childhood. They had been a close and tightknit little family. Her father had passed away when Clarice was relatively young and she became closer to her mother and siblings as a result. No way was Clarice going to introduce a child to anything less than a loving and nurturing environment.

Until she had witnessed Tara crying so pitifully for Arlon, she had not believed it possible that a child could develop feelings for him. Tara had succeeded in unlocking his heart where Clarice had failed. She realised that she felt outrageously envious. Understanding that allowed her to deal with it calmly and surely. Rather than resentment, she ushered in feelings of gratification and joy as she hugged Tara tightly. It didn't matter how it came about or who had reached Arlon on an emotional level, only that they had. It was a minor miracle and Clarice was not about to destroy the moment with petty jealousy.

"Listen, Tara. We have to be strong for Arlon right now. He's out there trying to help us all out of this predicament. In all that wind, lightning and thunder, he's fighting for us, for our survival. It's up to us to support him and give him all the help we can. Out there, we would only be in his way, and he would be worrying about us too much to keep his mind on the problem. If we stay inside the house, relatively safe, then we are giving him that support and peace of mind to let him get on with it. Wouldn't you much rather help him than cause him to get hurt?"

Tara nodded without facing her. The sobbing was slowly decreasing as she listened intently.

"I think that if you were out there he would be so worried and upset about your life being in danger that he would sacrifice himself and his job to get you back in here. Then there would be no one to help us out there."

"I don't want him to be out there," she said, as she turned to face Clarice.

"Neither do I, little one, neither do I. Sometimes, a man just has to do what he has to do to protect the ones he loves. And something tells me he loves you very much, Tara. You and me both. He wouldn't be out there facing that if he didn't."

"House is a bit shaky," warned Freddy, as he approached the pair in the hallway behind the rear door.

"Well, thank you for that wise opinion when we least required it," fumed Clarice.

"Hey?"

"Perhaps not everyone appreciates the absolute truth at a time like this?" said Clarice, pointedly indicating Tara with her eyes.

"Oh, yeah, rightyo," agreed Freddy reluctantly.

"How about a nice hot chocolate, princess?"

Tara nodded. Clarice led her by the hand towards the kitchen, past Freddy, who was shaking and scratching his head. Clarice lit a few candles to introduce a warm atmosphere to the gloomy interior. Outside, the wind howled like a wounded animal, shaking the walls as it attempted to enter from every crevice. Clarice shuddered with apprehension, expecting Arlon to perish in the onslaught without. It didn't seem possible that anyone could survive outside.

She wanted to open a window so she could keep a close eye on him with every fibre of her body. She even wanted to be out there with Arlon if the end was truly coming. But her wise counsel to the girl was of equal relevance to herself. She would only hinder his efforts. How he might challenge the events encapsulating the island, she could not begin to postulate. He was just one man alone against nature, and nature knew no opposition, no adversary of comparable ability.

They ate a frugal fare without conversation. The afternoon had grown darker and more ominous with every passing hour. Any conversation would have been drowned out by the steam train from hell roaring around the house. The diabolical and destructive winds threatened to tear down the miserable structure at any moment. On several occasions, Clarice fully expected the roof to be torn away.

She had to peer through the tiny window beside the rear door occasionally to ensure Arlon was still alive. She was under no illusions as to his chances. Even with Freddy's assistance, they were unable to budge the rear door against the might of the ferocious winds. Were it an inward opening door, as it should have been, based on the original plans for the house, they might well have perished in their efforts. The monstrosity attacking their domicile would have burst through the opening with demonic force, quickly dispatching the two insignificant humans, smashing them like bugs on a windshield between the solid door and the interior wall.

Tara had cried herself to sleep in Clarice's arms after finishing her meal and her second hot chocolate. Drawing comfort from her presence, Clarice did not make a move to deposit the child into her hammock for the night. She was content to cradle her in her arms for as long as the imminent danger persisted. Freddy had found a bottle of liquor somewhere, from which he gulped periodically, then burped. The sound of the burp was lost in the mêlée, but the wafting odour did not miss her. She recoiled each time a wave of the nauseating breath reached her delicate nostrils.

FIFTEEN

Clarice woke around midnight when she heard a small movement in the bedroom. Curled up next to her in their hammock was Tara, sleeping soundly. In the dim glow of the guttering candle, she made out the shape of a man's shadow creeping into the room. She was facing away from the door and feared it might be Freddy, though why she thought that she couldn't say. If it turned out to be the fisherman, he had no good excuse for being in their bedroom and he would sorely regret the intrusion.

She was shocked when she saw that it was Arlon moving slowly to the other hammock; shocked, because he appeared to be glowing; shocked because he seemed to be stooped and suffering; shocked because, when she saw him clearly, it seemed as though he had lost much of his hair and had the jaundiced appearance of a very sick person. She watched as he slunk wearily into the hammock, almost fast asleep before being fully ensconced within the cocoon of string mesh and blankets.

She decided to leave him be, to allow him to gain a few precious hours of sleep. Outside, the wind continued to rattle the roof sheets and threaten to do a big bad wolf, but it seemed less fierce than before. Clarice was greatly relieved to know that her man was alive. She was less relieved to know that something dreadful was occurring to him. Had she a perceptive mind to the existential, which she did, she may have concluded that some evil presence was possessing Arlon.

The faint glow emanating from him gradually subsided as he fell into a deep, sonorous slumber. Despite every nuance of Clarice's mind compelling her to remain awake and alert, she also found herself drifting off, with troubling thoughts, unable to sustain her wish. When next her eyes opened briefly, his hammock was empty.

It was morning and the terrible sound of impending doom had abated considerably. While a strong wind persisted, it lacked the intensity to sustain the awful fear she had felt before. Tara was no longer in the hammock next to her. She heard the child's voice from the direction of the kitchen.

She heard Freddy and Tara talking quietly as she walked down the hall after washing her face and brushing her teeth. When she entered the kitchen, she was surprised to see Tara smiling broadly as she wolfed down some dry cereal. Clarice had used the last of the milk in the girl's chocolate drink the previous evening.

"Good morning, Tara. Morning, Freddy," she said brightly, hiding her concern for everything happening around them. "Have you seen Arlon?" she asked of either.

"He went back outside an hour ago, Miss Clarice," answered Freddy in a grave voice.

Clarice glared at him to dissuade him from saying more. He appeared to nod his head as if he received the message but she couldn't be sure.

"Now, remember what I said last night, princess. Don't go outside to disturb Arlon while he's working."

"He's sick," said Tara sadly.

"Don't you worry about that. He'll be all right," explained Clarice, with doubts and concern gnawing at her.

"He isn't..."

"He's fine...or he will be," insisted Clarice, interrupting Freddy before he could say anything more to upset Tara.

Clarice was torn between going out to check on Arlon and keeping Tara inside. Leaving her with Freddy didn't sit well with her. She didn't fully trust the fisherman, not since Tara had revealed that she had caught him watching her and her mother bathing nude. That in itself caused concern. The fact that he then left them there without offering assistance increased her mistrust. He had proven himself to be unreliable at best and a craven coward at worst. He could not be depended on if push came to shove. She could not leave her child with such a man.

"Tara, if you've finished, I want you to come with me."

"Okeydokey."

Tara slithered from the chair to join Clarice in the hallway. They walked to the end of the hall. Clarice gradually tested the exterior door to the rear of the house. Finding little resistance, she opened it fully and exited swiftly with Tara in tow.

"Shit!" she exclaimed loudly.

"That's a naughty word," Tara admonished, having not yet seen what had made Clarice swear.

When Tara turned to see what Clarice was staring at, she opened her mouth in awe.

A bright shaft of iridescent blue and white light shone from the pair of rocks that Arlon was working on, straight upwards to a height of around a hundred metres. Hovering at the end of the beam was an oval pool of shimmering, rippling intensity. Every so often something minute and glowing could be seen emerging from the entity, disintegrating instantly as it transcended the plane of harsh blue light. As the pair stared in awestruck confusion at the phenomena, a larger object passed through the surface, exploding messily as it, too, passed through the perimeter of light.

Tara and Clarice both yelped involuntarily.

Arlon suddenly swivelled at the intrusion of noise. Unadulterated rage suffused his features. His eyes practically glowed with the same fierce, blue-white light as the emanations from the rocks. Very little of his illustrious blue-black hair remained on his pate. His bare, emaciated torso was bathed in a dirty sweat. His mouth was twisted into a cruel and harsh sneer.

Clarice suddenly understood that the rocks were emitting invisible radiation of sorts and it was making him ill, poisoning him, killing him. She did not know how it was happening or why, only that it was. Somehow, the rocks over which he obsessed were radioactive or similar. His prolonged exposure to them was causing him to become unbalanced mentally and destroying him physically. To Clarice, it seemed that Arlon was unaware of the effects. His mind had slipped so far that he was unable to acknowledge the harm it was causing.

Tara was desperately trying to run to him. Clarice was resolute in her determination to prevent the girl from approaching him. It wasn't safe. Arlon was no longer the man she once knew. He was damaged beyond hope of rescue, as far as she was concerned. He appeared to be almost demented with rage, under some dire influence. He stood statue still, staring at them as though they were the lowest form of life on earth, as though he wanted to extinguish them in the cruellest manner possible.

Then a wave swept over him, and he slowly emerged from his evil funk as recognition entered his glittering eyes. He released the hammer and chisel he had been holding in a threatening manner, visibly relaxing his entire posture to assume a non-aggressive pose.

"Hey there, Miss Blaze," he said suddenly, smiling broadly.

Tara ripped free of Clarice's hand, ran to Arlon and jumped into his outstretched arms. Arlon swung the girl around in a joyful reunion. Clarice was not sure what she was witnessing. He didn't appear dangerous any more.

"Arlon, I want you to bring Tara here at once!" ordered Clarice.

"Sure, sure," he said, swinging the child up into the air easily, then catching her as she descended. Tara whooped with joy.

"Arlon?" Clarice asked as he drew near.

Just then the apparition above them and the twin beams of light from the rocks crackled and faded into oblivion. The wind died almost immediately and everything reverted to a moderate state of calm.

"Yes, Clarice?"

"Was that..."

"Yes, I think it is...was...will be again."

"Tara, I want you to go straight inside. I have to talk to Arlon for a moment."

"But..."

"NOW!"

Tara ran.

"Hey, there's no need to shout at her like that," accused Arlon the moment she was out of earshot.

"A moment ago you were set to kill us, Arlon. I've never seen a look of such wanton hatred and evil in all my life. Look at you, you're a walking bloody zombie, death warmed up!"

"Now, Clarice. You're exaggerating..."

"No, I'm not. You aren't yourself, Arlon Grey. You're sick, and getting sicker. It's because of those things, those...rocks. Only they aren't just rocks, are they? They're some sort of radioactive mineral from another world or another dimension and they're killing you. They're poisoning you, Arlon, and causing you to become mentally unstable."

"You don't understand..."

"Arlon, I don't have to understand. I can see the evidence right in front of me. You're bald, for Christ's sake! You've lost weight and your skin looks like the work of a poorly-qualified embalmer. And..."

"And?"

"And...you're showing emotions."

"You're mistaken..."

"I am bloody not mistaken. You don't smile...ever."

"I do so, Clarice."

"Not with joy. Not that. I admit you've forced yourself to smile sometimes, but you've never exhibited the joy I just witnessed on your face when you saw that young girl. You always said that no one was able to crack your bubble, that your emotions were untouchable, especially by your parents, who refused to believe they didn't exist. I've seen hard evidence that they do exist and that young girl has unlocked them, apparently, or those...things have."

"Shouldn't that be a good thing, Clarice?"

"Not if it costs you your life. Nothing is worth that. I need you, Arlon Grey. I love you and my heart's breaking to see you suffer like this. What do you hope to achieve, anyway? What is it with these bloody rocks?"

"Well..."

"No, don't bother with that for the moment. I want you to come back inside and have something to eat. You need to regain your strength. How much sleep did you get?"

"Couple of hours," he admitted, with a shrug of indifference.

"You aren't going to be much good to anyone if you can't function any more. I insist that you come inside and stop whatever this is until you've recuperated."

Arlon and Clarice stood toe to toe without moving, staring into each other's eyes. Slowly, Arlon nodded his head in compliance. Before he took a step forward, however, Clarice stopped him.

"One thing, though. It's getting worse."

"Yep, I told you it would."

"Only, you're making it worse. At least that's what it looks like to me."

"Yep."

"What?" she exclaimed.

"You're right, I am making it worse."

"Then bloody stop making it worse!"

"It'll get worse by itself regardless, Clarice."

"Then let it happen naturally without speeding it up, for goodness sake."

"You don't understand..."

"Damn straight I don't understand, bucko!"

Arlon smiled.

"What are you smiling about?"

"You. I love when you get all tomboy on me."

Clarice was momentarily silenced by the shocking revelation. Further evidence of his disturbing behavioural alteration became apparent when Clarice happened to peer downwards. The bulge in his trousers indicated his arousal, something she had only ever witnessed if she worked hard to make it happen. It was a pleasant chore that she tackled with gusto on those occasions. This was not one of those occasions.

Arlon Grey did not get erections at the slightest mystical impetus apt to befall menfolk. The seemingly mindless and random reactions of the one-eyed trouser snake in normal men defied all possible explanation as far as Clarice was concerned. She was happy with Arlon's peculiarly narrow perspective in that regard. It gave her a perverse comfort to know that it required her particular loving ministrations to bring about that result in her man.

Everything was wrong about the scene before her. Everything about the man she had grown to love and adore was changing before her eyes. No longer did he behave in a manner to which she had grown accustomed and comfortable. Gone was the soft, deadpan, soulless voice. The face that once showed the least animation of any human she had ever known now displayed humour and excitement as well as lust. It was getting too much for her to take in. Her coping mechanisms were breaking down. She knew that Arlon was dying.

SIXTEEN

Twenty-four hours later, Arlon emerged from the main bedroom, where he had slept as though dead on the dried mattress upon the timber bedframe. Although the interior of the house had been mopped out entirely after the seawater inundation, it remained musty and retained that dank quality. He walked into the kitchen where the others were attending to breakfast. He seemed gaunt, though the jaundiced appearance had greatly diminished. His black hair had regrown in a short stubble, with a definitive silver/white streak over the ears.

Tara ran to him with all the happy exuberance of an eight-year-old without the weight of the world crushing her existence. Arlon had no recollection of calamities occurring during his absence from the world of the living. He heard and recognised nothing outside his vivid fantasies and dreams. While he did not immediately confer on the child an unabandoned welcome as he had the previous day, neither did he reject her or display his usual non-animated persona. Clarice observed the interaction with great interest.

"Hello, Miss Blaze. I hope you've been behaving yourself?" he asked rhetorically. "Hello, everyone. Anything happening that I missed?"

Arlon, released by Tara, who resumed her seat to finish her dry cereal and juice popper, made his way to the table. Clarice stood beside him. She pecked him lightly on the cheek, then gave him a brief inspection

"Hungry?" she asked him.

"Ravenous," he replied softly.

"You look so much better, Arlon. How do you feel?" asked Clarice as she repaired to the kitchen, where she began to cook some tinned Spam in a frying pan.

Reluctantly, she had resorted to opening the dreaded tins of Spam and canned ham from the walk-in pantry. Goods from the lower shelves had been contaminated by the six hundred millimetres of seawater that had surged under the doors to fill the house. Mattresses, furniture, cushions and the like had been soaked by the flood: all had been dried within the house during the last couple of days.

"I feel fine, Clarice."

Arlon had donned a white T-shirt and a pair of loose-fitting canvas shorts. On his feet, he wore a pair of leather sandals sans socks, which would have been his customary accoutrement with such footwear.

"No, Mr Arlon, nothin' outta the ordinary happened while yiz was asleep. Wind died down a lot as well."

"How long have I been asleep?"

"Just a day and a night, Arlon."

"You should've woken me, Clarice."

"I tried, believe me. You were out like a light, snoring your head off."

"How's the boat coming, Mr Boggs?"

"Not too bad. Should be done today, I reckon. Dunno about usin' it, though. High and dry."

"Can you get the tractor going?"

"Got the outboard goin', didn't I?"

"I don't know, did you?"

"Yeah, it'll do."

"Not sure that sounds confident enough for me to entrust lives to it," argued Arlon.

"Here, Arlon, coffee," said Clarice, handing him a mug of steaming black coffee before she returned to the kitchen.

"'Bout as confident as I can get under the circumstances," said Freddy.

"Forget the boat, will you, Arlon? I'm not going anywhere without you, and Tara has told me she can't face being separated from her new father, either."

"Father?" he asked Tara pointedly.

Tara placed her spoon gently on the table, taking her time about answering Arlon.

"I want you to be my daddy," she stated confidently.

"Aren't you being a little quick about that, Miss Blaze? Your daddy..."

"Is dead. He was mean to me and didn't like me very much. You said you wanted to be my daddy. Don't you want that anymore?"

He saw the bottom lip about to quiver. "Now, Tara, of course I want to be your daddy. It would be my greatest pleasure. I just don't want to replace your father before you've had time to grieve properly. I realise you need parents now more than ever, not just guardians who take care of your physical requirements. I was hoping that in time you might come to accept Clarice and me as your new parents, but I didn't think it would happen so soon, that's all.

"I wanted you all to leave if it became possible to prevent your demise on this island. That's why I wanted Mr Boggs to fix his boat. Won't you please go?"

"I think it's time for you to fess up, Arlon," stated Clarice, as she returned to the table with Arlon's plate of fried Spam on damper bread cooked in the Dutch oven on the gas range. "We need to know what you know, or even what you think you know. I want it straight, buster. No sugar-coating it, no unsaid stuff to spare our feelings."

"You all sure you want to know? Even if it sounds crazy as bat shit?"

Tara giggled. "Guano. It's called guano, not the bad word."

"Very good. Clever girl. Yes, it's called guano, and I shouldn't be using bad language in front of you, should I?" asked Arlon.

"I've heard it before," she admitted sadly. "My other mummy and daddy used to say bad things all the time when they were fighting."

"Well, you aren't about to hear it from me or Clarice. Although all married couples fight occasionally. It shows they care. So you all agree that you want to know what I think?"

All three heads nodded in agreement.

"Although I didn't think much of it straight away and couldn't make heads or tails of it in any case, I felt something the moment I first entered the shed after arriving here. The second I passed between those rocks I felt a distinct pressure variance. I didn't recognise it as coming from any particular source at the time, and I pushed it aside as having little consequence. It happened again the next time I found myself in the same position, and I noted it then. That was when the fossilised fish appeared. Or rather, that was when the fish I caught was transmuted into stone." Arlon corrected himself as he saw Clarice about to intervene with a statement about him not having caught a fish in the first place.

"You believe that thing changed the fish into a fossil?"

"If fossilised is the right term for turning something into stone, then yes. I think we can all agree that some form of interdimensional portal is occurring here?"

All heads nodded again, though not as confidently as before.

"Yes, I know how it sounds. I wasn't too keen on accepting the notion myself. I can't think of any other explanation for the appearance of the strange, unearthly animals we've encountered. The undersea eruption or disturbance theory didn't ring true the more animals we saw. The other weird thing about all this is the timing. It seems too recent for a major undersea disturbance so close to mainland Australia. Seemed to me that scientists would have been all over this island if that was the case.

"After the tidal wave took everything of substance away from the shed area except for the inoperative generator was when I first decided that my theory was correct. With nothing else to interfere with the energy field, I was finally able to ascertain that the rocks on either side of where the shed door used to be were what was causing the anomaly. I could feel and positively identify the waves of energy produced by them."

"And what's causing that to happen, Arlon? They're radioactive, aren't they?"

"In a way, yes, Clarice. Not from here, though. Not like anything on earth."

"Huh?" said Freddy in confusion.

"Freddy, you said the deepwater bay out there was caused by a meteor?"

"A bloody long, long time ago," he agreed.

"Exactly!" Arlon suddenly shouted, causing them all to jump. "Sorry, didn't mean to startle you. That's what makes what I'm about to say more realistic. The meteor crashed into this bay, causing damage at the time. It was probably quite large out in space, then it crashed through our atmosphere, subjected to incredible heat from the friction. The inferno reduced the meteor to a fraction of its original size before it smashed into the ocean here. The immediate cooling of the seawater on the super-heated fragment caused it to fracture into two near-identical pieces.

"The pieces were, eventually moved by tide and time to either end of the bay, where they lay for millennia gathering marine coatings which helped to keep them inert. The distance from each other, and the liberal outer layer deposited by eons of growth, maintained the passive nature of those elements.

"Now, what if, and this is pure speculation, what if that meteor was not from our universe? What if it somehow breached the dimensional barrier by the nature of its composition, or by travelling through a wormhole or portal produced by something else? Let's just accept for a moment that it didn't come from our dimension.

"Nothing happened in all the time those two pieces remained apart and covered. Then Ben and Gail Sandringham had the idea of lining the path to the shed with flotsam and jetsam washed up on the beach, capping it off with two almost identical rocks they found on either side of the bay. They used the tractor to haul their treasures up here, pushing and shoving the two rocks into their final resting place either side of the shed door.

"Suddenly, the two halves of the meteor detect one another again elementally, on a geological level defined by the other dimension. The two pieces are attracted to one another in some super-magnetic, interactive capacity because of the new proximity. I saw one place where Ben Sandringham may have been attempting to remove some of the growth on one rock. I think it was that small section of clear rock surface that became the catalyst for everything that happened thereafter."

"So all we have to do is separate them again to stop this?" asked Clarice incredulously.

"No. It took the planet surface and cool water on its super-heated surface to separate the pieces, Clarice. I don't think any power on earth will prevent the two pieces from doing what they're doing."

"Which is?"

"Reunification. The two pieces are being drawn inexorably to one another to become complete."

"If they don't?"

"I think the exposure of the bare surfaces to our dimension is what's causing these massive disturbances."

"Then why on earth are you out there trying to facilitate that outcome? Shouldn't we be covering the rotten things in concrete, lead or something?"

"Before your brother-in-law inadvertently chipped away some of the outer layers, that might well have been the ideal solution: cover them in as many different protective layers as possible and separate them to opposite ends of the earth, thereby neutralising them."

"Ya sayin' ya can't do that now?" asked Freddy, with growing interest and concern.

"I don't think so. Everything tells me that nothing will stop them from reuniting. I am trying to speed up that process to forestall the gross effects it may cause in the process. The longer it takes, the worse the disturbances get and the longer they last. The two elements are reacting with each other enough to produce these temporary portals everywhere. Each time one of those materialises, it come into contact with our dimension, and that's almost catastrophic.

"We've seen only the tip of the iceberg. The longer those two pieces are kept apart while in range of one another enabling the elements to react to each other, the worse it gets and the longer it lasts. I plan to chip away the coatings altogether and force them back together."

"What happens then?" asked Clarice in a whisper.

"Hmm, not sure you're ready to hear that bit."

"If you value your life you'll spit it out, bucko."

"One of two things...or maybe more, I don't know for sure. Either the unification of the two pieces will bring about an end to life as we know it by igniting this planet into a second big bang, or..."

"Jesus!" exclaimed Clarice.

"Or it may produce its own portal with which to return to the other dimension, leaving this one relatively unscathed. All in theory, of course. None of it's provable, none of it's covered by any modern science that I am aware of, and all, most probably, is a load of codswallop. I can't logically accept a single word of what I just outlined. It goes against everything I am and what I know. I deal in plain, simple facts as they present themselves, not all this airy-fairy bullsh...sorry, rubbish."

"Why go through with any of this, then? Putting your life in jeopardy for something you don't even believe in?" asked Clarice.

"The alternative, to do nothing, is anathema to me. While mankind has made an absolute mess of this planet and the people are sometimes evil, it's our world. It's all we have unless we want to leap into one of those portals and take our chances on what's on the other side. Not that we would last in that other reality, anyway. We'd most likely implode like those creatures we saw if we came into contact with the other realm.

"We have many, many lessons still to learn as human beings. We still have to evolve into entities that have no hate for one another, no need for jealousy or envy, no room for greed, power or domination. I have to believe we'll get there. I have to know there's something at the end of the rainbow for humanity, otherwise it's all a waste. This can't be all we have. The magnificence of music, painting, literature. I know there's beauty there. I see it in you, Clarice and Tara. I even see it in Mr Boggs when he isn't being a miserable coward and a liar. He has his moments. We all do. And that's what makes us special.

"I can't sit by and do nothing. It isn't in me to quit or allow myself to ignore what has to be done."

"What if it kills you, Arlon? I've seen what this is doing to you. You won't survive it," said Clarice, with tenderness and care etched on her features.

"We're here, Johnny on the spot, ground zero. We may well be the only thing standing between life and the total annihilation of everything on this planet. Either I try to do something to prevent this catastrophe, or there'll be nothing left for anyone."

"Why do you have to be the dead hero who saves everyone?"

"Because if I don't, it's over."

"Then let me do some of it."

"What?" asked Arlon with alarm.

"Look, if prolonged exposure to those rocks is causing you such harm, let me take some of the burden away from you. If we take it in turns we might not have to endure the full extent of the energy...thing, whatever."

"I can't let you risk yourself..."

"You already said it doesn't matter. If we don't succeed then there's nothing left. It all goes boom."

"Boom." Tara imitated Clarice.

"Oh, pumpkin, you don't need to be hearing this, do you?" asked Clarice rhetorically.

"I want to help, too," stated Tara emphatically.

"Ya all nuts. It's gonna kill yiz. Ya seen what it done ta him, lookin' like somethin' the cat drug in?" remarked Freddy, almost shaking with fear. "We gotta get goin' in me boat. Bondy'll get us off here."

The other three turned to stare at Freddy, making him squirm uncomfortably.

"Whatcha lookin' at me like that for? Jest sayin' what's right."

"Clarice? That's your answer. That's why I feel obliged to do something. Because cowards like him won't."

"Hey!" shouted Freddy indignantly.

"We have an eight-going-on-nine-year-old girl and a woman here with more gumption in their little fingers than you have in your entire body, Boggs. I may have premature in my announcement that you have good in you. You're so pathetic that I don't feel like doing anything to save your kind. It's for the others that I won't follow through with that, though. It's for these two magnificent human beings and the multitude like them that I'm ready to make any sacrifice to see them survive. This beautiful planet deserves every effort on my part to avoid the very real threat this thing poses. I don't intend to abandon it and humanity just because it gets hard, becomes dangerous.

"You go ahead and get to your boat. You won't be getting very far, I assure you. I only half-believed we would succeed in using it to get off the island. It was a great way to get your mind and body busy while I could concentrate on the real task."

"Arlon? You don't think we can get away?"

"Have a look at the wall of cloud surrounding us. We're stuck in some sort of climatic vortex that doesn't present like any natural weather pattern I'm aware of. I hoped it might dissipate enough for you lot to be away from here, but that doesn't seem likely. You shouldn't have the shutters open, by the way. That wind could pick up again at any moment. In fact, I can almost guarantee it'll be stronger, much more intense."

"Ya done me wrong, mate. Take back what ya said," threatened Freddy.

"Or what?" asked Arlon, in a voice so low and full of menace it had the fisherman baulking as he rose from his chair.

"Sit down, Boggs! You don't stand a chance in a confrontation with my future husband. He has more black belts in the martial arts than you can probably count. I've seen him tackle bigger and stronger blokes than you without raising a sweat. I'm scared as well. We all are. That doesn't mean we have to slink off like mangy rats leaving a sinking ship. Arlon's right. It's up to us to do everything we can to make this right. You make one move towards your boat, whether it works or not, whether you can get off this island or not, I'll take the spear gun and shoot a spear right into your worthless, yellow gut. Now sit down before I lose my temper."

Arlon and Tara both stared at Clarice agape as she sat down at the table with firm resolve, daring Freddy to make an inappropriate move. After a moment, Freddy resumed his seat, without making eye contact with anyone. Arlon gave a long, slow handclap in admiration for his wife-to-be. Tara joined him. Clarice grew red with embarrassment.

"Stop it, you two. Arlon, I meant what I said. I aim to take the next shift at whatever it is you're doing out there. Maybe we can do an hour each, or two? Tell me what it is we're doing, exactly."

Left with few options, Arlon accepted the proposal. "I'm chipping away the marine build-up on the rocks, especially around one section that I believe marries up to the other. You can easily identify the fracture line where the pieces would fit together again seamlessly once all the rubbish is removed. We don't have to remove everything, just from those areas."

"How do you propose to bring the two pieces together again?"

"If the tractor doesn't work, I saw a block and tackle set-up washed away past the back yard. I can anchor that to a tree stump and slowly winch one up to the other."

"What do you think will happen?"

"Best case scenario?" When Clarice nodded, he continued, "Nature knows best how to heal itself, and I can only assume that's the same for any dimension or reality. Unfortunately, until we can get them together, we're exposed to the emanations caused by the two halves as they strive to unite. Each new section that's cleared of debris exposes more of the alien surface to this reality, which reacts explosively in any number of ways. The disturbances will continue to get worse."

"Why isn't that happening now?"

"It is. Just because we don't always see the effects doesn't mean they aren't occurring. They could be affecting the ocean floor, triggering a volcano or an earthquake somewhere that isn't felt here. That weather pattern may be causing all sorts of havoc beyond this island that we don't know about. We're in the eye of that storm and it may be only a fraction of the tempest the rest of the coastline is experiencing.

"We don't know. We have no way of finding out, either, and I would never risk you out there in a flimsy little fishing boat. We're better off here. Make no mistake, though, this will get far worse before we're through. We may have to peg ourselves to the ground while we work out there. It's a bit like you'd imagine being in the middle of a tornado's funnel. It wants to suck everything up into the air. I had to keep hold of the rocks for grim life quite a few times."

"You agree to be helped, then?"

"I see the necessity. I don't like it, not one little bit. You're right, though. I can't do it by myself. It buggers me physically and, you say, mentally as well. I can't keep it up indefinitely. I have no choice but to accept your help..."

"Me, too," added Tara firmly.

"Only with one of us and for much less time. Thank you, Tara, for being such a brave girl. I'm very proud of you."

"S'pose ya want me ta take a turn, huh?" asked Freddy with scorn.

"Only if you volunteer. I'm not going to force you or give you a guilt trip for not participating. I think, in the end, you'll do that yourself when your conscience kicks in. I know you have a conscience; I've witnessed it once or twice already. Besides, you can do other things in here to support our efforts if you elect not to assist us outside. You can even take your chance in the boat if you want. I guarantee that no one will try to stop you."

"What about us, in that case, Arlon?" asked Clarice.

"Moot point as far as I'm concerned. Either way, win or lose against this thing, I don't think that boat will make it far. Even if we succeed, which is highly unlikely, the repercussions from what we do will be felt for months. All we can hope for in the end is an abnegation of the catastrophe that I foretold and a gradual reduction of the effects if that's achieved."

"How do you want to go about it?" asked Clarice.

"If we're going to be traipsing back and forth to the site, I have to put in place some safety measures to make sure that we don't fly off into oblivion. Have a good look around for another hammer and chisel, or a meat tenderiser and screwdriver. I need to locate some more rope or steel cable..."

"Saw some spare washing line under the tub in the laundry," offered Freddy contritely. "I could maybe help ya set up a safety line between the shed and the house? Ya could all then hook onta it like ya would on a ship at sea. I got a couple of safety tethers in the cabin of me bondy."

"Perfect. I'd be very grateful if you could give me a hand with that, Mr Boggs. There's plenty that you can do without having to be out there working on the rocks themselves. You can be our support staff. Every good work crew has an equally valuable support crew," agreed Arlon.

"Nah, can't have the little-un doin' that out there. I'll do me share and ya can leave the girl ta look after us."

"No! I want to help. I'm not a baby."

"Too right you aren't, Tara. You and I will go out together when it's our turn, okay?" suggested Clarice.

"No, that won't do, Clarice. Sorry. It'd be too much for you to battle the elements and keep hold of her as well. She can come out with me for half an hour at a time. Then you can come and get her. What do you say, Miss Blaze?"

"S'pose,' she agreed reluctantly.

"Tara, every little bit helps. You aren't a baby, but you aren't a grown-up yet, either. Your body won't be able to sustain as much punishment as ours. It's extremely dangerous and I wouldn't be able to forgive myself if I allowed you to suffer more than you had to out there. Trust me, your help is needed and appreciated and you will be able to come out more often if you don't stay out as long as the adults."

"Thanks," she beamed.

"You're welcome. Thank *you*," Arlon emphasised.

SEVENTEEN

The wind was building up to gale force again by mid-morning. Freddy and Arlon struggled to and from the shed site to secure the safety cable, anchoring one end to the house and the other to the diesel generator. Several other anchor points were placed around the two rocks for protection while working on them. The vortex continued to form around them, threatening to suck up into it anything that wasn't firmly secured to the ground.

Two parallel beams shot straight up from the rocks, though no portal had yet formed above them. Tara had been sent inside with Clarice once her shift had ended, without her realising it had only lasted ten minutes. Arlon chipped away at a section of one of the rocks, showing a blacker than black surface emerging from beneath the millennia of marine build-up. Despite the biting winds chilling the atmosphere, Arlon sweated profusely as he laboured, eyes burning with determination and whatever effect the rocks were producing in him.

The air crackled within the funnel, sending random sparks and bolts of super-charged energy about the area. Arlon did not know what would happen if a human were struck with one of the charges: nothing good, he imagined. He could not be certain of anything he told them, finding it difficult to digest the theory himself. He was working on bold hunches and instinctual impulses, all quite foreign to his way of thinking. He did not deal in hunches or guesses, did not recognise speculative sciences. His world centred on provable facts and evidence gained by process of elimination.

Worse still were the strange alterations to his persona as he worked on the rocks. His mind began to react weirdly to events and memories. He couldn't be certain, but at one point he thought he shed a tear about his estrangement from his parents. A myriad of cascading thoughts and recollections rushed through his mind, tearing him apart psychologically, dare he say, emotionally? He struggled to cope with the influx of feelings that savaged his brain.

He acknowledged to himself how wise Clarice had been to make him share the burden. He was incapable of sustaining prolonged periods of chiselling the crud off the rocks. It could take days for him alone to clear the sections at the fracture site on the two rocks; days that they might not have. The build in intensity was palpable. Portals would begin reappearing and reacting to earth's atmosphere; opposite would meet opposite with catastrophic consequences.

Another sound carried over the howling gale, eking its way into Arlon's consciousness. He knew it was a sound he should recognise, knew it should have a significance, but it was elusive and mysterious. Finally, the sound reached him...

"Mr Arlon, Mr Arlon." Freddy was shouting directly into his ear. "Ya hafta go back inside. Ya been here out here for over four hours already!"

It couldn't be true, could it? He'd sent Miss Blaze back inside with Clarice only a moment ago. It had to be an attempt by her to reduce his time, despite agreeing to the hourly schedule they'd implemented. Only when Freddy showed him the face of his watch did he believe him. He was shocked that so much time had passed. When he peered down at his work area, he was dismayed at the small amount of removal he'd achieved in all that time. It beggared belief. Slowly, reluctantly, he relinquished control of the hammer and chisel to the fisherman. The old man had to pry the implements out of Arlon's cramped and claw-like hands.

Arlon unhooked himself from his grounding pegs, transferred his tether to the safety cable, and then made his way back towards the house, fighting to remain grounded the entire distance. The house remained in place and relatively stable for the present, for which Arlon was immensely grateful. He didn't think they could survive being exposed to the elements for any length of time.

He looked back before entering the rear door to make sure Freddy was doing what he had promised. He was satisfied by the result. He hoped the rocks would not affect the older man too greatly. He reminded himself to keep an eye on him and relieve him at the first sign of struggle. He was pleased when he managed to open the door to get in out of the bitter wind.

Tara ran to him the second he entered and closed the door behind him. Arlon hugged her close, enjoying the warm and loving embrace of the freshly-showered child.

"Pee-yew!" remarked Tara, holding her nose.

"Hmm, I guess I could do with a shower, too?"

"Yup."

"How about you ask Clarice if she can make me something to eat while I take a shower?"

"Sure...daddy," she replied tentatively, half fearing a rebuke.

Rewarded with a huge smile from him, Tara felt secure in her sentiments. She rushed through the hallway to issue his demands of Clarice.

"Arlon? Hold on a moment," said Clarice as she joined him in the hall.

She drew up short when she saw the deterioration the rocks had caused. She sucked her breath in sharply.

"That bad?"

"You were out there far too long. I thought we'd agreed to an hour each?"

"I had no idea where the time went, honestly. When Freddy shouted in my ear I thought only moments had passed since you came for Miss Blaze. She seems none the worse for wear."

"Well, her half-hour was somewhat shorter than she was led to believe. I don't think she was affected by it. Not like you. You have to promise me that you won't do that again, Arlon."

"Now, Clarice..."

"Promise me. One hour maximum, and only three times a day. No going out there after everyone's asleep."

Clarice had her hands on her hips, which indicated that she would brook no argument. At those times, Arlon knew best not to push the matter. Before he could answer he was marched straight into the bathroom, where Clarice handed him a large bar of scented soap. Arlon relented.

As he soaped himself down in the hot stream he noted how thin he had become. They had all lost weight to varying degrees, but none more so than Arlon, who could see his ribs clearly; *far too clearly*!

"What the...?" he muttered, as he turned every which way to view himself.

Arlon was seeing through himself. He was able to see through the epidermis and underlying muscle and tissue to the bones, which appeared to be almost hairy from his fuzzy viewpoint. Arlon drew the shower curtain aside to look into the vanity mirror. Within the dark bathroom, his eyes glowed eerily with an iridescent blue sheen.

The moment he turned the overhead light on, the sheen vanished. Noticing the puddle of water gathering at his feet, Arlon quickly stepped back into the shower, where he could no longer see inside his body.

As his breathing gradually subsided, his hearing picked up sounds above the dozen or more freight trains racing around the house. The winds had reached gale force and were battering the house mercilessly. Yet Arlon somehow managed to pick up familiar sounds, voices, pulsating within his brain, moving in and out of auditory recognition as though someone was adjusting the tuning knob on a radio. Suddenly clear...

"Oh, Arlon, what's happening to you? I'm so scared..."

"I want to go home..."

"Never shoulda come ta this rotten island..."

He could hear them! Clarice, then Miss Blaze and lastly, Mr Boggs. No, he couldn't hear them. That would be impossible. Mr Boggs was outside and the other two were in the living room. He was hearing their thoughts! He was tuned into their consciousness somehow. As quickly as it came, it left him: no fuzziness or static, just a hollow emptiness. As his hearing returned to normal, or rather, as his consciousness became aware of its surroundings once more, Arlon regretted the loss.

He checked himself in the mirror again once he had finished showering. Nothing of the eye shine remained and he could no longer hear anything out of the ordinary. He towelled himself down thoroughly before climbing into the fresh clothes Clarice had hung over the towel rail for him. He knew he didn't have much left in the way of fresh clothing. They had packed only for a week and he hadn't envisaged a constant need for fresh apparel.

"Jesus!" Clarice exclaimed, when Arlon appeared in the living room.

"Wow," added Tara.

"What?" asked Arlon innocently.

"Did you pack a wig or something?" asked Clarice in awe.

"What?"

"Arlon, your hair. First, you lost most of it and you shaved the scraggly bits off. Then you had stubble coming through in record time, with silver streaks over the ears. Now your hair is almost to your shoulders with pure white streaks in the time it took for you to shower. Don't get me wrong, you look spectacular, but..."

"You can't be serious? I just looked at myself in the mirror and didn't notice anything...like *that*," Arlon admitted, running his hand through the long growth on his head, baffled.

"This is freaking me out, Arlon. Can't we just make a break for it in Freddy's boat?"

Arlon put his arms round Clarice. Tara ran to join them in a huddle. A noise at the rear of the house disturbed them. Freddy staggered up the hallway. When he reached the living room, he collapsed onto the cane lounge. He was drenched in sweat and his hair was falling out. His gaunt expression left no doubt about how he was faring.

"Hold on, Freddy, I'll get you something to drink," said Clarice, breaking away from Arlon's and Tara's embrace. "Arlon, sit, I'll make you something to eat."

"That...that tears me up inside. I feel like I'm dyin'," said Freddy in a whisper.

"Something tells me you weren't too fit to begin with and it's taking its toll on you far quicker than me," explained Arlon.

"I'll go back out as soon as..."

"Oh, no, you won't, bucko! My turn and I don't want to hear any argument. Soon as I've made you something to eat, I'll go out. Tara, are you hungry?"

"Nuh-uh."

"That would be 'no', young lady. Or, better still, 'no, thank you', not 'nuh-uh'."

"Sorry. No, thank you," said Tara, happy enough to comply.

"Well, have some water at least, okay, pumpkin?"

"Okay."

"I don't think Freddy should go back out there, Arlon," suggested Clarice.

"No, you're probably right. If we don't get this accomplished soon, though..."

"We can only do what we can do, Arlon."

"But, Clarice..."

"No buts. If this is going to be the end, then let me at least enjoy what time I have left to be with my family, okay?"

Arlon couldn't see her face while she was busying herself in the kitchen, but he could tell she was crying.

"Are we going to die?" asked Tara suddenly.

"Probably."

"Arlon!"

"No point in sugar-coating it, Clarice. In all likelihood, we will not survive this, Miss Blaze. That doesn't mean we don't stand a chance. That doesn't mean we should quit. It certainly doesn't mean we should give up hope. I intend to do everything I can in the time I have left to make this better, no matter what it may or may not do to me."

"Or us?" asked Freddy.

"Tell me something, Mr Boggs. If this island is in the grip of a cataclysm this planet might not survive, why are you so concerned with living? If you miraculously managed to survive, would you want to? Do you hear that force out there? No one is crossing into or through that. It's going to get worse, much worse," explained Arlon.

"Only got yiz word for that," argued Freddy.

"Granted. You only have my word for that and I can guarantee you that I'm guessing at best. I hope I'm wrong. I hope I come out of this looking like a complete and utter imbecile who's never taken seriously again as long as I live. If that's the worst that happens out of all of this, I can relax. What the world or you thinks of me is the last thing I care about. At the moment, I have only two interests. One is Clarice Manning, soon to be Clarice Grey, and the other is Miss Tara Blaze, soon to be Miss Tara Blaze-Grey, if she decides that she'd like to take on that name.

"Sorry, there is one more interest...earth. This is a magnificent planet with a wealth of beauty and a plethora of experiences to offer. I am of this earth, of this wonder that we call home. I'll be damned if I am going to sit by and watch it all go to shit. I am going to fight for those three interests, those three loves, with every last breath in my body. You go ahead and stay in here. You're too old and cynical to be of much use, anyway. Every time I think there might be something of value to you, in you, I'm reminded of how wrong it is to go against my first impressions. Clarice, I..."

Clarice was no longer in the kitchen.

When Arlon and Tara stood near the back door, peering through the dirty window, they could see Clarice hammering at the rock to the left of the pathway. All about her, chaos reigned. Objects and tree limbs hurtled about the funnel as easily as confetti from a party-popper. The sky had taken on a greenish-dark hue, while the air roiled in perilous fury. Thunder rolled in never-ending peals, while lightning crackled overhead in a blazing effect of strobing light.

When Arlon made to open the rear door, Tara halted him by taking his hand.

"No," she pleaded, with teary eyes.

"I have to..."

"Not now. Later. You have to eat and rest first. I'll go out with you again in an hour, Mr Arl...daddy," she insisted. "Only this time I want to stay for my full half an hour."

"Oh, you know, do you?"

"I can tell time," she said, with her hands on her hips.

"Wow, you look just like Clarice. I suppose you aren't going to give me a choice in the matter?"

"Nuh, uh."

"That would be a 'no', young lady. Remember?"

"Sorry."

"Come on, let me get something to eat so that I can be strong enough to relieve her when the time comes. You and me, kiddo?"

"You and me, daddy-o," she replied happily.

EIGHTEEN

"She's crying," said Tara in a panic as she approached the dining table.

Arlon, who had just finished eating, flew from the chair, almost knocking over the diminutive Tara in his wake. What Arlon observed, through the rear window through which Tara had been watching her new mother, disturbed him.

"I have to go out there," he said, as he crouched low to look directly into Tara's eyes.

"Me, too. I want to go," she pleaded with him.

"It isn't safe."

"I know, but she's my mummy now and I have to go."

"I can see that. Promise me one thing?"

"Okay."

"If you decide not to come back with Clarice as you should, will you promise that you'll tell me the moment anything happens to you out there?"

"Happens to me?"

"Hard to explain exactly. If you aren't behaving normally is the best I can do."

"Okeydokey," she acquiesced, not having the slightest idea what he meant.

The demonic wind sent icy needles into the pair the moment they exited the rear door. They tethered themselves to the cable set immediately before them. Arlon had to place Tara before him to push her along against the building maelstrom that threatened to launch them both into the air with the rest of the debris swirling about them.

Their voices could not be heard over the roaring gale. Arlon decided that he needn't bother trying to relate anything to Tara as they moved along the cable slowly. He could make out Clarice bent over the rocks, her shoulders bobbing to the convulsive sobs racking her body. Arlon hoped that she had not injured herself or been irreversibly damaged by the alien emanations coming from the twin rocks. The bright blue and white beams shone from the dual source with an eerie and ominous glow. For a radius of three hundred metres about them nothing but the house remained standing. Where trees had been flattened by the tsunami before, only their stumps remained. The entire area had been swept clean by the devastating forces triggered by the anomaly.

Painstakingly, Arlon and Tara finally approached Clarice, who was hunched over one of the rocks in a state of utter disconsolation. When Arlon's hand lightly brushed her shoulder she whirled on him with eyes shining blue, tears washing down her cheeks. He swept her up into his arms, held her for a long while as she wept. Tara laid a hand on her to add some comfort.

Arlon bent low to shout into Tara's ear.

"I have to take her back. I can't take you as well. Will you stay here until I get back?"

Tara nodded solemnly. Without waiting to be told, she picked up the screwdriver and mallet Clarice had been using to begin chipping away at the same rock. Arlon nodded with satisfaction, admiring the girl more and more. He had never come across a more likeable and courageous child. He doubted he ever would. He decided then and there that he would never try to father a child of his own, preferring to spend all of his time and devotion on this one precious life so deserving of better parents than the two she had before. If they managed to survive the battle they faced, he would be the best father he could be...no, better than he could be to this wonderful child.

Arlon ensured all the tether lines were safely secured and untangled, then staggered away with his burden. It was an effort against the immense forces raging about them. Arlon fought gamely for each step, utilising every ounce of his strength and energy to finally gain the rear door of the house. There he kissed Clarice passionately as she turned her teary face to his. Without realising it, his heart was breaking to see the woman he loved suffering. He didn't know why he understood her pain intimately. Curiously, he managed to convey that understanding and sympathy directly to Clarice, who smiled as he placed her within the open doorway.

Clarice attempted to smile as he shut the door. She watched him return to Tara through the window. She felt vastly improved once she was away from the rocks. If asked why she had been so bereft, she would have been unable to answer. If asked why she felt buoyed beyond believability, she would have answered in a millisecond that she knew she was truly loved and admired by her family. Her heart soared when she heard Arlon say those things she longed to hear. Only, he had never uttered a word. She heard him think it as clearly as she heard the winds crashing outside the door.

While the mixed emotions of devastation and euphoria battled for supremacy within her beleaguered brain, she knew with complete confidence exactly how much she was loved by the man who declared his inability to love. The remnants of the trauma she had experienced at the rocks struggled to maintain a grip on her emotions and gradually subsided, leaving her feeling bewildered and exhausted. Seeing Arlon reaching Tara's side prompted Clarice to venture back to the dining room, to regain her composure and refuel her system for the next bout.

Arlon and Tara worked at the twin surfaces a metre apart for more than half an hour. Then Tara suddenly giggled. Although Arlon did not hear an audible sound, he turned in her direction the second he detected a difference. Inexplicably, the child was now laughing. Arlon intuited the reason by way of the new link he shared with his family. He began to understand the reason for their odd behaviour and his own. It was time to return Tara to the house. While she continued to roll in mirth upon the ground, Arlon stepped over to her, picking her up easily in his arms.

"Are you okay? What, what...is she laughing?" Clarice asked, as they entered through the rear door.

"Yes, she is."

"Tara? What is it, what's so funny?" asked Clarice, taking the child from Arlon's arms.

"She won't be able to give you a good reason, Clarice. Just as you won't be able to give a good reason why you were crying before. I think I can give you all a reason for our odd behaviour, though."

"Come on, let's make you a well-deserved coffee and a hot chocolate for this one using the last of the milk," suggested Clarice as they walked down the hallway.

Tara's hysterical laughing had subsided into giggles by the time they reached the table where Freddy still sat.

"All right, you'd better tell us what's going on, Arlon," suggested Clarice, once the others were seated and she busied herself in the kitchen heating water and the milk.

"It's affecting and increasing everyone's strongest emotion. I finally understood when I saw the happy little chipmunk here giggling and laughing. Her strongest emotion at the moment is happiness, which the radiation amplified. Yours is deep-seated compassion, Clarice, making you weep uncontrollably, for us, for you, for humanity. Mr Boggs's greatest fears were pushed to the extreme by this thing, debilitating him to the point where he could no longer face it."

"And you?" asked Clarice.

"I'm the best equipped of all of you to handle more than my share. I had no emotions to begin with. I had nothing to overwhelm me. I gained emotions on such a minor scale that they only affected me because I had never before experienced them before. It wasn't a matter of amplifying existing emotions to the point where they crippled me, it was merely giving me a taste of something new."

"Why is it affecting us like that, Arlon?"

"I have no answer for that, Clarice. The waves of energy passing through us while we're out there are doing more than playing with our emotions, though. They seem to be invading us on many levels. They may even be reaching different parts of the brain, increasing our awareness, extending our abilities to a certain extent."

"What do you mean?" asked Clarice.

"I started to hear what people were thinking. When I was out there for a long time by myself, I started to see...*through* things."

"Well, that settles it, then. No more going out there for any of us."

"We can't stop, Clarice. At least, I can't. I agree that it's too much for the rest of you, especially for Miss Blaze. I'm the only one who won't succumb to the debilitating emotional effects it has on each of you. Besides, I think it may take only another hour to complete what I have in mind. We've managed to clear away those areas around the fracture site sufficiently to attempt the reunification of the two pieces."

"Arlon?" Clarice stopped him before he could exit the rear door.

"Yes?"

"If...if this is..."

"It isn't. I'll make this happen, Clarice."

"Maybe we can each take shorter shifts, so it won't affect us so badly?"

"Time's running out. Hear that wind? Getting worse. If I don't do something about it this house won't stand for long. I saw one of the roof sheets peeling away last time I was out there. The moment that wind finds a way through the ceiling, it'll destroy the place. None of us is safe, Clarice, and I think I'm the only one capable of withstanding the effects long enough to make a difference."

"I don't want to lose you," admitted Clarice tearfully.

"I don't want to lose any of you, especially you, Clarice. I want you to know one thing if...I want you to know that you reached me. You're the only one."

"No, that isn't true. Tara reached you long before I did. No, it's okay, better than okay. The tenderness and understanding you showed that little girl melted my heart, Mr Grey, and made me love you all the more. I can never be jealous or envious that she reached you first. I know you love me, Arlon. I felt it, saw it clear as day, in my head. You go out there and do what you have to do. Come back to me...to us."

"I'll fix it or fuck it, Clarice. That's a promise."

"Arlon Grey! You swore!"

"I know how," he admitted sheepishly.

After a kiss, Arlon stepped out into the maw of the monster. The sheer ferocity of the blast cast doubts in his mind whether he would reach the site of the rocks. The twin beams continued to radiate upwards, where they ended in a portal once more, creating an electric blue ambience within the swirling funnel. Lightning crackled ominously overhead, thunder rumbled and roared like a living leviathan.

Arlon fell to his knees to crawl along the cable, hoping to make a smaller target for the wind. It was slow going in the extreme. Several times lethal debris passed only millimetres above Arlon's head. Had he been standing he would have been cleaved in two or decapitated. The deafening maelstrom made thinking impossible, made movements seem eternal, made time stand still. Arlon lowered himself farther still to crab-crawl like a soldier under intense fire by a superior enemy.

When he eventually made it to the pair of rocks he was exhausted. A hundred metres above him the oval window shimmered brightly, its surface undulating and rippling with energy. Now and then a piece of debris would enter the portal and be disintegrated in a spectacular explosion, adding to the extremely volatile atmosphere.

Before Arlon was able to mount another attack on the pair of rocks, he felt something heavy land behind him. He did not want to turn around. He worried that any movement by him might be seen as hostile if a living thing had landed behind him. It seemed too heavy to be one of the purple spiders or penguins they had witnessed. He supposed it might have been another whale chunk...

An ear-shattering shriek caused his blood to freeze and his pulse to quicken impossibly. Arlon did not feel fear, yet he seemed to be quaking all the same. He was unsure about his options. If he turned and alarmed the creature that had just descended from the portal, he might not live to regret it. If he failed to turn he might miss an opportunity to evade his demise.

What he saw when he finally turned his head defied explanation or description: a blob, a glutinous, glowing blob. Then he detected movement, as the thing gradually unfolded itself much like its predecessors. The gargantuan entity grew more tentacles than Arlon could count, stretching to impossible lengths. Atop the nest of writhing limbs sat an enormous head with multiple eyes dotting its circumference. Two large antennae/feelers tested the air about the struggling creature.

It was predominately a fiery red, with spots and flashes of every other colour in the spectrum radiating throughout its body, fluctuating and pulsing in alternate patterns. The shrieks became longer, more urgent, louder. It was clear to Arlon that the creature was in great distress, possibly out of its natural element, such as water. Unable to cope with the enormous stresses gravity placed on its anatomy once out of the near-weightless environment it normally inhabited, the creature gradually collapsed in on itself. Finally, it slumped to the ground with one last convulsive jerk and a sigh, with the aroma of a thousand putrid, festering bodies.

Arlon wondered if it was the same thing Mr Boggs had seen, his kraken. Small wonder the man had abandoned ship if he witnessed that thing aiming for him. Arlon was immensely pleased that he did not have to fend off an attack from the beast. As he watched the behemoth revert back to nothing more than a gelatinous red puddle, a piece of debris struck the surface. The second the insides of the creature were exposed to an alternate reality, it exploded, sending globs of matter everywhere. Arlon was coated in the horribly-reeking mess from head to toe.

Movement of light intensity from the periphery made him glance backward. The rocks had started to vibrate and wiggle. The concentration of the vibrations increased alarmingly, causing the eons of collected coatings to come loose and fall off. Layer after layer of marine encrustations and sea silt shook free of the rocks, with shafts of bright blue and white lights projected outwards in every direction where the surfaces were fully exposed.

Arlon stepped back to witness what he knew would be the end, one way or the other. The blacker than black surfaces of the two rocks had folds upon folds and multiple ripples making up its substrate. From in between the folds and waves of material shone the blinding rays. The pair of rocks jiggled and waggled as they shed their layers, rotating and tumbling in place to remove every last foreign element.

Arlon guessed that he and the others had removed enough of the outer coatings to cause a reaction between the pair or a response to their environment. If the former, he held some hope of survival. He knew he should be attempting to place as much distance as possible between himself and the unfolding event. Instead, Arlon was cemented to the spot by his fascination and awe. He knew he had a ringside seat to a once in a lifetime, once in a universe's lifetime, spectacle. Nothing could move him at that moment.

Arlon felt a rejuvenation in his tired limbs and brain as he witnessed the miracle before him. The shards of piercing light knifed through him, roiling within him before exiting. They warmed and excited him beyond words. The cascading waves of pure energy passing through him invigorated every nerve ending and fibre of his body, now burgeoning with vitality. In the chaos of his mind he saw his life passing before him, the events that shaped his existence, the trials and tribulations, everything punching in and out of his mind's eye like a slideshow.

It was difficult to discern the outcome from the myriad of effects invading his system all at once. It was a hectic and insane journey of life in the physical and mental realms, clashing, coalescing, and cascading into one another. All about Arlon, the atmosphere adopted the bluish ambience of excited energy waves. Whether that spelled the end of all existence on planet earth, their particular part of the planet, or just the end of life on a tiny island, was impossible to predict. It all seemed to be leaning heavily towards a destructive result rather than the pleasant cessation Arlon had envisaged previously.

The two halves of the ancient meteor, now free of every speck of foreign matter, quivered and shook with a mutual attraction that caused them to eke their way towards one another. Whatever element it was that made them behave in that manner, be it simple magnetism or some other alien geological effect, the rocks slowly moved themselves from their year-long resting place.

What started with Ben Sandringham moving the rocks from opposing ends of the beach to their new positions beside the doorway to the shed, then chipping away at a small section of one rock to expose a surface to the atmosphere, where it suddenly became aware of its counterpart after millennia of separation, was reaching a cumulative finale in front of Arlon's eyes.

Shockwaves burst from the two halves as they slowly moved toward each other, sending undulations through the ground. Arlon nearly fell on more than one occasion. Squinting through the blinding blue and white glare, he watched in dread and fascination as the two pieces of impossibly dense material angled and rotated their positions until they were lined up unerringly with one fracture line facing the other.

In the wall of cloudy wind forming the funnel around the area, lightning flashed and crackled dangerously, illuminated brilliantly by the increasing radiance from the rocks as they drew inexorably closer to one another. Suddenly the rocks exploded forward. The sound wave resulting from the collision of the two rocks forced Arlon off his feet, knocking him heavily to the ground several metres distant.

The united meteor rose ponderously from the ground, hovering a few metres above. It began to spin on its vertical axis, spearing light every which way, forming a barrier of light. Arlon edged away from the circle forming around him until he was well outside its circumference. The roaring of the wind, the infernal rumbling of thunder, and the constant crack of the lightning striking the ground and spreading overhead in a complex matrix of jagged branches overwhelmed Arlon's senses.

The darker than dark ball at the centre of the confusion continued to spin, rotating on both axes, casting its rays in a profusion of blue and white until the barrier coalesced into a shimmering sphere around the central meteor. The surface of the outer spherical globe had the same appearance as the two-dimensional portals Arlon had witnessed. It glimmered and rippled with pulsating energy, while the ball within spun at impossible speeds. Just when Arlon believed it could go no faster it increased speed, again and again, until...

NINETEEN

Silence.

The curtain of swirling wind began to dissipate. The storm ceased all movement and sound instantly. The ball at the centre halted its manic rotations and the outer sphere of energy stabilised into a mirror-calm blue and white reflection. For the first time in many hours, Arlon could hear his breathing, gather his thoughts. Stars shone overhead in a clear sky. He had no idea the day had turned into night, no indication of time having passed.

Peering back towards the house, Arlon made out the faces of the others as they pressed themselves to the small rear windowpane with rapt attention. Tara seemed especially concerned for Arlon.

He feared that the eerie silence and the stillness might be a harbinger of the doom that awaited them all. The tension-filled moments in the silent void increased the group's apprehensions. Just as Arlon was ready to stand he detected a slight variation in the status quo. The outer spherical barrier began to expand around the centrally reunified meteor. Reaching outward to encompass everything, it enveloped Arlon within moments, removing all foreign matter from his body.

While all matter pertaining to the alien realm seemed to be consumed by the energy, all earthen elements remained untouched. The expanding energy mass soon encompassed the entire area, removing any signs of the other reality, hoovering up every last aspect of its dimension as easily as vacuuming the dust from a carpet. Arlon could only assume that every insect and molecule of interdimensional matter was being removed from the vicinity.

The bright spherical wall reached farther and farther outward until it seemed to envelop the entire island within its protective influence. Though Arlon and the others could not know, the phenomenon encompassed the entire region as far as the effects of the portals and its inhabitants had reached. It removed all traces of the upheaval's existence, every element that had reacted with the alien atmosphere detrimentally, and the influence it had on the ocean floor, its tectonic plates, its volcanoes, the ocean and its marine life. Gathering every last molecule of its dimension, the expanding wall of blue and white stretched from one horizon to the other until the earth was cleansed of foreign matter.

Gradually, the meteor began to rotate and spin on all its axes once more, as the outer energy field contracted. Arlon witnessed the external shield retracting until it surrounded only the glowing rock at its centre by a distance of no more than a metre. The rotations became insanely fast, unable to be followed by the human eye. The light increased in intensity until it blinded the humans with its glare. Sounds of gales and a hundred storms gathered until it imitated a dozen diesel locomotives all converging on the area; a hundred, a thousand, though not a breath of wind stirred.

The deafening cacophony of confusing sounds overwhelmed Arlon, sitting no more than a few metres from the spectacle. Clarice, Tara and Freddy remained glued to the small windowpane beside the rear door, unable to tear their eyes away from the unfolding event. Through slitted eyes, Arlon was able to make out the field of energy contracting more and more. The unbelievable sounds grew worse, the light intensified and the entire island was bathed in the effects. The impossible rotations of the meteor became nothing but a blur within the shield of decreasing light.

Closer and closer, the spectacle was roaring as though the bowels of hell had been opened to a trillion howling, shrieking souls crying out in terror; as though Dante's inferno had been breached and the entire underworld was voicing its fear as one.

Arlon became certain he was witnessing the end of life as he knew it.

Clarice gasped in fear and awe, holding Tara tightly, believing the end was at hand.

Freddy Boggs clutched his chest as the first telling spasms heralded the onset of a major medical episode.

Inexorably, the outer field converged on the spinning meteor until the two touched. It was the moment Arlon dreaded most of all. He felt sure a cataclysmic explosion would tear the globe asunder...

...It all winked out of existence as if it had never been. With it went every sound, leaving a blissful silence to settle on the scene and three of its shaken onlookers. The fourth member of their group was no longer capable of fear or thought. He slunk to the ground as his heart fell victim to the enormous stresses imposed on it. Unable to face the possibility of an apocalypse, Frederick Alexander Boggs capitulated to the demands on his weakened heart.

Epilogue

Only three people knew the truth behind the mysterious and bizarre events that took place off the mid-Queensland coast centred on the Whitsunday group of islands. Though a phalanx of scientists converged on the islands in the aftermath of the natural disasters besetting the islands and the nearest mainland communities, no evidence or explanation emerged as to the cause.

The simultaneous occurrences of cyclone, tornado, underwater earthquakes, possible underwater volcanic activity and the subsequent tsunami resulting from all that, baffled the top echelon of Australia's scientific minds. The media frenzy from around the world failed to elicit a plausible indication of origin despite the plethora of conspiracy theories circulating the globe about unofficial nuclear testing and the like.

Not a single shred of evidence remained on Cid Island to elicit a response from the men and women sent there to seek answers from what was assumed to be the epicentre of the phenomenon. The house standing on a lease belonging to Gail Sandringham, though having survived the onslaught of disasters, was eventually condemned as unsafe and demolished. Scattered debris from a metal shed and a fence surrounding the property were found littering the island and bay waters. Frederick Boggs was transported back to the mainland, where he was cremated and his ashes scattered upon the ocean as per his wishes.

On a sunny summer's day in Brisbane, several months after Cid Island and the surrounding areas had been cordoned off to the public, Arlon Bartholomew Grey entered into a marriage contract with Clarice Maude Manning, witnessed by all five of Clarice's brothers and her sister, Gail. Standing proudly between the pair as they recited their personal vows in front of the celebrant, Tara Blaze-Grey smiled effervescently.

THE END

Eye for an Eye
Featuring Arlon Grey

Josef Peeters

PROLOGUE

Deep in the temperate rainforests of Victoria's rugged hinterland, where crisp white peaks decorated the tips of the numerous mountains surrounding the area, in a ravine known to only a handful of locals, sat an elderly lady beside a babbling brook.

With only starlight penetrating the chilly darkness, Hilda Haggerty hummed softly as she held out her hand with a morsel to tempt the local fauna out of hiding. For nigh on eighty years, Hilda had maintained the annual ritual, travelling the length of her cleared property within the hidden ravine, to sit upon the stump at midnight on the eve of the winter solstice to await her guest.

From the time of her fifth birthday, introduced to her inaugural pilgrimage to the stump by her blessed father, Hilda had followed the routine set out by Jason Haggerty eighty times since. It was to mark her passage on earth, the day she entered the world. It was also the day she lost her mother. Ten years later, on the same date, she lost her beloved father in a logging accident.

Tragedy and birth, joy and heartache: two faces of the same coin flipped into the air on any given day to randomly reveal which face will decree another chapter in a person's life. Though the date held sad memories for Hilda of the loving father she lost and the mother she never knew, it also foretold of a special event that she shared with no other living soul after her father, one that brought immense joy to the old woman.

Her exhalations formed small clouds of vapour in the still night air. The temperature was below freezing, as expected for that time of year in the Victorian forest of towering mountain ash, some trees taller than seventy metres. A thick fog had yet to emerge above the frigid soil, where it stayed until well past midday during the depths of winter. Snow would descend on the slopes of her mountain, only a few hundred metres higher than her clearing in the deep ravine, immersed in shadow for much of the winter cycle.

By re-enacting the annual ritual, Hilda held to the promise she made to her father eighty years ago on the first night he carried her down the slope from their cottage to the stump by the creek. He placed the young, tired girl on the stump, wrapped in many blankets to protect her from the biting cold and rising damp. Without speaking a word, Jason made sure his daughter remained absolutely still and silent as the grave.

There they waited for the miracle that occurred each year at the same time, when humankind would commune with nature, when the Haggerty family of two repaid a debt they owed and paid homage to the creatures of the forest that blessed them with their trust. Her father explained to the young Hilda that no other human contact of the kind had ever been recorded in Australia's history. He invoked a pact of complete secrecy about their assignation upon the impressionable young girl, a pact that Hilda swore to uphold until her dying day and beyond.

She was the last Haggerty. The secret would perish upon her deathbed unless something miraculous occurred in the time she had remaining to her. Hilda doubted her old body was capable of reproducing and so held little hope of passing her secret on to her offspring, just as the recipient of the midnight tryst had done with hers. She couldn't determine exactly how many generations she had celebrated the ritual with over the ensuing years. Her old eyes had developed cataracts some time ago, ensuring that she could no longer distinguish individual markings as she once did.

Like the fogs that rolled in over the clearing each night, the mists had invaded her eyesight long ago, leaving her nothing but blurry white and indistinct shapes to witness on the eve of the anniversary. Hilda now saw only ghosts haunting her vision, spectral apparitions swimming before her day or night, wafting in and out of view, retreating to the periphery whenever she attempted to focus on an image.

Her other senses had taken up the mantle of responsibility to guide Hilda through her daily chores; senses sharpened to perfection over time; senses that transcended the norm, heightened and honed to a razor edge by necessity. She had acute hearing, exceptional olfactory perception, and an intuitive perspicacity that came from living alone for a lifetime. The gradual loss of her vision had not impaired the redoubtable Hilda Haggerty. It had enhanced her in many ways, beyond the belief of most, unacceptable to others and downright spooky to the rest.

Alone, in the dark, unafraid and highly attuned to her

surroundings, Hilda waited patiently on her stump beside the permanent creek, listening to the gentle splash as the crystal-clear waters washed against the many stones and boulders in its downward path. Much had occurred in the clearing of late and Hilda held fears that her guest might not appear, might no longer be able to appear. She felt intensely sad about that possibility. It would not be worthwhile continuing if she could no longer experience the event that had been such a large part of her existence.

All that she did, everything she accomplished each year, was designed to follow through with the promise made to her father: to continue the ritual he began in his youth, before she was born, before he met her mother. Her entire philosophy of life revolved around the anniversary of her birth, to continue the crucial act of reunification with nature.

Succumbing to lethargy and her aging anatomy, Hilda's eyes blinked in an attempt to remain awake. Gradually her eyelids descended as gravity and age took their toll. Unable to remain awake for the first time since being introduced to the sacred tryst, Hilda nodded off, releasing the morsel she held in her hand to tempt the creature from its forest refuge. It rolled from her wrinkled and liver-spotted hand onto the frosty grass at her feet. From there it continued for a metre down the slope before coming to rest against the base of another small tree stump.

Staring up blankly from its final resting place, the gelatinous globe remained until it was finally found and consumed by the secretive recipient hours later.

ABOUT THE AUTHOR

Josef, born in Düsseldorf, Germany, immigrated to Australia with his parents in 1964. A near lifetime of creative pursuits has culminated in his desire to produce entertaining stories. Josef lives with his wife in the tiny outback town of Moulamein, NSW, Australia, where they own and manage a small caravan park, while they each indulge in their own artistic endeavours.

www.ingramcontent.com/pod-product-compliance
Lightning Source LLC
Chambersburg PA
CBHW070018120726
47909CB00003B/977